E.R. PUNSHON
HELEN PASSES BY

ERNEST ROBERTSON PUNSHON was born in London in 1872.

At the age of fourteen he started life in an office. His employers soon informed him that he would never make a really satisfactory clerk, and he, agreeing, spent the next few years wandering about Canada and the United States, endeavouring without great success to earn a living in any occupation that offered. Returning home by way of working a passage on a cattle boat, he began to write. He contributed to many magazines and periodicals, wrote plays, and published nearly fifty novels, among which his detective stories proved the most popular and enduring.

He died in 1956.

The Bobby Owen Mysteries

E.R. PUNSHON

HELEN PASSES BY

With an introduction
by Curtis Evans

DEAN STREET PRESS

"To desire the desiring of her own beauty is the vanity of Lilith."

—C.S. Lewis

INTRODUCTION

"Well, you know," Bobby said, and there was a distinct touch of exasperation in his voice, "all this makes it very difficult. If everyone goes looney whenever they come near the girl, how are you to work out any reasonable pattern of behavior?"

LIKE THE LEGENDARY Helen of Troy--whose enchanting face, Christopher Marlowe tells us in his play *Doctor Faustus*, "launch'd a thousand ships and burnt the topless towers of Ilium"--the eponymous Helen of E.R. Punshon's twenty-third Bobby Owen detective novel, *Helen Passes By* (1947), with her matchless beauty arouses men (and even women) to decisive actions, some of which they might well come to regret later. As Bobby carries out his latest murder investigation in this novel, he is repeatedly informed how astonishingly lovely this Helen is--so much so, indeed, that she has utterly captivated every man who has beheld her. With a show of bravado Bobby declares that as a policeman he naturally is immune to such things ("Duty, you know, and all that"), yet during the course of Bobby's questionings the fabled lady somehow keeps eluding him, thus denying him the chance of putting to test his claim of immunity to her "all-conquering charms." If it ever comes to the point, however, will Bobby indeed be able to resist Helen's siren spell while bringing yet another murderer to justice?

The more prosaic (if practically important) matter which preoccupies Bobby Owen at the beginning of *Helen Passes By* concerns his now nettlesome employment situation in Wychshire. At the opening of the novel, Bobby, his patience exhausted over continual conflicts with the staid and conservative Watch Committee, has just offered to hand in his resignation as Wychshire Deputy Chief Constable. Happily Scotland Yard shortly afterward offers Bobby a position as a Deputy Assistant Commissioner, provided that he handle for the Yard a politically sensitive murder case involving Lord Adour of Adour and Avon, "a V.I.P. of the first vintage."

At the quaintly named Toad-in-Hole—a formerly tiny Seashire fishing village that since the outbreak of the late war has "grown into a busy port, if 'growth' is a word that can properly be used to describe such a shooting up, unparalleled since the days of Jonah's gourd"—

manufacturer Itter Bain, a partner in Bain Products, Limited (the other partners being Itter Bain's brother, Mauley, and cousin, Prescott), has been shot and killed; and circumstances suggest that Lord Adour might be implicated, the aristocrat having objected to the attentions Itter Bain was paying his daughter, Helen. (You see, she's very beautiful," explains the Scotland Yard Assistant Commissioner to Bobby. "Takes your breath away. Bowls you over. The K.O.") Inconveniently for the newly empowered Labour government, the late Itter Bain was a nephew of the leftist pamphleteer "Jack Cade Junior" (so named for the leader of a fifteenth-century English popular revolt), whose booklets "are said to have had a good deal to do with the Labour Party's winning the election," while the law enforcement man in authority in Seashire is Superintendent Seers, "the Toriest Tory in the country" who "seems to think it's socially incorrect to suspect a man like Lord Adour. ..." (In the mind of the highly traditionalist Seers, confides the AC, "men in Adour's position don't commit murders.") Dissatisfied with the lack of progress in the criminal investigation and distrustful of Seer's motives, Jack Cade Junior is threatening to make trouble over the whole affair in Parliament; and it is hoped in the government that a timely intervention by Bobby will smooth political waters that threaten most boisterously to roil.

Once arrived in Toad-in-Hole, Bobby takes lodging with the local police sergeant, Gregson, and his wife, the latter of whom plies the investigator with such delicacies as hot scones--upon which she has "lavished nearly the whole of the week's ration of butter" (rationing remained very much in effect in England during these postwar years of Labour government)--and regales him with accounts about her family that illustrate the late war's social impact in the United Kingdom:

> Bobby ... heard all about Mrs. Gregson's boy in Burma and how there he had become very pally with an American boy....Also Bobby heard about Mrs. Gregson's girl, Gwen, in the A.T.S., and how she had been given a "mention" for returning to carry on with her 'phone after a bomb blast had blown her twenty feet away. In Mrs. Gregson's opinion—and in Bobby's too—she deserved a medal, let alone a "mention," but Gwen said that if they gave medals in "ats" for things like

that, almost every girl would have one, and what would be the good?

The establishment of cordial relations proves more challenging for Bobby in the case of the imperious Lord Adour. The aristocrat is extremely protective of his daughter Helen, who potentially is an important witness in the murder investigation, and rather dubious about this quietly assertive new investigator: "All this was not quite what [Lord Adour] had expected—something more like Hawkseye the [dime novel] detective, of happy childhood memories, was what he had looked for. Not a man who could spot a [Richard Parkes] Bonington [painting] at a glance and showed no sign of being overawed by the other's title and social position."

Once again Bobby finds occasion to remind a literally entitled murder suspect that "It is the first duty of all police to be no respecter of persons." But Bobby must draw upon all his mental fortitude to solve what proves a particularly challenging case, involving not only a lord and his mesmerizingly lovely daughter, but a missing motor launch, a meddling journalist, a mysterious Frenchman, a plain Jane poor relation, a cadging old school chum and other vexing complications. This time around Olive, holding the domestic fort back in Midwych with the providential assistance of a new maid named Phyllis ("just released from Ack-ack service"), is present in the case only in spirit, when Bobby writes her a series of letters about his investigation, which are quoted extensively throughout the tale. Sadly, we never learn just what Olive thinks about Helen.

Curtis Evans

CHAPTER I
FAIRY TALE

SLIGHTLY RUFFLED in his usually fairly equable temper, the Wychshire Deputy Chief Constable, Bobby Owen, was walking back to his office after a meeting of the Watch Committee that had not been so calm and smoothly working as usual. The question of deaths on the road had been discussed—the figures had risen unpleasantly of late—and Bobby was discovering that one of the drawbacks of holding a responsible position is that of being held responsible for things over which you have not the least power or control. Very plainly had it been intimated to him that the duty of the police was to reduce road deaths to an absolute minimum, though of course without in any way interfering with the natural and inalienable right of the motorist to drive as fast as he liked, built up areas included, if the police weren't around. Bobby, goaded by criticism, had remarked that if he were given the power, he could reduce road deaths by seventy-five per cent, in a few weeks. Asked how, he had suggested prohibiting the use of the horn, since too many motorists drove on the horn and believed that by sounding it they automatically relieved themselves of all responsibility. A taximan, he had remarked, would sometimes drive all day without sounding his horn once.

This had not been well received. It had indeed ruffled some tempers considerably. It was stigmatized as reactionary. Something was said about Bolshevism, plain hints were dropped that though the Deputy Chief might have had his successes as a detective, this success had been obtained at the cost of some neglect in the administrative sphere. Instances were quoted of police duties less adequately performed than was desirable. Bobby retorted by quoting man-power figures. Impossible, he declared, to carry out duties there were not the men to perform. Thoroughly annoyed by now, he offered to resign, promised to hand in his resignation that very day, but had his hurt feelings and injured dignity assuaged by prompt, ample, and hurried expressions of confidence, even from motoring members of the Committee, still shaken to the depths of their souls by his audacious, unprecedented, revolutionary and totally impracticable suggestion.

"I didn't know you were like that, Owen," Sir Merrick Templemore, the Chairman of the Committee, remarked to him aside as the meeting was breaking up, and when Bobby asked, "Like what?" Sir

Merrick shook a doleful head and said people, young people, were never satisfied nowadays unless they were trying to stand the world on its head. Give him, said Sir Merrick, the good old days when things stayed as they were and people knew where they were, and Bobby did not try to tell him that such days had never been nor could be and now less than ever.

All the same, Bobby was still feeling a little ruffled as he walked away, for never before had he been subjected to so much criticism; criticism he resented all the more because an uneasy conscience suggested that possibly the lure of the problem to be solved, the criminal to be brought to justice, attracted him more than did the steady, solid work of administration, conscientiously and capably performed as he knew it to have been. Also there was the road deaths question itself, and none more troubling, more difficult, more pressing. Nor did he see what answer there could be, since the lives of children and speed on the road seem two incompatibles. It was for the community, he felt, to give to one or the other—in the new wartime slang—"first priority."

On these not too pleasant meditations a voice broke suddenly, a deep, melodious voice, a voice indeed like that of the organ in its full command of every note and tone.

"Dear old boy," the rich, full tones were saying, "this is a piece of luck. I am really glad to see you again," and the last words sounded like a whole orchestra welcoming its collective and dearest, long-lost friend.

Therewith, before he quite knew what was happening, Bobby felt his hand seized and held in a brotherly grasp. Thus roused from his thoughts, Bobby saw a smallish man of about his own age, a trifle seedy in dress—but what is that in these days of early peace?—and of an almost fantastic ugliness. His enormous head was set upon an ill-proportioned body, with arms too long and legs so short he waddled rather than walked. There was a slight cast in one eye, his nose was flat and squat and yet managed to be twisted, too; an enormous mouth showed large, discoloured and uneven teeth, his ears flapped like a young elephant's—the legend was that he could waggle them at will—his chin seemed to have been lost; and his complexion resembled that of an imperfectly poached egg, diversified by a mole or two and patches of reddish brown hair a blunt or careless razor had failed to remove.

No one, even those not possessed of Bobby's trained memory for faces, could have failed to recognize that strange, gnome-like figure and face—once seen, never to be forgotten. Bobby, though without much enthusiasm, said at once:

"Why, hullo, Wayling. It's a long time since I saw you."

"Not since we both went down," agreed Wayling, who incidentally had not "gone down," but been "sent down," as Bobby well remembered. "Dear old St. Barnabas," Wayling went on, still holding Bobby's hand in a warm and friendly grasp. "Best college ever. Don't talk to me about Balliol, All Souls, the House—you were there, weren't you?"

"No. They wouldn't have me," Bobby said, managing at last to release his hand from the other's clinging grasp; and he named his own college, libellously asserted to have the lowest standard of admission in all Oxford.

"Of course, of course," declared Wayling. "I remember now. Ah, well, we can't all be Barnabites. But I ought to be congratulating you. I saw in the papers you were a big bug now in the police. Bit of a surprise to find an old pal high up in the cops. Nice to know there's a friend at court, though, if you want one."

"Let's hope it won't be wanted," Bobby remarked with a sub-acid tone that Wayling, quick in the uptake as a cat after a mouse, did not fail to notice.

"Now, don't tell me," he remonstrated, "you still remember that old pack of lies about me and the empty till at the 'Fox and Grapes,' I did make a bit of a fool of myself over that barmaid, but the little brute took it out of me good and proper with all those lies she told. Oh, well, that's over and done with, and I had my lesson. Yes, yes, I had my lesson and I've profited by it. Dine with me to-night? I'm staying at the Midwych Central."

Bobby said it was very kind of Wayling, but Olive, his wife, would be expecting him, and he had some paper work to see to that he would have to take home. Wayling said they must arrange a dinner some other time. Unluckily, he was only in Midwych for a day or two and didn't know when, if ever, he would be back.

"If you take this new job on, though," he added, "we might fix up an evening somewhere, if you think Mrs. Owen would like that. I'm only a poor, solitary bachelor with a couple of rooms off Park Lane, so it'll have to be one of the cook shops—I prefer the Savoy myself."

"What new job do you mean?" Bobby asked suspiciously.

"Oh, haven't you heard?" Wayling asked, and laughed again, a pleasant, jolly, slightly embarrassed laugh. "Perhaps I oughtn't to have said anything. You're going to be offered a Deputy Assistant Commissionership at the Yard."

"Rubbish," said Bobby. "Where did you get that cock-and-bull yarn?"

Wayling threw back that enormous head of his and laughed once more.

"Dear old boy," he said. "Never you mind how I know. You just wait and see. It's over this Bain murder they want you."

"Deputy Assistant Commissioners don't take on murder cases," Bobby said sharply.

"They do, if they are Bobby Owen and the murder is the Bain murder," Wayling asserted smilingly; and his smile was one that somehow managed to transform his ill-formed, twisted features with an odd and baffling charm. "Just as Deputy Chief Constables don't take on murder cases unless they happen to be Bobby Owen, and even then they have to leave the administrative side to others just a bit at times."

This was a thrust that went home. Bobby knew, remembered, that Wayling had had the reputation of knowing all the secrets of everyone in Oxford, from dons to freshmen, with most of the citizens of the town thrown in. An exaggeration, no doubt, as was certainly the story that he was always hidden under every separate dinner table everywhere every night. Nevertheless, it was the case that somehow or another he managed to pick up every bit of gossip in the whole University. One explanation put forward was that all the women he met always told him everything within five minutes of their first meeting. Another exaggeration, no doubt, but not such a wild one this time. Anyhow, somehow or another, though the man was a complete stranger in the town, he had apparently already managed to get wind of recent Watch Committee criticism. Bobby looked at him sourly, but made no comment, beyond saying briefly that he must be getting back to his office.

"I've an appointment, too," declared Wayling. "Bit late for it. Any chance of getting a taxi, I wonder? They seem as rare here as in town. Well, awfully glad to meet an old pal again," and as he said this his deep, rich voice was vibrant with emotion. As they were shaking hands, he added: "By the way, old man, can you change me a pound note?"

As he spoke he produced, not without a certain flourish, five brand new one-pound notes. "Just got them from the bank," he said, "and I haven't another penny in the whole wide world. No change where I lunched and the tip took my last coin."

Bobby hesitated. The story might be true. Change was in short supply—shorter than ever now peace had caught the world on one foot and sent the world reeling with the shock. He fumbled in his pocket and produced a little silver. In a friendly, detached tone—that voice of his could convey every mood almost as clearly as print— Wayling said:

"Oh, don't bother if it's going to clean you out, too. I didn't want to have to offer a taxi-man a pound note. Most of them don't seem to know what change means. Five bob will do me. Let you have it back as soon as I can get to the Midwych Central Hotel—send the porter chap round with it."

Somehow, without Bobby quite knowing how, two half-crowns got themselves transferred from his hand to Wayling's pocket. Wayling said "Thanks awfully," waved a gay farewell and disappeared. Bobby walked on in thoughtful mood, and when he reached his office picked up the 'phone.

"Hullo. Is that the Midwych Central Hotel?" he asked, connection made. "Is Mr. Alexander Wayling staying with you?"

The voice at the other end of the line said it would inquire. A moment or two later the voice said, No, no one of that name was staying at the hotel. Were they to expect the gentleman?

Bobby said he didn't think so. Probably Mr. Wayling was staying somewhere else, and thank you very much. Therewith he hung up, reflected that Wayling was running true to form, that certainly the Deputy Assistant Commissionership at Scotland Yard was merely a fairy tale, meant to facilitate the transfer of that five shillings most certainly now due to be written off as a total loss.

"But he had five one-pound notes all right, brand new, too, as if they had really just come from the bank," mused Bobby and before he turned to his work, murmured, half aloud: "I wonder where he got them from?"

As the old books used to say, generally in italics, and rightly so: *Little he knew.*

CHAPTER II
AN OFFER

STILL ALL UNKNOWING, having indeed, for that matter, forgotten all about the mystery of the five brand new one-pound notes, Bobby arrived home that evening a little earlier than usual. Olive was in the kitchen, gloating in the company of Phyllis, the new maid, just released from Ack-ack service, over some real, genuine, absolutely fresh Dover sole sent—yes, sent—by the fishmonger. She heard Bobby's key in the door and came into the hall to greet him.

"I expect," she suggested, "you smelt 'em, and that's why you caught the early train for once."

"Smelt what?" Bobby asked; but Olive looked prim and wouldn't say, thus adding another mystery to that of the five one-pound notes.

Instead she remarked:

"There was such a funny little man came to see you this afternoon. Rather nice, but so ugly it almost took your breath away. He said he knew you at Oxford. He told me they want you back at Scotland Yard. Do you think it's true?"

"Good lord!" exclaimed Bobby, dismayed. "I hope Wayling isn't broadcasting that yarn all over the place. Probably all his own invention. How much did he borrow?"

"Bobby," gasped Olive, "how did you know?"

Bobby tapped his forehead impressively.

"Sheer brain-power," he said, "or, in other words, knowing Wayling of old. He touched me for five bob. How much was yours?"

"Only three and sixpence," Olive told him, a touch of triumph in her voice, since this showed she was one and six up. Then the fundamental honesty of her character made her add, ruefully this time: "It was every last penny of change I had. He was rather nice about it, though, and said it was quite all right when I told him how sorry I was it wasn't more." She paused and then, without either triumph or regret in her voice, but only deep dismay, she exclaimed: "Oh, Bobby, I had five one-pound notes and I can't find them anywhere."

"Oh," said Bobby, memory flooding back. "Brand new, weren't they?"

"Yes, why? I only got them from the bank this morning. How did you know?"

"As before, sheer brain-power," Bobby told her. "When did you see them last?"

"I thought I remembered putting them on the mantelpiece in the drawing-room," answered Olive uneasily, "but when I went to look they weren't there."

"Before or after?"

"Before or after what?"

"Before or after the Wayling episode?"

"Oh, Bobby," said Olive, all protest and dismay.

"Well," said Bobby, inexorable. "Was it?"

"After," admitted Olive. "I mean I only missed them after.
You can't think that nice little man—"

"Can and do," said Bobby, and went on with reluctant admiration: "He showed them me. When he was touching me for that five bob. Sort of guarantee. Asked me for change and produced those notes as proof of good faith. I wondered at the time where he got them from. Now," said Bobby bitterly, "now I know."

"Bobby," Olive exclaimed, all protestant and unbelieving, "it couldn't be that. Not that nice little man—not taking all my change with my nice new notes in his pocket all the time. Oh, Bobby."

"You said 'Oh, Bobby' before," Bobby pointed out.

"Did I?" said Olive. "Oh, Bobby, I'm sure it can't be that. Only if it is, I needn't feel worried about Phyllis. She's only been here since Monday and she does seem nice and willing, but I couldn't help wondering—not really wondering, only being a weeny bit uncomfortable. It's awful to think you very nearly suspected someone of stealing when they hadn't," and Olive looked so remorseful and unhappy that Bobby had to laugh, and then Olive was cross and said it was very unkind of him and nothing to laugh about. "I shall have," declared Olive, "to try to be extra nice to her to make up."

"She's not a bad-looking girl," Bobby remarked. "She wasn't alone with Wayling, at all, was she?"

"No. Why? She took him into the drawing-room and then came upstairs to tell me."

"He's a fast worker," Bobby observed meditatively, "but I shouldn't think that would give even him time enough."

"What are you talking about? Time for what?"

"To seduce her."

"Bobby!"

"Where Wayling is concerned," Bobby pronounced, "no man's purse and no woman's virtue can be considered safe."

"Bobby!!! How can you say such things? That nice little ugly man—"

"I know," interposed Bobby. "I know. Eyes like those of a faithful dog. A voice that wraps itself round your heart-strings. And so deliciously ugly and such a perfectly wonderful contrast, too—makes any woman look twice as beautiful as she really is."

"Don't be beastly," said Olive, indignant, and twice as cross as before. "It isn't that at all."

The 'phone rang and Olive said "Oh, dear," She always said, "Oh, dear," when the 'phone rang, and often enough with good reason. Bobby went to answer it.

"Deputy Chief Owen here," he said. "Who is speaking? Oh, Sir Merrick Templemore. Oh, yes, I know Wayling all right. He got five bob out of me this afternoon and four bob out of Mrs. Owen here at home." ("Three and six," interposed Olive. "Don't be jealous.") "Yes, that's true. ... We got off pretty cheaply. ... Ten pounds seventeen and fourpence out of you. ... How did he manage just that amount? ... Oh, I see. Trust him to think up something and turn even a debt to profit. ... Shall you prosecute? I think you could. ... I should strongly advise. ... Well, perhaps there's something in that. ... Of course, it would mean a lot of trouble and worry. ... Did he spin you that yarn, too? ... Rubbish, of course. ... They're as likely to offer me a Deputy Assistant Commissioner's job as the Prime Minister's ... part of Wayling's sales talk, so to speak. ... I'll give him something to remember if I can lay hands on him, only I shan't ... eels are static compared with Wayling ... The Bain murder? ... I don't know anything about it, beyond what I saw in the papers. ... No, I hadn't heard anything like that ... just talk probably.... You've quite decided not to prosecute ... Perhaps you're right; not worth powder and shot ... Thank you very much ... Goodbye."

He hung up, and Olive said:

"What's the Bain murder? Mr. Wayling said something about it, too."

"There was a paragraph in the papers," Bobby said. "That's all I know. A week or two ago. A man found shot dead and foul play suggested. Wayling always tries to make you think he knows all the secrets, and perhaps he'll tell you some day, and have you got such a thing as half a crown you could let him have till to-morrow? The Bain murder's nothing to do with me. Templemore seems to have taken that rot about the Yard rather seriously, though. There was a bit of a rumpus at the Watch Committee to-day over traffic control. I told them if they weren't satisfied I was always ready to resign, and Templemore was saying he hoped I didn't mean it. Quite nice about it. Most likely he was thinking of Wayling's rot about the Yard offer."

"You don't mean you want to resign, do you?" asked Olive, slightly dismayed.

"I'll think about it," Bobby promised her, "when the Yard comes through. Committees have to be kept in order. I know'," he added slowly, "children's deaths on the road are enough to make anyone feel a bit hysterical."

Olive asked: "Did Mr. Wayling really manage to get all that money from Sir Merrick? Sir Merrick's rather nice, but he is careful about money, isn't he?"

"You have to be more than careful when Wayling's around," Bobby told her. "He worked it all right. He met Sir Merrick some time ago somewhere in Town. Most people meet Wayling once or twice. He takes care they do. After that, after he's touched them, he takes care they don't. It was more than a hundred he owed Sir Merrick—not cash apparently, a gambling debt. So now he's turned up with a cheque in full settlement, plus five per cent, compound interest. Sir Merrick thought that jolly decent, but he couldn't possibly accept compound interest. He explained to Wayling that he wasn't a moneylender. So after they had argued a bit he managed— of course, with great difficulty—to persuade Wayling to accept a counter-cheque for the ten pound odd that was supposed to stand for the compound interest. Now he has discovered that his own cheque was cashed by Wayling as fast as a taxi could get Wayling to the bank, while Wayling's cheque has just been returned, marked 'R.D.' Smart work. Oh, and Wayling had five and nine out of Templemore, too, to pay for the taxi to get him to the bank before it closed. Good day's work—you and me and Sir Merrick and I dare say one or two others as well."

"Such a nice little man he seemed," murmured Olive and looked quite sad.

The 'phone bell rang. Olive said, "Oh, dear." Bobby answered it.

"Trunk call," he said.

Presently he went to find Olive. She had been called away for consultation by Phyllis, who had never before seen Dover sole; of the whole vast finny tribe, she knowing none but cod. Bobby said to Olive:

"That was the Yard. They want me to call to-morrow. Something about the Bain case. And would I like my name considered for the vacant Deputy Assistant Commissionership?"

"Oh, Bobby," said Olive.

CHAPTER III
A MISSION

"IT'S LIKE THIS, Owen," said, the Assistant Commissioner, leaning back in his chair. "The Bain case is worrying the Home Office, and the Home Office is worrying us. If you agree to help us, we think it would probably be better if you came in as from the Yard. I dare say the Home Office could fake up some sort of authority for you, if you prefer to stay on at Midwych. But Commander Seers will probably be more co-operative, less unco-operative might be a better way to put it, if you show up as a Yard man, as a Deputy Assistant Commissioner rather than as a Deputy Chief Constable when Seers himself is a Chief Constable all on his own. These Service blokes have a great feeling for seniority. One grade up and you're a demigod. One grade down and you're a doormat. I don't know where in the hierarchy chief constables and deputy A.C.'s stand. If we sent a mere Chief Inspector, Seers would simply ignore him. You've never met Seers, have you?"

"I don't think so," said Bobby. "But what's behind all this?"

"Politics," said the Assistant Commissioner gloomily.

"Politics," repeated Bobby, profoundly shocked. "Politics," he repeated, indignantly this time. "What's politics got to do with police?"

"Yes, I know," agreed the Assistant Commissioner. "We all feel that way. All the same. Well, now then. Heard anything about the Bain case?"

"Only what's been in the papers. I didn't pay much attention. It seemed straightforward enough. Man found shot dead in a wood, wasn't it? Poaching?"

"Not our pigeon," the Assistant Commissioner went on. "Seers says he has no intention of calling us in. The *Seashire Herald*—influential locally and even more than locally—sent a reporter to ask him why not. Seers told the reporter to go to the Devil, and he would be run in for obstruction if he didn't clear out. Sent a constable to see he did clear out. They were on private property at the time. Great mistake to treat the Press like that. Only way to approach the Press is on your hands and knees. The Assistant Commissioner paused, and a yearning look came into his eyes. "I never see a reporter," he said, "but I wish I were the Gestapo and knew the address of the nearest concentration camp. But I'm not and I don't, so I suck up to 'em instead."

"I know," said Bobby sympathetically. Then he remembered that we are living in the Hollywood age. "You're telling me," he said.

The Assistant Commissioner looked alarmed.

"I say," he said, "all that's strictly between ourselves."

"Cross my heart," said Bobby.

"As a result," the Assistant Commissioner continued, "the blasted paper is hinting pretty broadly that Seers is protecting a Certain Very Important Person—a V.I.P. in social, financial and political circles all at once. And they hint he is acting under pressure from what the Russians would call Dark Forces. Seers is consulting his solicitors about a libel action. No good, of course. The Editor has his stuff carefully vetted by a leading K.C. But think of the scandal! Think of the gift such a libel action would be to the extremists. It might affect votes, and the mere thought of that would send any government into hysterics."

"Yes, of course. So it would," agreed Bobby. "But I'm still a lot in the dark. Who is the Very Important Person? Do you know?"

"Lord Adour of Adour and Avon," said the Assistant Commissioner.

"Oh," said Bobby, impressed.

For Lord Adour of Adour and Avon was a Very Important Person indeed—a V.I.P. of the first vintage. His pedigree went back to Adar, the Saxon thane, who, according to legend, was the lover of Queen Elfrida and instigator of the murder of Edward the Martyr in A.D. 979. Besides, the pedigree was certainly authentic up to the time of Charles II, when the wife of a Charles Adour, a barber, had been one of the favourites of that merry monarch. Beyond that date the authenticity of the pedigree was probably more open to doubt. However, taking advantage of his good fortune, Charles Adour had flourished exceedingly. Many of his descendants had shown an equal business ability. A peerage came their way. Coal was discovered on some of their land. Property they had in the city of London increased a thousandfold in value while they sat by and watched. The present Lord Adour had continued the ancestral interest in coal, had extended it to iron and steel, and had many interests on the Continent. As a result, he had suffered heavy losses at the outbreak of the war. In politics, too, he had been active and influential, and though he had been a strong supporter of the unhappy Munich policy, he had occupied important positions under the Coalition Government, rendering valuable services. After the unexpected result of the 1945 General Election, he had publicly announced his readiness to accept the verdict of the nation. In return for this magnanimity, the Labour Government, determined to be equally magnanimous, had continued to avail itself of his services, though this had exposed them to some criticism from some of their more zealous supporters. All this Bobby knew and remembered, and the more he remembered it, the less he liked it.

"Politics must be kept out," he said with great decision and emphasis.

"Of course they must," agreed the Assistant Commissioner warmly. "Read any of Jack Cade Junior's stuff, by the way?"

"Well, no," said Bobby. "I've seen the things of course—piles of them everywhere. I remember catching one of my men reading some of the stuff. I ticked him off. I told him he could read them till he was blue in the face off duty, if he wanted to, but on duty, in uniform, no police officer had ever heard of politics. Real name is Robinson, isn't it?"

"Sammy Robinson," confirmed the Assistant Commissioner. "Those booklets of his are said to have had a good deal to do with the Labour Party's winning the election. Well, Jack Cade Junior—Sammy Robinson to his friends—is the uncle of the murdered man."

"Oh," said Bobby startled. "Awkward. All the same," he repeated more firmly than ever, "politics have got to be kept out."

"Of course they have," agreed the Assistant Commissioner, more warmly than ever. "Only Jack Cade Junior is doing his blasted best to bring 'em in. He says he'll bring it up in Parliament, make a national question of it. Seers says: Let him and be damned to him. Very proper attitude on Seers's part. Only if it does happen to be true ..."

"If what happens to be true?" Bobby asked.

"I don't suppose it is for a moment, not for one moment," declared the other with great emphasis. "But ... well, there you are. Seems someone has got to look into it. And now Seers has put up the back of the *Seashire Herald*, and there's a suggestion the Editor may get hold of one of those crime-investigating blokes from one of the big national papers. Can't afford to let one of them poke it out if there is anything to poke out. Of course, Seers sticks to it there isn't. Says there's not a shred of real evidence against Lord Adour."

"If there isn't, why worry?" asked Bobby.

"Yes, I know," agreed the other, but somewhat uneasily. "Only, Seers has made up his mind and a closed mind is—well, a closed mind. If Seers had seen Adour committing the murder, he wouldn't believe his own eyes. Bain was killed by a charge of small shot fired at close range. Adour admits he was in the neighbourhood. He admits he had his gun with him. Quite natural at this time of year. Adour farms a biggish bit of land and many farmers take a gun out with them, much as you take an umbrella in Town. His story is that he saw a rare bird of some sort or another—he is president of the local bird-watcher society. He says he saw the bird, put his gun down against a tree, hurried home to get a camera to take a snap, came back with it, bird disappeared, hunted round a bit on the chance of spotting it again, had no luck, and went home, forgetting all about his gun. When he remembered and went back for it, it wasn't there. Seers accepts the story. He seems to think it's socially incorrect to suspect a man like Lord Adour of lying. Seers suggests the murderer saw the gun, saw his chance, and that's that. He is concentrating on finding the gun. Fingerprints, he hopes. Of course, there's no proof Adour's gun was in fact used. What Seers really means is that men in Adour's position don't commit murders. He's quite sure of that. But when you're quite sure you're right, you're not too likely to find anything to prove you wrong, are you?"

"You aren't," agreed Bobby, "and you won't. Any reason known for ill-feeling between Lord Adour and the dead man? Is anything known about him—Bain, I mean. Apart, of course, from being a nephew."

"Engineer by profession. Started as a ship's engineer. Left the sea to start on his own with his brother and a cousin who had a small capital. Bain's Products, Limited. They've done very well out of the war. The dead man is Itter Bain. He looked after the engineering end. His brother is Mauley Bain. He is the production head. The cousin is Prescott Bain. He provided the capital and runs the financial side. The works are at Drinks, three or four miles up the Adour River. Drinks was a big port in mediaeval times till the river mouth silted up. The small fishing village there, Toad-in-Hole, has been developed into an important wartime port the Germans never seem to have found. Takes fairly big ships. Helped Bain Products a lot because of transport. Loaded their stuff on a barge down the river and straight on board ship. Itter Bain helped with the plans for the layout of the new docks and so on. Lord Adour scored, too, because he owns all the land."

"Was there any friction between them?"

"Not as far as is known. No reason apparent why there should be. Their interests didn't clash. They ran together. Then there's the girl."

"What girl?" Bobby asked.

"Helen Adour. Ever heard anything about her?"

"No. Why? Should I?"

"No, no. Very nice girl. Keeps the publicity hounds at arm s length. Won't be photographed, except keeping strict control of the copyright. The society papers have done all they know to get her, but she's not having any. You see, she's very beautiful. Takes your breath away. Bowls you over. The K.O. You don't believe it at first, not till you've looked again."

"Is it genuine?" Bobby asked doubtfully. "I mean, does she really dislike publicity, or is it just a dodge to get more? That's not unknown."

"I think it's perfectly genuine in her case," the Assistant Commissioner replied. "I rather gather from what I've heard that she has some sort of idea that she must keep her beauty private, that if she makes a public show of it or uses it for any sort of personal advantage, then she will lose it. Or it may be she is jealous of it and wishes it to be for herself alone."

"Sounds an odd sort of notion," Bobby said doubtfully. "A pretty woman generally likes to be looked at, doesn't she?"

"Helen Adour isn't pretty," the other answered slowly. "Hers is more like a beauty from another world. I think sometimes it terrifies. It upsets people."

"Oh," said Bobby, not knowing what to make of this. "I see." But he didn't, not in the least. "Was Itter Bain affected like that? In love with her at all?"

"Oh, yes. Badly. Everyone is, once they've seen her. I am. The women, too. There's no competition. The girl's hors concours. Besides, she keeps everyone at arm's length. Not interested. I expect she will be some day, but not yet. Seers is, head over heels. That's another complication. He means to keep her name out of it. Or die. Officially or otherwise, for her sake. Glad of the chance for that matter, glad and grateful. They do say it's the middle-aged who catch it worst if they catch it at all."

"You don't mean there's any suggestion of a love affair between them?"

"Oh, no," said the Assistant Commissioner and looked quite shocked. "Seers is most respectable. Thick-headed and pig-headed, but that s all. Besides, you might as well try to have a love affair with the Matterhorn—lovely and remote. That's Helen Adour. And both to the ninth degree. There does seem to be some local gossip that Itter Bain had been more troublesome than most and that Lord Adour had been obliged to warn him off. It may be only gossip. But it isn't gossip that the *Seashire Herald* is on the warpath and means to get ahead of us if it can. And I'm inclined to suspect Sammy Robinson is behind the *Herald*. Sammy has connections with the Press, and he could easily get hold of one of these crime reporter blokes. You can see for yourself, Owen, it simply won't do to let them get in ahead. If the *Herald*, with the aid of Sammy's man, manages to rake up something to suggest Seers had been failing to push the inquiry with vigour— I don't believe it for a moment, not knowingly or willingly, that is—because a man of Lord Adour's position was involved, there would be the very grandfather and grandmother of all possible scandals. It might get us all the sack, every man jack. It might have political repercussions. One of Jack Cade Junior's pet ideas is that the police ought to be under direct proletarian control. In fact, if Sammy, blast him, brings it off, if he can make out any sort of case against Seers, who is a perfectly honest, straightforward, pig-headed old Tory jockeyed into a job he isn't fit for by family influence, there'll be merry hell to pay—and you and me to foot the bill, because of course the Home Office will leave us holding the baby. How about it?"

"Sounds interesting."

"Going to take it on?"

"Oh, yes, I suppose so," Bobby said. "Can't turn jobs down because you don't like the look of them."

CHAPTER IV
A DOUBTFUL DOSSIER

BOBBY, LEAVING THE YARD, heavy with a sense of the difficulty and the responsibility of the task laid upon him, was stopped by the constable at the door.

"Beg pardon, sir," he said. "There's a gentleman been asking for you. I told him to fill in a slip, but he said he would wait. Very talkative gentleman. I had to tell him I was on duty."

"You don't know who he was, I suppose?" Bobby asked. "No, sir. I asked if you were expecting him and he said, Not yet, but you would be. I don't know what he meant. That's him, over there."

A tall, good-looking young man, in a blue serge suit, shabby but then that is normal in these piping days of peace—hatless, but with hair so plastered with hair oil one could see it glisten across the street, with a thin, smiling face and a general air of brisk self-confidence, was coming towards them. He said, beamingly, as one greeting an old and long lost friend.

"The great Bobby Owen, I believe?"

Bobby said severely:

"My name is Robert Owen. We will cut out the great, it you please. It is not impressive. I don't think I know you. Have you any business with me?"

"Well, that's what I'm here for," retorted the other, unabashed. "I'll walk along with you if I may. My name is Haile, Harry Haile, H-a-i-l-e, not H-a-l-e. How about a drink? Could you spare a minute to come round to my club—the Garrick?"

"I could not," said Bobby with still greater severity.

"Just as well," said the other cheerfully. "Especially as I don't happen to be a member. I knew you would refuse so I knew it was safe to ask."

"If there is anything you want to say, please get on with it," Bobby said impatiently, and would have cut the interview short then and there had he not known by long experience that valuable information does sometimes issue from the most unlikely beginnings.

"Oh, I have, lots," Mr. Haile responded. "I'm on the staff of the *Seashire Herald.*"

"Indeed," said Bobby. "Do you mean you are in the employ of Mr. Samuel Robinson, who writes political pamphlets as Jack Cade Junior?"

Mr. Haile looked slightly taken aback—a rare phenomenon with him, Bobby guessed. But he recovered so quickly that if Bobby had not expected and been on the lookout for such a reaction he would never have noticed it.

"The Yard always up to date," Haile murmured. "Does it matter? I think not. You can't wonder if Sammy is interested in the murder of a nephew. He has no children, you know. Itter Bain and his brother, and their cousin Prescott Bain, are his only relatives. He feels it a duty to see the murderer is brought to justice, and you can't blame him."

"It is our duty to do that," Bobby said coldly, "and he would be wise to leave it to us. We shall do our best without fear or favour. If you are in touch with Mr. Robinson, you can tell him so from me. You may also warn him that if he intends to try to use what's happened to bring pressure on the Government to do what he and his friends want, he may find himself heading for trouble. I believe some of them think the present Government too moderate and that a stronger line should be followed."

"I say," muttered Mr. Haile. "You do know it all, don't you?"

"No," said Bobby. "I know nothing about politics, for instance. The sole interest of a detective is to find out the truth; and if politicians or anyone else get in the way, they are liable to be hurt."

"Thanks for the warning," said Mr. Haile, quite perky again. "We are all liable to get hurt, aren't we? Even crossing the road."

"Have you really anything to say?" Bobby asked. "I've no time to spare."

"Not very forthcoming, are you?" Mr. Haile observed with a touch of reproach in his voice. "It struck me that, perhaps, as we are both on the same job, it might be a good idea if we pooled our ideas—gave each other mutual help. What we both want is to find the murderer of Itter Bain. What about it? I think I've already some information you would find useful."

Bobby was not quite sure whether to be amused or annoyed by the calm audacity of this proposal. Very nice and convenient, indeed, for Mr. Haile to be working with and under the aegis of police authority and yet remain entirely free of all responsibility.

"Mr. Haile," he said, speaking with a somewhat stagey solemnity, "I call upon you in the King's name to come to my assistance."

"What on earth," exclaimed Haile, staring bewilderedly, "what on earth does that rigmarole mean?"

"It means," Bobby told him, and now speaking naturally, "that I am reminding you that if you have any relevant information and keep it to yourself, you are committing an offence of which you have now been officially warned. It is your duty, the duty of every citizen, to give police officers every possible help. Or you risk becoming an accessory. I have no intention of giving any information to irresponsible amateurs. I have no right to, for that matter. It would be a breach of duty. If you would like to join the police force, though, you can get information at any police station."

"Well and truly snubbed," sighed Mr. Haile. "It was more Sammy Robinson's idea than mine. Still, anything is worth trying once. That's my motto. Well, I'll be seeing you. So long. I'll give you a bit of information though. It's a warning, too."

"Well. What?" Bobby asked sharply.

"Scored a rise at last," said Mr. Haile, beaming again. "May save me from being ordered off under threat of a charge for obstruction. Commander Seers is an old fool to get across the Press for nothing.

Very sensitive, the Press. What was I going to say? Oh, yes. Keep an eye on Mauley Bain. Took his brother's death hard. A black temper, and means mischief. If Mauley gets it into his head he knows who the murderer is, he may just possibly try to settle accounts for himself. It's on the cards. Awkward, though, if he happens to hit on the wrong person.

"Thank you," Bobby said. "I'll remember, and I'll not forget either that it came from you. Can you say anything more definite?"

"Afraid not. It's more a sort of general impression. Mutterings over a glass of whisky and that sort of thing. There's the money side too. Itter was the engineer and the firm will find it hard to carry on without him. It may mean selling out—probably at a loss. I don't think either Mauley or Prescott, the other two partners, are up to coping with the turnover from war production to peacetime activities—if any. If I hear anything more, I'll let you have it. I don't want another killing any more than you do. By the way, you hurt my feelings a lot when you called me an irresponsible amateur. Flat libel. I was three years crime reporter for the *Morning Announcer* before the war and I've been with the Secret Service since. Anyhow, if we can't be allies, I'm glad we've got as far as non-belligerency."

Therewith he nodded farewell, waved to two passing taxis, neither of which took any notice of him, as he was not an American soldier, and then jumped on a passing bus, only to be at once sternly ordered off again by the girl conductor as the bus was already fully loaded. But Mr. Haile had a way with him, a way more successful with girl conductors than it had been with Bobby, and she was still indignantly—more or less indignantly—rejecting his blandishments and repeating her orders when the bus stopped, some passengers got off, and so Mr. Haile was allowed to remain. Though with a warning that no more of his impudence was wanted.

For his part, Bobby, not quite certain what to make of Mr. Haile, but quite certain it would be well to keep an eye on his activities, went back to the Yard and asked to be supplied as soon as possible with any available information concerning Mr. Henry Haile, formerly on the staff of the *Morning Announcer* and during the war a member of the British Secret Service.

Then he returned to his hotel—"priority" had secured him a room—and early next morning took the train to Toad-in-Hole the little fishing village now grown into a busy port, if "growth" is a word that can properly be used to describe such a shooting up, unparalleled since the days of Jonah's gourd. There lodgings had been arranged for him in the house of a Sergeant Gregson, of the local police, no other accommodation being available in a neighbourhood as overcrowded as any where wartime activities have caused a concentration of population. Bobby was a little doubtful of his probable reception, for he had no reason to think his errand would make him popular with the Toad-in-Hole constabulary. But Mrs. Gregson, who welcomed him, seemed a pleasant and capable woman, the rooms appeared comfortable, and Bobby was inclined to think he was going to be much better off there than in any of the hotels where scarcity of staff and superfluity of guests have produced conditions of doubtful ease.

The first thing he did was to arrange, not without difficulty, a meeting with Commander Seers for the next morning. It was an interview, Bobby felt, that would have to be conducted with great care and tact. Any false word, gesture even, and he might easily have Seers not merely as the disgruntled and unwilling colleague he was almost sure to be, but actively hostile.

No use, though, decided Bobby, in crossing that bridge till he came to it, and he settled down to give a very careful reading to the dossier—a very extensive one—of the case. The various reports did not add very much to his knowledge, and he read them with an increasing dismay. To him they seemed amateurish and superficial to a degree. Obvious points had been entirely overlooked. Unimportant details had been worried over with a consequent dreadful waste of time and energy. The doctor's report was clear and efficient, but for the rest "slipshod" was the word that came into Bobby's mind. Only too plainly the work of those who had no experience in the handling of serious and difficult crime. A trail cold through the lapse of time and confused by previous incompetent inquiry was not, Bobby told himself ruefully, a very hopeful one to follow up. But one small point did emerge that he supposed might be of interest. The rare bird of which the mere sight had been enough to make Lord Adour stand up his gun against a tree and run off full speed to the house for his camera, proved to have been a kingfisher. Bobby knew very little about birds, but he was inclined to wonder whether a kingfisher was so rare a sight as all that, or the urge to secure a photograph of it so entirely overwhelming. A point to be considered.

The list of the objects found in the dead man's pockets seemed of equally little interest. Among the items was a cigarette case, engraved "From J. to I." Who was "J."? Bobby wondered, and decided to keep the initial in mind. The inquest on the dead man had been purely formal and had been adjourned in the usual way "for the police to complete their inquiries" and to permit burial to take place.

Presently he put the papers aside and went out to have a look round the town, to make himself acquainted both with its layout and with the "feel," so to say, of the place. Among the placards on walls and hoardings which he read with care in order to get an idea of local activities, he found one advertising a meeting of the Communist Party, Chairman, Mr. Prescott Bain. So evidently one at least of the Bain nephews followed in the footsteps of Mr. Sammy Robinson, that formidable and untiring pamphleteer of the extreme left, "Jack Cade, Junior."

But so far nothing to suggest that politics came into the murder in any way, however much politics might be threatening to affect the conduct of the investigation. But they wouldn't, Bobby told himself with determination, not so long as he had anything to do with it.

He went on towards the harbour, created almost in a night, up-to-date and efficient with all modern appliances, so tremendous is the power of modern methods, once allowed full, unfettered opportunity. It was growing dark now, and through the increasing gloom, for shortage of coal had reduced the town's lighting to something not very much better than the wartime black out, Bobby saw a man coming towards him with long, slow strides that yet somehow, though they seemed so unhurried, so deliberate, brought him nearer with unexpected speed. He was at Bobby's side almost as soon as Bobby was aware of his approach, and for a moment their eyes met, the stranger's stare so intent and searching it was almost like a blow. Then he went on his way, with the same apparent deliberation that masked the same swift ease of movement and almost at once was hidden in the falling night. Bobby was left with a memory of two unwinking, staring eyes that seemed both indifferent and uneasy, and to be so because they saw so much so quickly; with a memory, too, of that slow prowl which seemed so like the quiet pacing to and fro of a leopard in captivity.

"I wonder who that was," Bobby murmured, and found, oddly enough, without knowing why, a conviction in his mind that the other had been well aware who he was himself.

On a sudden impulse, Bobby turned to follow. But he had already disappeared. There was not even the sound of a footstep to tell which way he had gone; it might have been merely a vision or a phantom that had passed that way. At a little distance, though, when he walked on, he saw a policeman talking to a girl. The girl went away as he came up. In the policeman he recognized his host, Sergeant Gregson. Gregson seemed to be afraid that this important unknown from London might think he had been gossiping on duty or even flirting. He explained:

"Young lady from London, sir. Miss Lambert. She's staying at the nursing home up there on the cliff. She lost her fur the other night and we got it back for her. She was saying how obliged she was."

"Oh, yes," Bobby said, little interested in any Miss Lambert from any nursing home and her lost fur. "Did you see anyone go by just now?"

"No, sir, no one," answered Gregson, shaking his head. "Only Mr. Mauley Bain. Wool-gathering he looked, same as usual, since his brother's death. Very thick they were and he's never been the same since."

CHAPTER V
TACT

NEXT MORNING, in the small car which had been provided for his use, Bobby went off to pay his visit to Commander Seers. His reception was most correct and as genial as the North Pole.

"I was informed by the Home Office that I was to expect you," said the Commander. "I have asked if I may be also informed of the reason for so unusual a proceeding. I have had no reply; merely an acknowledgement."

"I do most thoroughly understand, Commander," Bobby answered earnestly. "That is why I felt I must hurry over at once to report"; and this word "report," carefully chosen by Bobby, began immediately to fulfil its purpose of oil on stormy waters.

Next Bobby proceeded to hint that all the blame was due to the meddling of politicians, concerning whom he uttered a few words of most severe criticism. This was a second dose of oil on a troubled sea, for the Commander detested politicians whom he classed as "scum" and "scoundrels," though from the category he quite unconsciously excluded all on his own side. These he regarded not as self-seeking politicians, but as self-sacrificing patriots. But he still talked of resignation as the only course open to him and at the demand for a public inquiry, his friends, in spite of his own protests, were saying they would certainly demand when Parliament reassembled; even if they had to move the adjournment of the House to consider the matter. The Commander mentioned several of these friends, all in the V.I.P. category or near it, but Bobby felt pretty sure that he had no intention whatever of resigning if he could possibly help it. He was plainly far too conscious of the difference between a retired Commander on half-pay and a retired Commander who was also the Chief Constable of the county. The impression Bobby gathered was of a capable administrator, a strict disciplinarian, a man whose whole conception of police work was of upholding established law and order and who was very much at a loss when called upon to deal with anything outside ordinary routine. Especially when serious crime was involved, since that was something of which he had no experience. Bobby had also already gathered that the Commander was very well liked by his men, who, as they said, knew where they were with him, were always sure of his full support, and could, moreover, when necessary, bamboozle him to their heart's content. Few chief constables, or deputy chief constables for that matter, reflected Bobby, had such valid claims to the respect and affection of their men.

Seers was apparently well aware of the rumours that there was evidence of Lord Adour's guilt and that it was being suppressed. It was a story, declared Seers, to be treated with the contempt it deserved.

"The plain fact," he said, "is that there does not exist even a shred of evidence to suggest so much as a shadow of suspicion. And absolutely no motive, no conceivable motive. The two had very little to do with each other. Lord Adour is a man of the highest character and position. A sahib," and Bobby realized that this last word represented the highest tribute Commander Seers could pay to any man. "Mr. Itter Bain," the Commander went on, "was an extremely clever engineering chap," and this again was said much as would have been said "a highly efficient buffer" or "a most capable chauffeur." He went on: "They were neighbours, of course, and met occasionally—local affairs and so on. But that was all."

The Commander went on to make it clear that in his view the murder had beyond doubt been committed either by a passing tramp, or, though this was less likely, by a disgruntled workman.

"There is a certain amount of communism in the neighbourhood, I am sorry to say," said the commander sternly. "If I had my way, it would be dealt with. Unfortunately, there has been encouragement. Prescott Bain is Chairman of the Party."

"Oh, indeed," said Bobby. "I saw Mauley Bain last night though not to speak to. A formidable personality, I should say. Brooding apparently. What is Prescott Bain like? He is a cousin of Mauley and the murdered man, isn't he?"

"A little bounder," pronounced the Commander. "I had lunch with him once. One has to do these things. Duty. You could hear him eating soup all over the room."

"Dear, dear," said Bobby, and tried to look suitably distressed. "Did this communist business cause any ill feeling between him and the others?"

"Not that I know of," admitted the Commander, though reluctantly and as if he found the fact hard to believe. "They never seemed much interested. Of course, there's their uncle in the background. An agitator of the worst type. But very likely they want to avoid quarrelling with him. There has been some difference of opinion, I understand, but not over politics. Apparently the concern is in difficulties through the cancelling of war contracts. The other two say Prescott has badly over-spent and over-borrowed from the bank. Prescott says that if so, the reason is that Itter Bain drew such large sums to spend on his new ideas and experiments. Very heated at times they grew, I'm told, blaming each other. I should have felt the strongest suspicion but for the one thing I don't think it is possible to get over."

"What is that?" Bobby asked, not without some faint idea at the back of his mind that he might find a way where the Commander saw none.

"The two of them," explained Seers, "Mauley and Prescott I mean, were both in conference with two of the London and Coastal Bank people the whole of the afternoon of the murder. I've seen the two bank wallahs myself. They are quite clear about it. It's an alibi there's no getting over."

"Seems so," agreed Bobby, though with an inward resolve to test it for himself.

"I repeat that, in my considered view," declared Seers once more and in a tone which suggested that those who differed were guilty of a degree of insubordination not far removed from mutiny, "it is perfectly plain what happened. Lord Adour saw a bird that interested him. He stands his gun against a tree, leaves it there, and hurries back to the house for his camera. I've handled that gun myself. A lovely bit of work. Many men would be willing to give a hundred, cash down, for it—and ask no questions. Very wrong, of course, but one can understand," and indeed the good Commander looked very much as if such a temptation he himself would have found difficult to resist.

"There are public paths through the spinney. There comes along a tramp, or, possibly though less probably, one of the new workmen all this war work has brought here, and very doubtful characters among them, too, I can assure you. We've had some trouble. Very unlike our own people, very decent and respectable, all of them. Well, this tramp, or whoever it is, is coming along one of these public paths and he sees the gun. Plainly visible and plainly forgotten. He recognizes its value, naturally, and is making off with it when Itter Bain, who happens to be there, tries to stop him—and gets shot. In the scuffle perhaps. In a way a kind of accident, not intentional. That is the line I am working on," and quite plainly his voice challenged Bobby to find or suggest one one-half as good. "There is," Seers went on, "the possibility that the murderer was a man with a grievance from the Bain works. Start stuffing working men's heads with all this communist rubbish and very soon they want it put in action, and, if you don't, then you're a tyrant yourself and you've got to be liquidated for the sake of the cause. I'm working on that, too." Bobby had to admit that both of these were theories it would have been wrong to neglect. But so far, nothing whatever to support them. He said:

"Is it known what Itter Bain was doing in the spinney at that time of the afternoon—especially if there was an important conference going on at the works?"

"My information," explained the Commander, "is that Itter left the money side entirely to the others. He expected to be supplied with all he needed for his work. Apparently he was sure that his new patents, or whatever it was he was busy with, would soon put everything all right financially and meanwhile he didn't want to be bothered."

"Rather a lordly attitude," Bobby commented. "It could explain why he wasn't at the conference with the bank people, but hardly why he went for a walk instead. One would have expected him to be busy in his workshop. Or why his walk took him to this spinney where he was murdered—Coldstone Spinney, it's called, isn't it?"

"Well, he seems to have had a habit of going for a walk to think things out when he was in any sort of difficulty," the Commander explained. "Not uncommon. I do it myself. Clears the brain, I find. The fresh air sweeps the cobwebs away."

"I suppose there's that," agreed Bobby. "Was this spinney a favourite walk of his? Is there any reason why he should have gone there rather than anywhere else?"

The Commander was very plainly beginning to grow restive under this persistent questioning. He hesitated a little before replying and then said, though reluctantly:

"Well, I suppose it's possible—we have had cases of youngsters hanging about in a most objectionable way. Trying to get a glimpse of Miss Adour or even in the hope of finding an excuse for speaking to her. Trespassing sometimes even. There has been some sort of suggestion that Itter Bain too—But it's very unlikely. In any case, quite immaterial why he happened to go that way for his walk. It's quiet."

"You don't think, then," Bobby said, "that much importance need be attached to these stories about Itter Bain having been annoying Miss Adour."

"No, no. Nothing in all that," declared the Commander. He paused and seemed to become lost in distant thoughts. His small, sharp eyes took on a far-away look, a little smile twitched at the corners of his mouth, his ruddy, strongly marked features seemed almost to melt together in a kind of suffused glow. He took on an almost ludicrous resemblance to a dog pleading for another lump of sugar, but knowing well it is much more likely to be ordered out of the room. The faintest sigh became audible before he went on: "Of course, Miss Adour does sometimes have a little trouble with the sort of unlicked cub who can't keep his head when he meets a pretty girl." The Commander was looking very severe now. One felt that in imagination he was handcuffing that unlicked cub and packing him off to gaol till he knew better. He continued: "Miss Adour is quite capable of looking after herself. A thoroughly nice girl. Very different from the girls of to-day; simple, unspoiled, doesn't even know her own good looks. More like the girls of my mother's time than the trousered, smoking, drinking hoydens you meet to-day."

Bobby didn't ask how the Commander knew what girls were like in his mother's time. He said instead he wished it had been possible to fix the hour of death more closely. The Commander repeated that the doctors refused to commit themselves. The body had not been found till the next day, and unfortunately there had been during the night heavy rain with a sudden fall in temperature and then strong sunshine in the morning. None of the doctors could be persuaded to go beyond what Bobby had already noted in the medical reports—that death must have occurred between two and five in the afternoon. Various people had heard various shots. But none had paid much attention, since the sound of shooting is not rare in country districts at any time. Or it might have been the military, since there were still soldiers in the vicinity. No one could be very definite about the time and there was nothing to identify any of these shots with the one fired by the murderer. The Commander mentioned that he himself, during a long motor drive he had made on the afternoon of the murder, had heard shots at intervals, but could not remember exactly when or where. And heavy rain, coupled with much excited coming and going after the discovery of the body, had destroyed any chance of finding significant footsteps or indeed any other clue of any value. A bleak prospect it offered, Bobby thought, this cold trail already so much confused.

Admittedly both Lord Adour and Helen had been in Coldstone Spinney that afternoon. So had other people. All had been impartially questioned. Some must have passed close to the body without perceiving it. Two of the paths crossing the spinney were not much frequented by the public in general. Of these one was between Kindles, Lord Adour's residence, and the main Drinks and Toad-in-Hole road, and one, crossing the first path, led to River Farm, owned and worked by Wing Commander Martin Winstanley, recently discharged with wounds that still left him limping. His discharge had also been in part a result of the effort to increase food production, as since the death of Martin's father a year or two previously, the farm had suffered from the lack of a master's eye. As an old and rude and still true proverb says: "Best of dung is the master's eye." Apparently, indeed, Winstanley had been warned that unless he returned to give personal supervision and see that production was increased, he might find someone else installed in his place.

All this the Commander explained, adding that after a most promising start, the Wing Commander had seemed to lose drive and interest. The Area Agricultural Committee was said to be taking a serious view. Recently the death of two valuable pedigree Holstein cows who could, it was believed, have been saved had more care been shown, had threatened to bring on a crisis.

"A serious loss, those two cows," the Commander commented. "Milk seems to be priority number one just now. The Agricultural Committee is very peeved about it. They used pressure to get Winstanley back on the farm and they feel he's letting them down."

Bobby asked what Winstanley was like. The Commander answered gravely that Winstanley was a very decent sort, very decent sort indeed. But not quite out of the top drawer. Definitely, not out of the top drawer. In the Commander's opinion, it had been a piece of unwarrantable impudence for Winstanley even to think of himself in connection with Miss Adour.

"Oh, he is a victim, too?" Bobby asked.

Seers had the air of regarding this as a rather too frivolous way of putting it. Not that Miss Adour had taken it at all seriously. As was her wont, she had merely smiled and passed undisturbed upon her way. Lord Adour had, however, felt obliged to drop a gentle hint to Winstanley that any thought of marriage was hopelessly impossible. Not that this meant that Winstanley had been annoying Miss Helen in any way. It had merely been necessary to suppress him gently and show him how fantastic were any hopes he might have permitted himself to entertain. In this connection, the Commander repeated with even more emphasis than before that Lord Adour took great care of his daughter, and would certainly not hesitate to give a good dressing down, or even a sound thrashing on occasion, to anyone who attempted to annoy her. But he wouldn't have shot such a person. Inconceivable. Inconceivable, for that matter, that anyone would dare to annoy Miss Helen. Anyone at all, drunk or sober. Bobby asked why it was so inconceivable, and was answered by a blank stare, a shrug of the shoulders, and a fresh assurance that no one would ever try. With that Bobby had to be content.

Seers had by this time talked himself into a fairly good humour and had been, moreover, much placated, and his injured feelings soothed, by the respectful interest with which Bobby had listened to him and by the obvious importance Bobby seemed to show to everything said. So now, as it was getting near lunchtime, Bobby received an invitation to stay to that meal. He accepted with just the right air of being both grateful and flattered, and Seers began to think that, though this Yard fellow was a nuisance, after all it wasn't his fault. He had to go where the Home Office sent him. Anyhow, Seers reflected smugly, he hadn't asked for help, and he would take good care not one penny went from the local police rate to pay Mr. Bobby Owen's expenses. The Home Office had sent him and the Home Office could pay.

"By the way," he added, "Collier is here, one of the Public Prosecutor back-room boys. Do you know him?" and Bobby said he did, and would be very glad to have the pleasure of meeting him again, and the Commander looked very much as if he had found that pleasure one of a somewhat doubtful savour.

CHAPTER VI
WAYLING REAPPEARS

MR. COLLIER GREETED Bobby as an old friend, and Bobby greeted Mr. Collier with that wary and suspicious deference any police officer shows towards any official of the Public Prosecutor's department, rather like that shown by a worker in any of the arts to a critic.

Lunch itself proved an excellent meal, with fish that had that morning been swimming in the sea, and wine the Commander produced with a shy and proud smile. It was Australian. The Commander had begun to drink it in a spirit of grim and devoted patriotism, and for once, surprisingly in this imperfect world, grim and devoted patriotism had been fully rewarded. Now the Commander was finding himself suspected, most unjustly, of having large investments in the Australian wine trade.

"Old Spikes was here to dinner the other day," he told his two guests, the reference being to a well-known admiral. "He fancies himself no end as a judge of wine—on his club's wine committee and all that. I gave him a glass of this and asked him to name it. He said it was a Chateau, but he couldn't name it. New to him, he said, but as good as any. He wouldn't believe it was Australian till I showed him the bottle. And I'm not sure even now he isn't half inclined to believe there's a catch in it somewhere," and the memory of this mild triumph so pleased the Commander that he almost forgot his grievances and almost smiled on Bobby, but less so on Mr. Collier.

Of this more favourable atmosphere Bobby took full advantage. The skill with which he accepted the Commander's ideas, turned them upside down and inside out, and then returned them to the Commander as his own indubitable offspring was much appreciated by Mr. Collier. Afterwards, though, he modified his approval by remarking to Bobby that his procedure had been a trifle crude and could only have succeeded so well with a born sucker like Commander Seers. To which Bobby retorted that we are all of us born suckers on one side at least, and probably more. Mr. Collier had no reply to make.

In this favourable lunchtime atmosphere Bobby took an opportunity to mention the kingfisher incident which hitherto he had avoided for fear of exciting still further the Commander's prejudices and so perhaps putting Lord Adour still further on his guard—if indeed there was any justification for the vague suspicions that seemed current. Casually, Bobby asked if the kingfisher had been seen by others and was it such an extremely rare bird? Professing— quite truly—great ornithological ignorance, he said he had always supposed the kingfisher was fairly common. The Commander explained that there had been complaints that the recent industrial activity in the district, and some consequent pollution of the river, had driven away a pair that had become before the war almost a kind of communal pet. Sometime previously a claim had been made that they had returned. This had been denied, and so Lord Adour, seeing the bird, had wished to obtain a snap as conclusive evidence.

Unfortunately, the bird flew off before the snap could be obtained. Very casually, Bobby elicited the information that no one else had seen the bird either that day or subsequently. It appeared also that Miss Adour had been equally interested at the reappearance of the kingfisher, but she had been too late to catch a glimpse of it. Probably the bird had been disturbed when Lord Adour deposited his gun against a nearby tree and hurried off to get his camera.

Later on, when Bobby and Mr. Collier had taken their leave and were driving off together, Mr. Collier asked why Bobby seemed so interested in the kingfisher incident and Bobby said he didn't know exactly. All incidents connected with an obscure and difficult crime were interesting, and Mr. Collier grinned and said, of course, Bobby was fully entitled to keep his thoughts to himself. So Bobby said sadly that so far he had no thoughts either to keep to himself or to give away. What did Mr. Collier himself think of it all?

"Not my job to think about it," Collier answered promptly. "We aren't an investigating body. All we do is to lick into shape the stuff you give us."

"I know," said Bobby bitterly, remembering how often his reports had come back to him spattered all over with such red ink comments as: "This is irrelevant,"

"Such statements are wholly inadmissible,"

"Requires further confirmation,"

"Not evidence as it stands," and so on and so on.

Mr. Collier grinned again. He knew exactly what Bobby was thinking. He said:

"Notice how Seers went all goo-goo whenever that Adour girl's name was mentioned. I thought he was going to cry."

"Have you met her?" Bobby asked.

"Not me," said Collier; "and don't mean to if I can help it. Safety first is my motto. I'm a married man."

In a more serious vein he went on to say that his boss, pally with all the big legal noises in the new Government, had been told there was real anxiety in high political circles over possible Bain case developments. Behind the scene activities—and how formidable and even disastrous these can be—were going on with the aim of forcing the hand of the new Government and obliging it to adopt measures for which, in its view, the country was not yet ready, which indeed might have very unpleasant consequences at the next election. Jack Cade Junior's writings were extremely influential. He had an extraordinary knack of putting forward the most extreme ideas in the most mild and even deprecatory language imaginable. If he and the group working with him, with the further assistance of the indignant and resentful *Seashire Herald*, managed to get it widely believed that "hidden forces," now exposed by their efforts, had been at work to influence the police and protect a man of high social and financial standing, then their position would be greatly strengthened.

"Of course," Collier added, "so far as Sammy Robinson alias Jack Cade Junior is concerned, there's a certain amount of family feeling involved. He was on quite friendly terms with his nephews. His nearest relatives. He has no children."

"Going to make things difficult," Bobby remarked. "I believe he's got a man working for him he's managed to get pushed on the *Seashire Herald* staff."

"Oh, he's out for blood all right," Collier agreed. "The ultimate aim is to get the police nationalized, so to speak. Under complete central control, that is. None of your troublesome local independence. One government, one police. It could easily be taken as the first step towards a political police."

"Good God," exclaimed Bobby, whose hair was nearly standing on end at the mere thought of such an unholy mingling of police and politics, abhorrent to gods and men alike.

"Oh, it's on the cards," Collier assured him. "Of course, in these days anything is on the cards. Luckily, most of it stops there. The new Government," he went on, speaking without sympathy, "is up to its eyes and over in trouble. I won't say they'll be grateful, because, of course, governments know nothing about gratitude. It's something quite outside their scheme of things. But if you can handle the job O.K., they may remember you next time they're in a hole and want someone to pull 'em out again. Mind you, they don't care a twopenny damn whether Adour is guilty or not. Purely a side issue. What is important is that there shan't even be rumours that Adour's political or social position or his money have given him any protection whatever."

"I see," said Bobby, reflecting ruefully that the very last thing he had ever expected was to be mixed up in what seemed very much like a backstairs political intrigue. "You don't think," he asked, "that Seers would willingly protect anyone he thought might possibly be guilty?"

"I'm perfectly sure he wouldn't," Collier answered. "He has far too strong a sense of duty. Can you imagine a devout Roman Catholic suspecting the Pope of heresy? As soon imagine Seers suspecting a peer of the realm of crime, especially a peer with a pedigree going back to Saxon times, even if the College of Heralds does rather look at it down its collective nose. Seers doesn't even know he is the Toriest Tory in the country. He just considers himself a sensible, reasonable chap thinking naturally in the same way as all other sensible, reasonable chaps."

They parted then, Collier going on his way and Bobby driving only a short distance before parking his car by the side of the road, near Coldstone Spinney, though this was really more a fair-sized wood of elm and beech than what is usually understood by "spinney." It had been originally planted by Lord Adour's grandfather to give protection to the house from the sea breezes that came in just here through a gap in the high cliffs that in a general way afforded shelter to this low-lying land near the banks of the small Adour River. Leaving his car there, Bobby entered the wood and visited first the scene of the crime, where a roped-off space still indicated the spot where the body had been found. There he looked about for a little, though he discovered nothing of any interest. He decided that later on he would return and make another and more careful examination. Then he walked on towards River Farm. At a turn of the path he met Wayling, slouching along in a more dispirited and aimless way than was usual with him, generally avid in pursuit of either a loan, a drink, or a woman.

"Hullo. Is that you?" Bobby exclaimed. "What are you up to now?" he asked suspiciously.

"What do you mean? Up to what?" Wayling asked, looking offended. "Well, was I right or wasn't I?"

"You were well-informed, anyhow," Bobby agreed. "See here, Wayling, are you mixed up in this business in any way?"

"Of course not," Wayling answered indignantly. "Damn it all, Owen, can't you ever stop being a policeman, not even when you meet an old pal?"

"Not when I'm dealing with a murder case and meet the old pal near where it happened," Bobby retorted. "What about that five pounds, by the way?"

No man since the world began has ever looked more bewildered than did Alexander Wayling at this question. He stood and stared and searched his mind and memory. Apparently in vain.

"What five pounds?" he asked finally.

"The five pounds you pinched when you called at my place," Bobby told him.

"Oh, that," exclaimed Wayling, suddenly enlightened. "Was it five pounds? Surely not. I don't know how it happened ... just one of those things. I say," he added earnestly, "I do hope Mrs. Owen wasn't inconvenienced?"

"I've a jolly good mind," Bobby exclaimed angrily, for now he was really annoyed, "to give you the thrashing you deserve."

"Now, now," protested Wayling, like one speaking to a fractious child, "you can't do that, you know. Deputy Chief Constables, prospective Deputy Assistant Commissioners, can't do that sort of thing. Couldn't possibly afford a summons for assault. I'll send you a cheque to-night."

"The same sort you gave Templemore?" Bobby inquired.

"Did you hear about that?" asked Wayling in return, his expressive voice vibrant with indignation. "I do think Templemore behaved extraordinarily badly. I asked him to wait twenty-four hours till I had paid in the funds to meet it with. What did he do? Instead of waiting, he rushed the thing through and it was sent back. Quite inexcusable on the bank's part, but you know what pedantic, red-tape places banks are. I've been advised to sue Templemore for damages for harm done to my reputation. My solicitor tells me I should have an excellent case."

Bobby gasped and gave it up. He felt the incredible Wayling was too much for him.

"What are you doing down here, anyway?" he demanded.

"Having a day or two's holiday by the sea. Jolly little place, Toad-in-Hole. I don't mind telling you there's a spot of business in it, too. It's dead as a port, of course. Stone dead. But some big people in the City I'm in touch with are considering developing it as a really high-class seaside resort. No trippers, you know. For the best people only.

I don't know if it'll go through. I'm not bothering much. A holiday with me first of all. Business is just a side issue. After all, after six years of pretty strenuous war work, one does need a bit of a rest."

"War work?" repeated Bobby. "You? What war work?"

"Oh, very hush-hush," Wayling answered, and this time his voice sank to a thrilling whisper. "The story can't be told even yet."

"Come off it," retorted Bobby rudely. "All you've had to do with war work is to dodge it. Do you know anything about the people round here? If you do, I may forget about that five pounds."

"You may forget it," Wayling said with dignity. "I shall not. I always make a note in a book I keep for the purpose. I'm afraid there's no information I can give you. I'm only a visitor here. How could I get to know anything?"

"From the barmaids in all the pubs in the place," Bobby told him. "Barmaids know it all and you are on kissing terms with them all before you've been in a town half a day. Do you know anything about Wing Commander Winstanley? Is that where you've been, to River Farm?"

"Oh, you're on him, are you?" Wayling asked. "How did you hear? Been cultivating barmaids, too? What would Mrs. Owen say?"

"Don't play the fool," snapped Bobby. "You had better remember this is a serious matter and I'll stand no nonsense. Now then, out with it."

"It's nothing much," Wayling answered, sulky and a little frightened; for Bobby's voice had had an edge to it, and this was unfamiliar ground. Wayling knew all the answers, when it was a woman, a drink, or a loan. But serious crime was different. Of that he had no desire to be suspected, and Bobby's voice and manner had all at once taken on a new tone and aspect, grim and formidable. Wayling said: "I did hear at the 'Fisherman's Arms' that Itter Bain and Winstanley had had a bit of a turn-up. Winstanley got the worst of it. Knocked out. Both the Bains—Itter and Mauley—are, were, real toughs. Mauley settled one dispute at the works by offering to fight the men's leader, a shop steward. Bare knuckles. The shop steward fancied himself no end and took it on. He got a bad licking in ten rounds. Mauley was so pleased with himself he gave the men what they wanted, and there's been no more trouble."

"Mr. Mauley Bain sounds interesting," Bobby remarked and remembered the warning Haile had given him. "I shall have to try to get a talk with him. Does he seem to take his brother's death hard?"

"He's drinking a bit—sulky drinking, if you know what I mean. A thing I hate," declared Wayling. "Wrong. Mischievous. He uses the 'Good Haul' generally. That's the newest pub. The 'Fisherman's Arms' is the old one, but the beer's the same in both. Equally bad."

"Barmaids equally kissable?" Bobby asked.

"If a girl isn't kissable," said Mr. Wayling slowly and thoughtfully, "well, what is she?"

Bobby attempted no answer to this profound and searching question. Instead, he said:

"Do you know what Winstanley and Itter Bain quarrelled about? Was it over Helen Adour? Have you met her, by the way?"

Wayling did not answer directly, but his whole expression slowly changed. It was a cloudy, heavy day, but for a moment Bobby thought it must be some stray beam of sunshine that had so illumined his companion's twisted, ill-proportioned features. That rich, deep voice of Wayling's sank almost to a whisper, yet a whisper vibrant with emotion as he said, as if intoning a prayer:

"Once or twice. Once I walked up from the village with her. When you're with her, when you've been with her, it's all different, the world, everything. It's like sunshine and fine music all around and you hardly know the earth's there you're walking on."

"Good Lord," said Bobby helplessly, and Wayling seemed suddenly to be recalled to himself.

"If you laugh, I'll kill you," he snarled, and hurried away.

CHAPTER VII
RIVER FARM

"Miss Adour must be a remarkable young woman," Bobby mused as he watched Wayling's disappearing figure till the trees hid him from sight. "I'll have to try to get a look at her myself as soon as I can."

The footpath he had been following ended now abruptly at a gate, on it a notice:

"PRIVATE. TO RIVER FARM ONLY."

As River Farm was his destination, Bobby opened the gate and entered the field to which it admitted. A number of sleek-looking black-and-white cows were grazing there; the Holsteins, he supposed, over the handling of which there was, he gathered, some dissatisfaction in agricultural control circles. Bobby stopped to look at them admiringly. An elderly man was coming towards him, apparently, from his dress, a farm worker of a superior type, a foreman or bailiff probably. He wore no welcoming smile. It was in a distinctly sulky and resentful tone that he said:

"We was expecting you. We heard you was snooping around."

"If I am," retorted Bobby, "it would do you no harm to be civil." To this remark, he added one of his most intimidating frowns. Then he said sharply: "Where is Mr. Winstanley? I wish to see him."

"Wing Commander Winstanley," answered the other with more than a little emphasis on the title, "is up at the house. He's expecting you. He can't get around like he used to with that game leg of his; and if it wasn't for the R.A.F. and the likes of him, where would be the likes of us?"

"That's quite true," agreed Bobby more gently; for this was clearly a loyal servitor, and a loyal servitor generally means a good master.

"Them's the cows," said the man, nodding towards them.

"Oh, yes," agreed Bobby, slightly puzzled by this abrupt change of subject. "Look very nice, too. This path takes me to the house, doesn't it?"

"That's right," said the other. "Man and boy I've worked on this farm fifty year come Michaelmas, and head foreman now, and I'll say this any day to any man. The young master's got an eye for the land as good as what his dad had, and his dad's was better than most anyone I ever heard tell of." Then he said: "But young's young all the world over, master or man, and when a young woman the likes of her passes by, isn't it nature as a young man'll stand and stare and forget ought else?"

"No doubt," Bobby agreed. "What do you mean? Is it Miss Helen Adour?"

"It isn't to be wondered at," the foreman went on. "I'm not saying myself, and me a grandfather, as when she passes by it isn't as it is when the moon and the stars come out on a night that's been all darkness and cloud."

"Why are you telling me this?" Bobby asked.

"So as you may understand, if so be you want to," came the slow reply. "The Wing Commander, he has the feel of the land in his bones, same as with only a few. Leave him be, till the fever that young woman has put in him has gone again, and there'll be no more need for the likes of you." The speaker turned away and then turned back again. He said: "There was some of the lads as talked of putting you in the horse pond. I told 'em it was a bit of all right itself but they wasn't to go for to do it, along of breeding more trouble, and them as tried would get the sack."

"They would get a bit more as well," Bobby said grimly. "I don't advise them to try that game."

"Says you," retorted the other with an unexpected lapse into film language, imperfectly understood, and walked briskly away.

A good deal puzzled, slightly amused, wondering why his attention had been drawn so abruptly to the cows, Bobby walked on. He was becoming quite eager to meet a young woman whom he was beginning to think of as ever more remarkable. She could apparently, simply by passing by, charm poetry from an elderly agricultural worker; turn a young farmer's head; make a tough old Chief Constable go "goo-goo", as Mr. Collier had said; and, most remarkable feat of all, produce a show of sincerity of feeling in Alexander Wayling. Soon the farmhouse came into view, a long, low white building with what farmhouses often lack, a well-kept, carefully tended lawn and flower garden in front. It was, as Bobby learnt later, the creation of the Wing Commander's mother, and had been kept up, both by her husband and by her son, in her memory. When he knocked the door was opened by an elderly woman, apparently a housekeeper, whose probably in general, pleasant, rosy features were now wearing what Bobby felt was an unfamiliar scowl. Bobby found himself forced to the conclusion that at River Farm he was not popular, and he did not feel it was a good sign. When the visit of a police officer is so plainly unwelcome, there is often a good reason. The woman told him, looking the while sternly over his head as if she found the sight of him too unpleasant to bear, that the Wing Commander would join him immediately, and therewith showed him into a room Bobby guessed must be the farm office.

There was about it a business-like and efficient air. A typewriter, a card-index cabinet, files, a safe, all the usual appurtenances of an up-to-date office were in evidence. There was a small private telephone exchange, connecting up apparently with the various farm buildings. A bookcase contained a number of agricultural works and there were neatly arranged piles of farming journals. With these last was a smaller card index, which Bobby guessed referred to specially interesting or important articles. Nothing much of a personal nature. Severely business-like. Not, Bobby reflected, typical of a young man liable to be swept out of his depth by the passing of any young woman, however attractive. The door opened. A young man came in, and stood silent, looking at Bobby with no more welcoming an air than had been shown by his foreman or his housekeeper. A handsome lad, Bobby thought, but with a strained, uneasy look in eyes that had so plainly been once fearless and steady, but now flickered restlessly hither and thither, on constant guard against the unexpected. There was an occasional twitching at the corners of his mouth, too, that Bobby did not much like. The young man came further into the room. He was limping badly. He said abruptly and not too pleasantly:

"I've been expecting you. Have a cigarette?"

He offered his case and when Bobby thanked him but declined, lighted one himself, his hands not too steady. Bobby was watching him closely. Why was it, he wondered, that all these people were expecting him? Was it because they knew something they felt was certain to be a subject for inquiry? Winstanley said as abruptly as before:

"The cows are in the spinney field."

"Cows?" repeated Bobby. But now he was beginning to understand. "Cows? But—"

"Yes, cows," snapped Winstanley, interrupting. "C for Charley, O for oxen, W—"

Bobby interrupted in his turn.

"You said you were expecting me?" he said. "Why?"

"Because of your 'phone call, of course," Winstanley retorted. "What else?" Then there began to dawn on him what Bobby had already guessed. He said: "You are the Area Committee bloke, aren't you? About the Holsteins? As if a loss like that wasn't bad enough itself without being worried into the bargain. They seem to think I did it on purpose."

"I've come about something more serious than cows," Bobby explained. "I've been sent by the Home Office to make further inquiries about the recent murder of Itter Bain. There seem to be complications beyond this area that will have to be followed up in other districts. I have to try to co-ordinate them. In this neighbourhood, of course, the investigation remains in the very capable hands of Commander Seers."

"Capable my foot," retorted the Wing Commander. "Seers is an old duffer. All he thinks about is 'Eyes right, spit and polish.' Have a cigarette?" Bobby again begged to be excused, and Winstanley, who had put down the cigarette he had just lighted and then apparently forgotten it, started another. "I've had one of your lot here already," he said. "What's the idea of somebody else coming? I've told all I know. It isn't much."

"What do you mean, another of my lot?" Bobby demanded sharply. "Do you mean another police officer has been to see you? Did he give you his name, show any authority?"

"Why? Was he a fake?" asked Winstanley. "A biggish chap, about your size. I think he said his name was Haile, something like that."

"Did he claim to be a police officer?" Bobby asked, and looked grim, for to make such an unauthorized claim is a serious offence.

"I don't know if he actually said so," Winstanley replied, a little doubtfully. "I'm not sure. I took it he was one. He said he was looking into Itter Bain's murder. That's a police job, isn't it? He talked a lot."

Bobby decided that probably Haile had managed to convey the impression that he was acting in some sort of official capacity without in so many words claiming to be an officer of police. He had been careful, most likely, to avoid any risk of prosecution. All the same, Mr. Haile would get a stiff warning next time Bobby met him. A swift worker, Bobby thought, and was not too pleased. Haile might prove an embarrassing factor. The Wing Commander was speaking again. He said:

"I knew the chap's face. I had seen him before knocking about here. I thought he must be one of your plain-clothes cops." Then he said resentfully: "I don't see why you blokes come worrying me."

"Haile has nothing to do with us," Bobby said. "I'll speak to him about it if I come across him." He paused. Haile had said nothing about having ever visited this district or knowing any of its inhabitants. Why not? He would have to be questioned on that point, too. Bobby continued: "I have called because there is information that you and the dead man quarrelled and had a fight."

"Heard about that, have you?" Winstanley grumbled. "What about it?"

"What was the quarrel about?" Bobby asked.

"Oh, I don't know," Winstanley answered vaguely. "One thing led to another. That's all."

"Hardly all, is it?" Bobby asked. "Couldn't you remember a little more clearly?"

"It wasn't anything really," Winstanley insisted. "Itter had had a drink or two, I think. I expect I was in a bad temper. About those blasted cows and the Area Committee worrying. I think we got on to Channel tides. Itter Bain had gone in for yachting lately. He bought Lord Adour's motor launch. A lovely little boat. It must have cost him something. You get interested in tides when you are flying to France. Makes a difference if you go in the drink. Have a cigarette? Oh, I asked you that before. Sorry."

He had been starting to help himself to yet a third, but now realized that he already had one between his lips and looked confused. Bobby was fairly certain Winstanley was not being entirely frank. The quarrel had been about something very different from tides—an impersonal subject.

"It was in Toad-in-Hole, wasn't it?" Bobby asked. "Had you gone there to meet Bain?"

"Good lord, no. Why should I?" Winstanley said, surprised. "Quite accidental. He was coming out of the 'Good Haul,' I think it was, as I was passing."

"You'll excuse my being personal," Bobby said. "I'm told both Itter Bain and his brother are first-class amateur boxers. Wasn't it a little rash to take him on when it's quite plain that your leg is still troubling you?"

"Oh, well, I dare say it was," Winstanley admitted, grinning a trifle ruefully. "I suppose I thought that if I was half a cripple he was more than half drunk and that evened things up. It didn't." He grinned again, even more ruefully. "I didn't last too long," he said.

"Not surprising," Bobby commented. "Being half crippled can't be much of a help to your foot work. I suppose you wouldn't care to tell me the truth, would you?"

"What the hell do you mean?" demanded Winstanley very angrily indeed.

"Just that," Bobby answered. "Wasn't your quarrel about Miss Helen Adour?"

"No, it wasn't. How do you know? It wasn't, anyway. You've no right to say that. Leave her name out of it, can't you?"

"No, not if her name's in it already," Bobby answered.

"Well, it isn't," Winstanley snapped. "How did you know?"

"My dear Wing Commander," Bobby protested, "is it difficult to guess that when two young men start fighting, the reason is more likely to be a pretty girl than Channel tides?"

"I suppose that's damn clever," Winstanley muttered. Then he said: "She isn't a pretty girl, I wish she was."

Bobby did not ask for an explanation of this cryptic remark. Instead he said:

"Miss Adour was here on the afternoon of the murder, wasn't she?"

"Yes. She wanted some more eggs. For cooking. She's a dab at cooking. She likes new laid eggs for it. Cooking and sewing, she's a double ace at 'em both."

"Oh, yes," Bobby said, interested, for these were the first definite traits he had learned concerning her, who hitherto had appeared merely as a disturbing influence, passing by. "Did she get her eggs?" he asked.

"Well, I had to tell her I couldn't give her any more. She had had a good many already and I was short. I had been short before. I expect the Area Committee blokes have got that marked up against me, too."

"What did Miss Adour say to that?"

"Nothing. She never does. She went to the packing shed and took what she wanted. Rather more, if anything."

"What did you do?"

"Nothing. What do you expect? I couldn't knock her down and take them back by force, could I? I told her she mustn't. She didn't take any notice. She never does. She just went home again."

"I see," Bobby said. "Did you go with her?"

"I walked through the spinney with her," the Wing Commander admitted. "You do get some rough characters hanging about sometimes. Men brought down to work at the new docks and wharves. Or at the Bain works. There've been complaints. I understood those were the lines you police blokes were working on. I thought I had better walk with her part of the way."

"Carrying her eggs for her?"

The Wing Commander first scowled and then grinned.

"So would you," he said.

Bobby grinned, too, but all the same was very conscious that this meant that Winstanley had been in the spinney about the time of the murder. Suppose the two young men had resumed their quarrel, re-kindled and inflamed by the opportunity and privilege Winstanley had enjoyed of acting as escort. What more likely? Suppose Winstanley had seen Lord Adour's gun left leaning against one of the trees and had used it to revenge himself for the thrashing he had apparently received on an earlier occasion. Or to save himself from the humiliation of another thrashing, if Itter had threatened it—an Itter stung to fresh jealousy by the sight of his rival again in Miss Adour's company?

Bobby asked a few more questions. He learned nothing fresh. He tried to get the exact time of this passage through the spinney but without success. No one ever knows the exact time of any event whatever, and if they do there is always someone else to contradict them flatly. Winstanley had seen no one, either going or coming. Bobby got the impression that nothing much under the size of an elephant would have impinged upon a consciousness entirely absorbed with Miss Adour's mere presence and proximity; equally entirely absorbed, when returning, in that entrancing memory. Certainly, declared Winstanley, he had no recollection of hearing any shot. Probably he wouldn't have noticed it if he had heard. One often hears shots in the country.

Bobby gave it up then and departed in a somewhat troubled mood. He made his way back through the spinney to where he had left his car and then decided that his next call had better be at the Bain works, where perhaps he might, he thought, be able to learn something from Mauley Bain of the rivalry between his brother and the Wing Commander.

CHAPTER VIII

BAIN PRODUCTS, LTD.

THE SMALL TOWN of Drinks was distant from its port of Toad-in-Hole about eight miles by the high road. The distance was less by the river or by the path along the river bank. During the war, following the establishment and growth of Bain Products, Ltd., the population of Drinks had more than doubled, with the usual pressure on accommodation. Now the number of inhabitants was beginning to shrink again, but it was still a busy, prosperous little place, though contemplating with some unease the grim prospect before it now that peace had broken out so suddenly.

Bobby had no need to ask his way to the Bain factory. The buildings were conspicuous on the outskirts of the town. Alighting from his car at the factory entrance, he asked for Mr. Mauley Bain. He was directed to the offices, standing apart from the main workshops and bearing a large sign, "Administration." Making his way thither, Bobby had to pass under a window, through which came to him the sound of voices raised loud in dispute. No words could be distinguished, but the tone was unmistakable. The voices ceased on the sound of a door banged with violence; and Bobby, who had walked on a little, saw through another window how, in a large outer office where clerks were at work, pens and typewriters paused, heads were raised, smiles were exchanged, looks were directed towards a door marked "Private," as though through it the neighbouring storm might presently burst. A row between the bosses, Bobby decided; and the staff in part amused, in part afraid, lest any of the storm should come their way. Bobby had the feeling, too, that sounds of such angry disputes were no great novelty. The outer door marked "Administration" was flung back and there emerged a flushed, angry-looking, youngish man, of middle height, whose plump, evidently well-nourished body made a contrast to a lean and hungry-looking face with a small red mouth and above it a hooked and disproportionately large nose. Certainly not Mauley Bain, and yet with somehow, somewhere, about him an odd resemblance to the prowling, predatory figure Bobby remembered going so menacingly by in the dusk of the oncoming evening. Something in the way the rather small head was set upon the shoulders perhaps, or possibly in the way in which the big nose seemed to thrust itself so aggressively forward. Bobby took a chance, and, when the other gave him a frowning, questioning glance, as much as to ask him who the Dickens he was, and what the mischief was he doing there, he said:

"Mr. Prescott Bain, isn't it?"

The other nodded and tried to look more amiable, though without much success. Bobby had the impression that he was holding himself in check in case the visitor should prove to have come on some possibly profitable business errand. If not, probably wrath would relieve itself in a vigorous and emphatic outpouring. As formidable in his way, this Prescott Bain, but not in the way of violence, probably, as that slow-pacing angry figure Bobby remembered so well. Prescott said:

"Yes. Well? Do you want to see me?"

"I am from the Home Office," Bobby explained. "This is my letter of authority. I have been sent to try to co-ordinate the inquiry here into the death of Mr. Itter Bain with other inquiries elsewhere, with which it may turn out to be connected."

"What other inquiries? In what way?" Prescott asked doubtfully, "I don't understand that."

"I am afraid I can't go into details," Bobby answered. "At present they must remain confidential. Indeed, it may turn out that there's no such connection at all. Hereabouts, of course, very good progress is being made under the very efficient, capable direction of Commander Seers."

"Oh, is it? That's news," snapped Prescott, apparently rather glad of the chance to let off a little steam. "If you ask me, Seers is an incompetent stuck-up old ass who hasn't an idea what to do and wouldn't want to do it if he had."

"Oh, why not?" Bobby asked.

"Better ask him," Prescott retorted. Then he said angrily: "Sahibs stick together." After another pause, he said: "Everyone knows who killed Itter."

"Do you?"

"Yes, and I'm not saying—libel, slander, or something."

"No," said Bobby. "Privileged. Anything said to a police officer in the course of a criminal investigation is privileged. And to hold back anything that is known is a very serious offence. I'm sure you don't wish that. I'm sure I can rely on you for every help you can give us. The least thing you know or suspect ... ?"

"I don't know anything beyond what's common knowledge," Prescott retorted. "Even that old muddled-headed ass of a Commander knows it. Itter has a row with someone and that someone goes out for an afternoon stroll, taking a loaded gun with him. Itter is found dead and the gun can't be found. It was last seen, according to the story, leaning against an oak where it had been put because there was a bird to be photographed. Circumstantial evidence and you can draw your own conclusions. So can I. Seers says there aren't any. You don't catch Seers running in one of his pals if he can help it. Sahibs stick together."

"Circumstantial evidence is always strong," Bobby agreed. "Facts can't lie, but they can easily be misinterpreted. It's always very dangerous to say, 'The facts show it must be so,' because some other entirely overlooked fact may show up everything quite differently. There is satisfactory proof that Lord Adour came running back to the house for his camera, which doesn't seem the conduct of a man who has either just committed a murder or is meaning to commit one. At any rate, a jury wouldn't be likely to think so."

"You mean a jury wouldn't be likely to think a peer of the realm could commit a murder," Prescott sneered.

"I don't much think a jury would require stronger evidence against a peer than against anyone else," Bobby said. "Anyhow, that's not the business of the police. All I have to do, all Commander Seers has to do, is to make sure that the evidence is strong enough to justify a charge. That ends our responsibility. You said something about your cousin having had a row with Lord Adour, whose name, by the way, you never mentioned."

"I know better," Prescott interrupted bitterly. "You have to be careful how you talk about your betters."

"Miss Adour's name has been mentioned," Bobby went on, ignoring this. "I've had hints that Mr. Itter Bain had been paying her attentions that weren't much appreciated."

"Oh, yes, that's so," Prescott agreed. "He wasn't good enough for Papa. Told so plainly. We aren't in the sahib class. Papa rather than the girl. I don't know what she thinks. You never do. She's pretty enough to turn anyone's head. She turned Itter's all right. Not mine. I've more sense, but then, of course, I'm not a thruster like Itter and

Mauley. What they want, they think they've a natural born right to. So they go and get it. Or try."

Bobby could not help wondering if Prescott had kept his head quite so thoroughly as he protested was the case. Was it once again "Methinks he doth protest too much"? Bobby said:

"Is Lord Adour generally popular, do you think? I'm told there's a fairly strong Communist Party here."

"Oh, yes, strong and growing," Prescott agreed. "I'm a member. They've made me Chairman. Why not? Look at Russia. Put sahibs where they belong, and pay a manager at the rate of eighty times a worker's basic rate. That's good enough for me. I don't draw eighty times what we pay our odd-job men. I wish I did."

Was this another instance of Helen Adour's all-pervading influence? Bobby wondered. Was it a sense of a social gulf between them, and a perhaps sub-conscious desire to abolish it, that had made Prescott turn communist? Odd, Bobby thought, if another of this young woman's remarkable feats had been to turn an ordinary business man into a communist. He left the subject then and asked instead:

"Did Mr. Mauley Bain keep his head, too, or was he another of the lady's conquests?"

"Better ask him. I don't know," Prescott answered, scowling. "He keeps most things, anyway. I can't say about his head."

"Do you think," Bobby asked next, "that the disagreement or row or whatever it was between Itter Bain and Lord Adour went deep? I hear Itter had just bought a motor launch from Lord Adour. So they were on terms to do business together. Lord Adour asked a big price, didn't he?"

"Two thousand pounds," Prescott said angrily, "and I never knew a thing till it was done. Two thousand pounds," he repeated; "and the business needing every penny if we're to carry on till the peace gets going—if it ever does. Every single war contract down the drain."

"I know things must be very difficult with such a sudden change," Bobby agreed. "Impossible to tell where you are. Do you mean the launch was paid for out of company funds, and it wasn't a private purchase?"

"He had some tomfool scheme in his head. He never said what it really was," Prescott said, and looked sulkier than ever as at a very sore memory. "He got me to sign the cheque. It's agreed I sign all cheques. I was pretty sick when I found what he had used the money for. The launch is the company's property now. You can have it for half what Itter gave."

"I am afraid thousand-pound motor launches are a bit beyond me, Bobby answered with a laugh. "Very nice to have one, though. Has it anything to do with the ill feeling between you and your cousins?"

"What do you mean?" Prescott asked, looking very startled indeed. "What ill feeling? There isn't any. Have any of the staff been talking?"

"Not to me," Bobby assured him. "Not to anyone that I know of. I've never even spoken to anyone in your employ. But I do know there have at times been angry scenes between you and Mr. Mauley Bain."

"Well, there haven't," Prescott declared emphatically. "I mean, nothing to speak of. We don't spend all our time billing and cooing, if that's what you mean."

"Very well," Bobby said. "I suppose you and he are the principal owners of the business now."

"Except for the Coastal Bank," growled Prescott. "What's it got to do with you, anyhow? Are you investigating Itter's murder, poor chap, or our business affairs?"

"The brother of one of you, the cousin of the other, the partner of both has been murdered," Bobby answered gravely. "My job is to bring the murderer to justice. Anything, anything at all, I can learn about him may help, may be very important. If it proves irrelevant, you may be sure I shall forget it. We are taught to forget in the police. The elephant never forgets, they say. A policeman never remembers, once his case is over. I am sure you wish to help. I am sure you want your cousin's murderer brought to justice. I'll ask you another question. I don't think you've told me all that's in your mind. Won't you say what you really believe? Was Itter Bain really infatuated with Miss Adour?"

"I don't know what I do believe," Prescott answered. "I don't think I believe anything—except that Itter's death puts every thing in the melting pot. What do you mean, infatuated? He wasn't. Infatuated's all rot. It wasn't like that with any of us. Can't you look at a pretty girl without being told 'infatuated'? Look. I've had enough. You can go and talk to Mauley now. Put him through it like you have me," and therewith Prescott turned and walked briskly away.

Nor did Bobby try to stop him. Their talk had been interesting, even enlightening. Probably best, though, not to press Prescott any more for the time. But it did seem as if these talks were helping to clarify the picture—or, rather, for there was as yet no picture visible, to dispel a little the surrounding, concealing darkness.

CHAPTER IX
SILENT THREAT

PRESCOTT BAIN was soon out of sight, and Bobby entered the office building and asked if he could see Mr. Mauley Bain. He gave his name without explaining his business—he said it was private—and was duly shown into the room whence, as he judged, had come the sound of quarrelling voices he had heard. Mauley Bain, a tall, powerful-looking man, was standing by the window, his back to it; and somehow, even in that simple attitude, managed to convey an impression of a hidden strength of passion, held fiercely in restraint. A capable face, Bobby thought, with strongly-marked features and deep-set, smouldering eyes, but more perhaps emotional than intellectual. A man to beware of, Bobby decided. Best, he was sure, to be wary of any man who could stand so still and so quiet and yet convey so odd an impression of being ready and prepared for instant, angry movement. It seemed as if his every muscle was tense for action. Bobby was reminded again of that tall, striding figure which had passed him in the dusk the night before, as one seeking a prey, but now waiting a victim. The voice though was a surprise; coming from that deep chest it emerged thin and reedy. As Bobby entered, Mauley said:

"I've heard of you. I was expecting you. Don't they think old Seers any good any more? He strikes me as well on top of his job. There's nothing much he misses."

"I'm sure there isn't," agreed Bobby heartily. "The utmost confidence is felt in Commander Seers." (Bobby salved his conscience by reflecting that he didn't say by whom that confidence was felt, and it certainly was felt by Commander Seers.) "There seems an unfortunate misunderstanding about that. The simple fact is other considerations have arisen, and inquiries have had to be extended in other ways. I am here to co-ordinate them as far as possible."

Mauley Bain did not look much impressed, nor did he relax for one moment his attitude of tense preparedness. He said abruptly:

"Well, what have you found out?"

"Not much," Bobby said placidly. "That's why I'm here. To ask if you can tell me more."

"No," Mauley answered. "No," and thin as was his voice, almost a squeak, he managed to make it sound as though through it distant thunder rumbled.

Bobby decided again that it would be very necessary to go carefully with this man. He was plainly under a considerable emotional strain. Well, that was not to be wondered at. His brother had just been murdered in mysterious circumstances and there had been various indications that all was not well with the business. That, of course, was the case with many businesses, affected by the sudden change-over from war to peace and the abrupt cessation of all war contracts.

"May I sit down?" Bobby inquired amiably, as Mauley showed no sign of either taking a chair himself or offering one to his visitor.

Mauley did not answer, and Bobby, taking silence for consent, lowered himself into a somewhat rickety armchair by the big writing table. He wondered if the armchair was psychological. All the other furniture in the room was good, new, substantial stuff. Most business men like to make their visitors as comfortable as possible, with the underlying idea of coaxing them, as it were, into friendliness and acquiescence. Psychology, of course, though often quite unconscious psychology. Did Mauley, on the other hand, with his aggressive and domineering personality, prefer that his visitors should be less at ease than himself, so as in this way to establish and express his superior status? Psychology, of course, once again, though yet again probably unconscious psychology. Bobby told himself that in Prescott Bain's room, the chair for visitors was probably of extreme comfort, the best that money could buy. Where Mauley's inner personality would express itself in an attempt to domineer, Prescott would try to wheedle. Though one had to remember, too, that, as Bobby understood it, Prescott had charge of the business side, and would therefore often have to deal with important and influential people. Mauley was General Manager and would therefore have more to do with the issuing of instructions—and rebukes—to subordinates.

Slowly, and even his slowest movements managed to convey an idea of controlled speed, Mauley moved from the window to take his own place at the other side of the big writing table.

"May I smoke?" Bobby asked.

Mauley opened one of the writing-table drawers and produced a box of cigarettes. Bobby was, however, already lighting one of his own. Without a word, Mauley replaced the cigarettes and closed the drawer. He was still, consciously or unconsciously managing to convey a hint of hidden menace lurking in every movement he made. He had seated himself as if preparing an attack, he had taken out the cigarettes as if producing some lethal weapon, he had replaced them as if seeking some weapon still more deadly. Yet Bobby did not feel there was anything intentional in all this. An unconscious revelation of angry and troubled emotions held still in strong restraint. An interesting and formidable personality, that at least was certain. Bobby said:

"In my experience—I could say in all police experience—people who quite honestly and sincerely believe they know nothing do often in the end provide the most useful and valuable information. I hope you won't mind if I ask you a few questions, even though you don't quite see what they have to do with it. What I'm aiming at is trying to get the background clear. It is only against a clear background that a clear picture can be framed and only when a clear picture has been obtained, can one begin to understand what has happened."

Only the dark, deep-set, intent eyes of the man on the other side of the table showed that what Bobby said was heard. But for those watchful, angry eyes Bobby would have felt as if he were talking to a statue, even if one liable to leap into life at any moment. Bobby went on:

"I think I saw you last night. I was having a stroll round the town. I think you passed me coming up from the harbour?"

"What about it, if I was?" Mauley said. Then he said again: "What about it?" When Bobby, since so far as he knew there was nothing about it, made no attempt to answer, Mauley added: "I had been to have a look at the *Seagull*—the launch Itter bought from Lord Adour. The engine's out of order, so I didn't go on board. Broken down. No use going on board her, if she won't go."

"I suppose not," agreed Bobby. "Now, if you wouldn't mind answering just one or two questions, it might help. Could you tell me whether Mr. Itter Bain had any enemies? Had he recently quarrelled with anyone, for instance?"

"He was always quarrelling with everyone," Mauley answered. "The Bain temper was never remarkable for sweetness. Mine isn't. He and I often rowed. What about it? You don't murder people because you've had a row with them." He smiled grimly. "Plenty of murders if you did."

"What about your workpeople?" Bobby asked. "Any ill feeling there?"

"Lots. Against me," Mauley said, and smiled even more grimly than before. "It's my job to keep their noses to the grindstone and they hate it, and me, too. If any of them are on the mat, that's for me again. They all hate Prescott as well. Who wouldn't? He's scum. Not so much as they hate me, because they don't have so much to do with him. If there's something new they don't like, it may be Prescott's idea, but it's for me to put it across. Of course, there's the office staff. I expect any of them would gladly murder Prescott any time they got the chance."

"But it's Itter who has been murdered," Bobby remarked. "Itter was as popular as any boss could be," Mauley said. "The only thing he really cared about was machinery—and money to try out his new inventions. He would talk to any of them—odd job man or foreman— about machinery for hours at a time. They all knew that; and, if they wanted a spell, they would try to get hold of Itter and ask him some fool questions about some gadget or another. Then he would take the blessed thing to pieces as likely as not to show them just what he meant, and then I would come along and curse them both. You can guess which of us was best liked. Itter spent most of his time messing about in his own workshop on the top floor. If he had been more in the other workshops, I don't believe we should ever have got a contract out on time. Satisfied now? You knew all this before, didn't you? There was one of your fellows who came poking round here the other day."

"Who was that?" Bobby asked sharply.

"Haile, I think his name was. Wasn't he one of your people?"

"Did he say he was? Did he say he came from the police?"

"Well, he said he was carrying out an investigation into Itter's death."

"I'll talk to him as soon as I can get hold of him," Bobby said ominously. He felt Mr. Haile was going to cause a good deal of trouble. "You have no suspicions against any one person?"

"No," said Mauley and paused, those dark, deep-set eyes of his fixed on Bobby till he felt them almost physically, so strong was their steady stare.

"Go on," Bobby said softly. "You mean ...?"

"I mean I don't suspect, because I know," Mauley answered slowly. "Damn you, I never meant to tell you that."

"Why not?" Bobby asked. "Who else but me? I stand for the Law."

"That's why," Mauley said, and his unblinking stare never changed or wavered. "The law be damned, and you, too. What good's the Law? I don't suspect, because I know. But that's all. I mean there's nothing I can show to prove I'm right. I know I know and I know I'm right. I shan't say anything till I've made up my mind what to do. Then you'll know," and these last words were said so quietly, in so still and thin a voice, that to Bobby it was as though he heard a deadly threat roaring through them.

Very clearly Bobby remembered the warning Haile had given him. Mauley had sunk into silence, and Bobby was silent, too. Now, silence is a thing few can bear for long. In silence and in stillness lie the dread of the Unknown. Of the Unknown that encircles all human life. Often had Bobby found advantage in remaining silent and still, waiting, waiting till the strain became too great to be further borne. But Mauley Bain seemed unaffected. He sat as still, as silent, as did Bobby himself. But for that unchanging, watchful gaze one might easily have thought that Mauley had lost all consciousness of his surroundings. It was Bobby who at last broke the spell of that strange stillness by a slight movement, and Mauley looked and said:

"That's all I have to tell you."

"There's something rather important I have to tell you, though," Bobby said. "You told me just now that you wouldn't say anything till you had made up your mind what to do."

"Well?"

"There can be no question of your making up your mind what to do. You have only one thing to do. To come to me or some other responsible officer of police and say what you know or think you know."

"The Law again?" Mauley asked and spoke with deep contempt. "The official view? What do I care? My view is that whoever is responsible for Itter's death, for my brother's death, is going to pay, Law or no Law, proof or no proof. If you can do your stuff, well and good. I don't much expect you will. It may not be possible. I must get my mind clear. What have I to do with the Law? I tell you plainly my brother's death is going to be paid for, one way or another."

"And I tell you even more plainly," Bobby said, "that if, as I think you mean, you may take the Law into your own hands, then the Law will deal with you as with any other criminal." Mauley might not have heard, so little notice did he take, so unchanged remained that sombre, unwinking stare of his, and it was in a very troubled mood that Bobby, since it seemed there was no more to say, took his leave. That night Bobby wrote home to Olive. Part of his letter ran thus:

"... It's all going to be difficult. There seems no chance of finding any physical clue. No good solid stuffy like fingerprints or bloodstains you can slap down on a table for everyone to see. All psychological stuffy and that's always tricky. Show a jury a fingerprint and they're impressed, though it's no proof of action, only of presence, which may be innocent. Talk psychology to them and all they want to do is to say 'Not guilty' before they get too bored to say anything at all. Even the weapon used can't be found. Lord Adour's gun probably, but no proof even of that; and, if it is where I think it is, it never will be found. On the face of it, it all centres round Miss Helen Adour, a young lady who seems to be able to set any man standing on his head merely by passing. I am very anxious to get a talk with her to-morrow, and then I shall be able to form my own opinion. But something quite different may be what someone or another once called 'the efficient cause.' Money? It seems Bain Products is in difficulties with the change-over to peace conditions, and apparently Itter Bain was wanting more cash all the time for his inventions. Yet he spent two thousand pounds on buying Lord Adour's motor launch. Why? And why does the launch keep popping in and out of the story as if it had something to do with it, though obviously it hasn't.

"As for the personalities involved—I can't call any of them suspects yet—I'm beginning to wonder about Haile. He's been very busy, and I was thinking of trying to have him called off, but I'm feeling now it may be as well he is here where I can keep an eye on him. If Martin Winstanley is telling the truth, he has been in this neighbourhood before, so why did he keep that back when he was talking to me? Winstanley himself is a bit of a dark horse. Identity of time, place and opportunity is admitted; so is motive. But identity of time, place and opportunity applies both to Helen Adour and to her father. And both may be thought to have motives. Lord Adour is said to have objected to Itter's bothering Miss Adour and to have warned him off. Itter may have replied by threatening violence, Lord Adour uses his gun. His running back to the house for his camera and his story about the kingfisher could be merely camouflage. Or Helen Adour may have met Itter, found his attentions a little too pressing, picked up her father's gun to frighten him away, and the gun may have gone off again. Prescott Bain had a quarrel with Itter over the money Itter spent on the motor launch. Did that quarrel lead anywhere? Is his alibi as good as it seems? Mauley Bain is a strange and, I think, rather formidable character. He will need careful watching. He means mischief. What and why? Why isn't he content with what we are doing instead of apparently wanting to act on his own? And, finally, I told you, I think, I met that scamp, Wayling, here. Does he come into it somewhere, I wonder?

"I don't like it, Olive. I don't like it at all. No good, sound, plain evidence, not so much as the smell of a fingerprint. Nothing but psychology and an atmosphere of doubt, menace, and suspicion."

The remainder of the letter is of a private nature.

CHAPTER X
SALE OF A MOTOR LAUNCH

IT WAS STILL EARLY next morning when Bobby presented himself at Kindles, a comparatively small but comfortable-looking house, dating from Georgian days, though with a certain number of modern amenities added from time to time. It faced south, the situation affording a glimpse here and there of the sea, obtained through a fringe of ancient trees that marked the boundary of the large garden that was indeed almost a small park. Since the outbreak of the war this had been chiefly devoted to vegetables, though the spacious and lovely lawn in front of the house had been left undisturbed. Beyond the garden and its fringe of old and stately trees lay two fields, part of the Kindles property, but now let to Martin Winstanley of the River Farm. Originally pasture, these fields had, under the stress of the drive for more food, been ploughed up and cropped. Further on again was Coldstone Spinney, though this was really more a small wood than a spinney.

A very pleasant little place, Bobby thought it, as he motored up the long semi-circular drive to the house, though certainly small for a man of Lord Adour's social standing and reputed wealth. Ten or eleven rooms in all, Bobby thought, trying to count the chimney stacks and making them eleven. But then, as Bobby knew, as most people knew, the Adour town house in the London West End had been wiped out by a direct hit from a German bomb, and the stately Adour country home in the Chilterns was still in the possession of the military authorities, who could give lessons to the most persistent and enduring of limpets. It was general knowledge also that Lord Adour's business interests had been largely on the Continent with the big French and German industrialists, and that therefore he had been badly hit by the outbreak of a war, in the possibility of which he had refused to believe up to the very last moment.

Bobby was admitted by an elderly maid, who showed him into a room probably originally intended for the breakfast-room, but now looking half library, half study. There the maid asked him to wait while she went to announce his arrival. A very comfortable room, Bobby thought. Well-lined bookshelves and one or two good pictures on the walls; a Bonington, Bobby decided, and two others that looked like Cromes, though whether "Old" Cromes or by the younger man, Bobby could not tell. The owner, however, would be perfectly sure they were the work of "Old Crome," whose output does seem somewhat remarkably larger than that of his less-talented son. Two comfortable armchairs stood by the fireplace and two smaller ones by the window. An enormous writing table occupied the centre of the room. On it were basket trays for letters and neat piles of documents, carefully docketed and secured by indiarubber bands. The work table, in fact, of a man much occupied with affairs. A lower shelf of the nearest bookcase held a number of box files and in one corner stood a card-index cabinet. A typewriter and a telephone completed the impression of the busy, tidy, slightly fussy, methodical temperament of the room's occupant. On one of the chairs was lying also a swansdown cape, presumably left there by one of the women of the household, the almost legendary Helen Adour no doubt.

Not much sign, though, of any interest in sport, either fishing or shooting, such as might have been expected from a man who, as a matter of habit, picked up his gun when he went out. But these two sides of life, business and sport, might be kept rigorously in separate compartments. Or, indeed, the gun could be something of an affectation, that of a city man living in the country and determined to be as countrified as any farmer of them all. Or it might be a return to early habits before the young Adour, heir to country estates and responsibilities, had become absorbed in city life. All possible explanations, Bobby thought.

He walked over to the bookshelves, giving them a rapid and comprehensive glance. Neat and tidy rows of volumes, arranged, he thought, more with an eye to size and binding than to subject. They were so tightly packed it was clear they were not often disturbed. It would be a struggle to get any one of them free. Not a bookish man, Lord Adour, apparently. There was one exception, though, for one shelf showed signs of use. One book was even standing upside down, a pleasant break in the monotony of so much careful planning. It was a shelf on which all the books it held dealt with seamanship, navigation, yachting. One was an old-fashioned manual treating of "Great Circle Sailing." Then there was the last, the pre-war, issue of *Lloyd's Yacht Register*; the year-book of a well-known yachting club; and so on. There was a business-like-looking chart case, too, and Bobby noticed that one chart had apparently been consulted recently, as it was lying on the top of the case. Clearly Lord Adour had been enthusiastically interested in cruising, and Bobby wondered what had made him sell his launch to the dead man.

The door opened. Lord Adour came in, a tall, thin man with a long, thin, worried-looking face in which incongruously were set two round and childlike eyes. Bobby turned. He had not attempted to touch the chart, and just in front of him hung the water colour he believed to be a Bonington.

"I am admiring your Bonington," he said. "It is a Bonington, isn't it?"

Lord Adour slightly surprised, admitted that it was indeed a Bonington, and even a good Bonington, and remarked that not so very many people could tell a Bonington at a glance.

"Oh, well," Bobby explained, "he did a lot of his stuff round that part of the French coast, didn't he—Calais, Boulogne and so on? Rather desolate and lonely, much of it, and must have been more so in his time, but I suppose it appealed to him. And then his father lived somewhere there, I think. Are those other two Cromes? They look like it."

"Yes, 'Old' Crome," said Lord Adour, and began to look a little doubtful. He consulted Bobby's card he still held in one hand. "You are Mr. Owen?" he asked. "The detective officer from Scotland Yard?"

"Well, as a matter of fact," Bobby explained, "it was the Home Office who sent me along, though Scotland Yard was asked to suggest someone, I think. Of course," Bobby explained, "they are frightfully busy themselves. At the Yard, I mean. When these foreign bigwigs come over, the Yard has to work forty-eight hours a day—or so they say, though they may exaggerate. But they have to make sure there's no shooting, which seems the favourite form of argument in Europe just now."

Lord Adour was evidently still slightly worried, a little doubtful. All this was not quite what he had expected—something more like Hawkseye the detective, of happy childhood memories, was what he had looked for. Not a man who could spot a Bonington at a glance and showed no sign of being overawed by the other's tide and social position. However, he invited Bobby to occupy one of the large and comfortable armchairs, seated himself at the writing table, and said:

"I've been expecting you for a day or two. I put it to the Home Office very forcibly—I went to Town for the purpose—that they must do something to stop the very unpleasant talk that was going on. I imagine you will have been informed of that?"

"You mean the gossip that you yourself committed the murder and that Commander Seers knows it but is shielding you out of class feeling and prejudice?"

Lord Adour's round and childlike eyes opened wide. They looked hurt—or was it frightened? But which? And why? Bobby was finding his lordship more difficult to sum up than his room and surroundings had suggested he would be. Lord Adour said: "I suppose I need hardly tell you that the suggestion is merely absurd?"

"Oh, no," declared Bobby heartily. "Just as I am sure you won't misunderstand me if I say that I shall have to keep the possibility in mind." This remark did not appear to be much approved of, and in the round and childlike eyes there showed plainly a flicker of unease. "Murderer or not, he has something to conceal," Bobby thought, and went on aloud: "I've read the statement you made to Commander Seers. He tells me it was entirely spontaneous. He hardly put a single question."

"That is so," agreed Lord Adour. "Seers is very conscientious and in his own way very capable. But he is certainly rather set in his ways, and I do feel that now he is somewhat out of his depth. That is one reason why I used what influence I have to get assistance sent. I strongly object to spending the rest of my life under suspicion as a murderer. I don't want it said I should have been hanged if I hadn't happened to be a peer. I should have thought this Government would be only too glad of a chance to hang a member of the House of Lords. Communists are in strong force about here and more so than ever since Prescott Bain joined them. They've made him Chairman. Absurd. Most mischievous. I suspect them of starting all this objectionable talk."

"Of course, I know and care nothing about any political side to it," Bobby declared with emphasis. "If I do hear any loose talk going on, I'll try to stop it. I am sure Commander Seers will, too. I'll remind people that only statements made directly to a police officer are privileged. Anything else is slander or libel, and actionable."

"Only makes more talk if you go to court," complained the other.

Bobby agreed that that was so, and went on:

"There does seem to be a general belief that Mr. Itter Bain was bothering Miss Adour, that you objected strongly, and that you told him to keep away. The idea seems to be that you might have seen him in Coldstone Spinney, told him again to keep away, and that a quarrel resulted and ended fatally. I'm told Itter Bain had a very violent temper and was quite capable of using physical violence or threats. It seems to be suggested you might have acted in self-defence."

"Nonsense," Lord Adour said. "I hope you won't pay any attention to such rubbish. Rubbish on the face of it. Everyone knows Itter Bain had the devil of a temper and rather liked a fight when he got the chance. He was a fine boxer and more than a match for most. But he would never have thought of anything like that with a man of my age—I think I may say, of my standing. And I shouldn't have given him the opportunity. I certainly asked him some time ago to make his feelings for Miss Adour a little less obvious. I said it was doing him no good with her. I told her she felt strongly about it." Lord Adour paused and shook his head. "Young men are so very apt to lose their heads over Helen," he said. "It's not the first time I've had to try to warn off youngsters making a nuisance of themselves. I can't see it myself."

"See it?"

"What it's all about. Of course, Miss Adour does certainly inherit the Adour good looks. Anyone can see that. It runs in the family." Lord Adour paused and looked complacent, and Bobby wondered wildly if his lordship included himself. Bobby emphatically did not. If Helen Adour were really so extraordinarily good-looking, she must be a throw-back to an ancestor—a somewhat remote ancestor, Bobby thought. "Even Jane has her share," Lord Adour concluded.

"Jane?"

"A relative—a cousin. She is staying with us at present. A great help."

"Oh, yes," Bobby said. "There is one other point I should like to mention. I noticed that in your statement Miss Adour's name does not appear, and that there's no hint of any—well, tension on her account."

"Yes, I did want to speak to you about that," Lord Adour said quickly. "Commander Seers agreed it was quite unnecessary and indeed undesirable from every point of view that my daughter's name should be mentioned. Most undesirable," he repeated firmly. "I am sure you will agree. Miss Adour dislikes all forms of publicity. She is constantly receiving requests to allow herself to be photographed. I've been told privately that one or two Academicians would be only too glad of a chance to paint her portrait. I'm happy to say she always refuses. She even had a most insolent letter from some firm of soap-boilers offering quite a large cheque if she would say she used their particular brand. I asked my lawyers to reply. Both she and I detest this modern vulgarity of ceaseless advertisement. I rely upon you entirely."

"Lord Adour," Bobby said gravely, "you can rely on me for one thing and one thing only—to do all I can to discover the truth concerning Itter Bain's murder. Miss Adour's name will certainly not be mentioned unnecessarily. No one's will be. But no more will any name, either yours or hers or that of anyone else, be kept for any reason out of any report in which it would otherwise appear. It is the first duty of all police to be no respecter of persons."

Lord Adour stared at Bobby angrily, or was it with more than anger? Vicious indeed might be thought the best description of the look in those round and, Bobby now felt, deceptively childlike eyes. There was even a new sharpness in his lordship's voice as he said after a pause:

"You misunderstand. I am sure you will always do your duty, and I was not aware I had suggested anything else. I spoke as a father and the father of a young girl."

"Very natural," agreed Bobby; "and I hope and trust you won't find any reason to complain. All I mean is that duty must come first. There is just one other point—quite a small point. I think I am right in saying you had no business dealings with Bain Products?"

"None whatever."

"I understand you recently sold a motor launch to Itter Bain?"

"Yes. Why?"

"Was there any special reason for the sale? Was there any dispute or difficulty about the transaction?"

"No. Why should there be? I don't quite see the relevance of all this," and Bobby felt that there was uneasiness over this turn in the conversation. Lord Adour's eyes were flickering to and fro with sudden brief concentrations on Bobby, as though trying to perceive what was in his mind and why these questions about the sale of the motor launch. Lord Adour went on: "I sold the launch because I have not been able to use it and because I very specially didn't want Helen to use it while there are still mines knocking about. Bain offered me a good price and I accepted it. I don't know why he wanted the thing. I suppose he thought he would like an occasional cruise. I believe he did say something about some idea of his for increasing the power of marine engines. I don't know. I'm quite ignorant about engineering."

A shadow fell across the window. Bobby, from where he was sitting, had not seen who it was. Lord Adour said:

"Ah, there is Helen passing by."

CHAPTER XI
PLAIN JANE

"OH YES, WAS IT?" Bobby said, a little disappointed that he had missed this opportunity of getting a glimpse of the young lady. "By the way," he went on, "there are one or two small matters I would like to ask Miss Adour about. Matters of routine. Do you think that would be possible? There are a few points on which I would like her personal opinion."

Lord Adour had no air of welcoming this suggestion. Was it really necessary? he asked. Bobby thought it desirable. Lord Adour hoped it was realized how deeply Miss Adour had suffered, both from the shock of the event itself and from all the talk and gossip that had been going on. Bobby said he did indeed realize it. Both Lord Adour and Miss Adour had his deepest sympathy. But there it was. A murder had taken place. Unhappily, the victim's name and that of Miss Adour were being mentioned together. One never knew, once gossip began, where it would end. A touch here and a touch there, and some most monstrous fabric would come into existence, in time to be accepted as the truth. Didn't Lord Adour think it most desirable, both in his daughter's interest and his own, that the whole business should be cleared up as soon as possible? Lord Adour agreed that that was what they both desired more than anything else. But there was still reluctance in his voice as he repeated that he didn't see how Miss Adour could possibly help. Bobby said he thought her personal impressions might be valuable. Lord Adour continued to hesitate. Bobby judged it necessary to put a sharper edge to his voice. Lord Adour said that, of course, if it was really necessary, there could be no possible objection, and he would go and find her at once, if Bobby wouldn't mind waiting a moment or two. Therewith he departed, with a final assurance that he wouldn't be long.

"Which means of course," Bobby said to himself, "that he intends to warn her to be careful what she says. Now, does that mean they have something to conceal? And if so, what? A love affair? With Itter Bain? With someone else? Or is it something to do with the murder?

Or is it only to tell her to come in full war paint, so as to stand me on my head, as apparently happens to everyone else?"

He got up and went again to the shelf on which were ranged all those works on seamanship and navigation. They interested him. Why had Lord Adour, so keen a pre-war yachtsman, decided suddenly to sell his motor launch just at the moment when yachting was about to become possible again? And why had Itter Bain bought it and been willing to pay what to Bobby seemed so high a price? Double its market value, apparently, to judge from Prescott Bain's offer to sell it for half the price paid. Of course, Prescott Bain's offer might have been more an expression of annoyance than seriously meant. All of it susceptible of perfectly simple and innocent explanation, no doubt. One should not, Bobby told himself, attach too much importance to such incidents. Yet against the background of a murder, who can say what is innocent and simple and what is far otherwise?

Only, again, if Lord Adour were giving up yachting, as the sale of his launch indicated, why had he procured what looked like a set of brand new charts? Charts, too, that Bobby was fairly certain were not yet generally on sale. Lord Adour must have gone to some trouble and probably pulled a few strings to get hold of them. It seemed inconsistent, and Bobby disliked inconsistencies. He had once been told that to dislike inconsistencies was to dislike life, which is wholly composed of inconsistencies. To which he had retorted that the inconsistencies of life are resolved as soon as understood, and it was the business of a detective to resolve those he met with in committed crime. He picked up the topmost chart and looked at it. During the war it would have been a gross indiscretion to have in one's possession, so near the coast, any chart or map of any description. No harm now, of course. Bobby noticed that the chart he was looking at was one only recently printed and certainly not as yet on general sale. Lord Adour must have secured it privately through some friend or another. Why not? Very possibly in recognition and recompense for others he might have handed over to authority at the outbreak of war, when every chart was worth its weight in banknotes. The chart was one showing a part of the Normandy coast, and on it faint pencil lines had been drawn, indicating apparently a course to be followed. Not a course, Bobby noticed, that led to any of the ports or coastal towns, but, as it seemed, to a spot remote and lonely, far removed from any village, even from any house.

Bobby began to look thoughtful, even worried, and the longer he looked, the more worried he felt. Easy, though, to draw imaginative inferences from pencil lines on a chart. He laid it down and went back to his seat. The door opened and a young woman came briskly in and then paused.

"Oh, I'm so sorry," she exclaimed. "I thought Lord Adour was here. They said he was looking for me."

A presentable young woman enough, Bobby thought. A pleasant, sensible face, the best features the bright, clear eyes, of so deep a brown they were nearly black. There was a dimple, too, in the small, well-shaped chin that looked as if it were waiting eagerly for a chance to join in a smile. But certainly, to Bobby's mind, this young woman was no world-beater; nothing about her, he thought, calculated to set every young man who came near "standing on his head."

"I think Lord Adour has gone to see if he could find you," Bobby said, rising from his chair. "I asked him if I might have the pleasure of a few words with you about this unfortunate affair."

"With me?" the girl said, and seemed surprised. "Do please sit down. But why with me?"

"Possibly you would rather wait till Lord Adour is present?" Bobby suggested. "I think it would be better. I must introduce myself though. My name is Owen and I've been sent by the Home Office to see if I can help Commander Seers in his investigation of Mr. Itter Bain's death."

"Oh, yes, I know," the other answered eagerly. "I heard someone was coming. Oh, I do hope you can do something. It's been awful for us all. People stare so, and you know they are all talking all the time. Oh, and the reporters." She paused for a moment as if horror and dismay could no further go. "Uncle's most terribly upset and Helen, too."

"Uncle?" Bobby repeated. "Oh, I'm sorry. ... I thought you were Miss Helen Adour?"

"Oh, no," the girl answered and began to laugh—a pleasant, low, bubbling laugh in which the dimple joined, hurrying to seize the opportunity it had been waiting for. "I'm just Jane. Plain Jane. Dear me, I ought to be most awfully flattered. No one has ever taken me for Helen before. She's beautiful," and there was almost a touch of awe in the girl's voice as she said this. Then she said: "That's what's so upsetting."

"Stupid of me," Bobby said apologetically. "I'm so sorry."

"It's not her fault, you know," Jane went on, pursuing her own train of thought. "She never takes any notice of men. I don't honestly think she ever notices they are there even. And then all this happens, and I do think it's such a shame the way people talk. She can't help it if men go all soft and silly."

"No, of course, no," agreed Bobby, but wondered; for beauty may not be able to help being armed, but all the same may have a say in the way in which those arms are used.

"You can understand it," Jane said. "She is so lovely. I mean, girls see it, feel it, too. They don't compete, they just sit and wonder. I know I do. Even really pretty girls, too, not only just us others. It makes you think of being in church or sunsets or of great music. And then this happens and people talk and stare and talk, and I think it's beastly, and I do hope you can stop it. Even if Mr. Bain did shoot himself, how could Helen help it? You can't marry a man simply because he says he'll kill himself if you don't."

"Had Mr. Bain threatened that?" Bobby asked.

"They all do," Jane said comprehensively. "On our doorstep as often as not."

"There was no weapon found near the body," Bobby reminded her.

"You mean Uncle's gun? Couldn't someone have gone off with it? It would be worth a lot of money, especially just now. Uncle paid a lot for it before the war, he told me. I expect it would bring double to-day. There are the men working at the docks and at Mr. Bain's place and there have been a lot of complaints. Pearson says some of them would rob a blind man of his last penny."

"Who is Pearson?"

"He's our chauffeur and gardener, too, and now he's everything else as well. He says that's how it must have happened. He says he's worked it all out. Mr. Bain shot himself—'temporary insanity,' they call it. And then one of these men at the docks or somewhere found him and saw the gun Mr. Bain had used after Uncle put it down when he ran back for his camera. Whoever it was would pick up the gun and then he would think about his fingerprints being on it, and the gun being worth a lot of money; and he would think how much easier and safer it would be to go off with it than to stop there and be suspected perhaps. Pearson says he's worked it all out, and he's as sure as sure that's how it happened."

"It might be possible," Bobby said cautiously, though he didn't think so. "I must ask Pearson if he has any more ideas."

"You'll have to be careful," Jane warned him. "Pearson's an awful old crab-stick. Uncle wants to pension him off, but he won't go. He won't tell you a thing if he doesn't want to."

"I'll remember," Bobby promised; and then Lord Adour returned, and looked surprised to see Jane.

Jane explained she had been telling Mr. Owen he simply must find out the truth, and Bobby said he had promised to do his best. Lord Adour said he hadn't been able to find Helen, and Jane said she might have gone into Drinks to do some shopping or she might be sitting quietly in one of her cubby-holes.

"She likes to get away and sit all by herself somewhere quiet," Jane explained. "I think it's so as to be away from people because she gets so sick of being stared at as if she were on exhibition in a museum or somewhere."

"Do you think you could find her?" Lord Adour asked.

"I could try," Jane said doubtfully, "but it's rather difficult if she doesn't want to be found. She sits so quiet and still."

Jane went away then on her errand, taking with her the swansdown cape with the remark that it belonged to Helen and Helen had been looking for it. When she had gone, Bobby said to Lord Adour that he hoped he would be allowed to have a talk with Miss Helen later on, if she couldn't be found now. Perhaps an appointment could be made. He would make his convenience suit that of Miss Adour. Meanwhile, might he trouble Lord Adour to come with him as far as Goldstone Spinney and there point out exactly where it had all happened? Again Lord Adour didn't seem to like the suggestion very much. He said he believed the spot where the body had lain had been marked off with tape and with pegs to show the precise position. Bobby agreed that was so. Most efficient work on the part of Commander Seers, if he might say so. But still it would be a great help if he could be shown exactly where Lord Adour was standing when he saw the bird that had attracted his attention and put down his gun, and how that position was related to the spot where Itter's body had lain. Still somewhat reluctantly, Lord Adour agreed, and the two of them left the house together.

CHAPTER XII

PRECISE POSITION

THE DISTANCE WAS not great across the garden and the two fields beyond to where the spinney lay, its shade cool and pleasant now that the sun had come out suddenly with abrupt and unexpected warmth. Bobby, to relieve the tension as he and Lord Adour walked along, made one or two casual remarks about the pleasant surroundings, but did not draw much response from a companion who was clearly not inclined for conversation. When they reached the spinney, Bobby asked one or two questions about the direction of the paths that traversed it. Lord Adour answered as briefly as he could, but sufficiently clearly. He showed, too, how the path to River Farm, taken by Helen Adour as she went for the eggs she wanted, ran a good twenty yards or so from the spot where Itter Bain's dead body had been found the next morning.

"Malicious suggestions are being made, I know," Lord Adour said resentfully, "that Helen must have seen the body as she passed by. You can see for yourself that no one walking along the path could possibly have noticed anything, even if the body had been there at the time, and there's nothing to show it was. It probably all happened much later."

"All the times are very uncertain, I know," Bobby agreed. "Times almost always are. No one notices the exact time unless there's some special reason, like the dinner gong going or the factory whistle sounding. You can sit in a room with a striking clock and never hear it, or remember if you did. Accustomed sounds are very often unheard sounds. Neither Mr. Winstanley nor Miss Adour in her statement seem to be able to say more than some time about the middle of the afternoon."

"Well, I can't either," Lord Adour commented. "One doesn't go about with a stop-watch. Even Jane isn't sure, and she's a very accurate sort of person. It's unlucky she didn't go on to the farm with Helen."

"Oh, did they start out together?" Bobby asked, casually enough, but interested, for this was something new.

"Jane was going to call on Mrs. Eaton, so they took different paths through the spinney. Jane went that way to Toad-in-Hole and Helen took this other path to River Farm. Mrs. Eaton is the Vicar's wife," Lord Adour added.

"Did Miss Jane—I don't think I know her other name?"

"Felgate," Lord Adour said.

"I was wondering if Miss Felgate came back the same way?"

"No. She returned by the river path. She told Commander Seers when he asked her. It's a little further, but it's more open."

So Commander Seers had questioned her, but had not thought it necessary to include her statement in the dossier of the case. Not quite satisfactory, Bobby thought. His mind flew back to that cigarette case with the inscription "From J. to I." Did those initials mean from Jane to Itter?

"Were Miss Felgate and Itter Bain friendly?" he asked.

"Well, they haven't seen much of each other since they broke off their engagement," Lord Adour said, "but they kept perfectly good friends. They soon made up their minds it was a mistake on both sides."

"Oh, yes," Bobby said, and yet he wondered.

So Jane Felgate and Itter Bain had been engaged at one time. That explained the cigarette case. Was it possible the parting had been less friendly than Lord Adour believed? Than it had appeared on the surface? Had Jane Felgate acquiesced in fact so amiably in her displacement? Or had she nursed her anger against the man who had thrown her over? Some truth, Bobby believed, in that old, well-worn saying about the woman scorned. If, that is, Jane Felgate had been scorned. Possible the scorning had been on her side. But how to tell? She did not look like a murderer, but then murderers so seldom do. Bobby remembered the description he had once been given by a colleague of quiet, pleasant-spoken, meek, subdued little Dr. Crippen. Not that Jane Felgate in any way resembled that picture. A young woman of considerable force of character, he was inclined to think, as he remembered her direct gaze, the strong lines of her mouth and chin. There's another old saying, too, that has truth in it: "Still waters run deep." Well, it would have to be followed up, he decided. Not very likely there was anything in it, but in a case like this, not even the faintest possibility can be neglected.

By now they had penetrated well within the spinney. Lord Adour showed, with a slightly impatient air, as of one who felt all this was a rather foolish waste of time, exactly where he had been standing when he had seen the kingfisher. The spot was a small glade or clearing facing south. Lord Adour pointed out the tall beech tree at a little distance on which the kingfisher had been perched. He had been able to see it clearly. To the right lay the River Farm path, cut off by a fairly high growth of young trees and a screen of undergrowth that had been allowed to spring up in these war years when there was no spare labour to keep it orderly and trimmed. Directly on the left, behind yet another tangled growth of bush and bramble, was the spot where Itter's dead body had lain.

Bobby looked around gloomily. The thought in his mind was that originally the place must have been fairly plastered with clues of one sort and another, all quickly destroyed by the excited running to and fro that had followed the discovery of the body. He told himself that if he had been on the scene in good time, probably there would have been no mystery at all. Now the mystery was likely to remain one, insoluble. Nothing to be done now about those vanished clues.

One thing was however perfectly clear. The suicide suggestion put forward by the redoubtable Pearson was not acceptable. The shot killing Itter had undoubtedly been fired at close quarters, but equally certainly at a distance of ten or twelve feet. And within ten or twelve feet of the dead body there was no support on which could have been fixed any mechanical arrangement whereby the gun could have been fired from a distance. Nor any reason why a man contemplating suicide should have arranged anything of the sort or, again, any reason why any thief, removing the gun, should have removed also all trace of any such contraption.

"Do you think you could show me exactly where you put down your gun?" Bobby asked his companion.

Lord Adour answered wearily that he didn't think so. He had just put it down. He hadn't noticed. Against a tree, he supposed. Almost certainly against a tree. Certainly not on the ground. Nor yet on the top of any of the bramble bushes near. So against a tree. Impossible to say which tree, though. He couldn't even remember whether he put his gun down when he first saw the bird and crept cautiously nearer to make sure, or when he decided to run back to the house for his camera. Was it of any importance, he asked, and his tone clearly implied that it most certainly wasn't—mere fussiness and red tape. Bobby said that most likely it didn't matter in the least, but all the same he would like to know, because you could never tell. Lord Adour looked rather helplessly round the circle of trees, mostly young beech with a few older ash. Then he said:

"There's someone watching us over there. I can see his shadow behind those trees."

"Yes. So there is," agreed Bobby, annoyed, for he had been aware of the fact for some time but had been hoping for developments, which now would not happen, now that Lord Adour's loud voice and pointing hand had shown their knowledge.

He went towards the indicated spot. There was no one there. He had not expected there would be. But he could see a figure going swiftly away, a figure easy to recognize as it passed, sombre and heavy, before a background of greenery. No mistaking that long, menacing stride, that form surrounded, as it were, by an aura of purpose and threat. Bobby turned back to Lord Adour.

"It was Mauley Bain," he said.

"What's he want?" Lord Adour said, and there was uneasiness in his voice. "I've seen him hanging about here before. He never speaks. What's it for?"

"Well, it's where his brother was murdered," Bobby said. "There may be some instinctive feeling that he'll find something here to tell him who it was."

"I've heard he's been making threats," Lord Adour said. "I hear he's been saying that if the police can't, he will."

"So I believe," Bobby agreed. "I've warned him already. I will again. I'll tell him that if I hear any more of that sort of talk, I'll have him bound over. That is," Bobby added more doubtfully, "if we could show cause. The magistrates mightn't want to take it too seriously."

Lord Adour looked as if he took it seriously enough. Evidently he thought Mauley's threats might have a personal bearing. Then he said:

"I remember now. When I put the gun down it nearly toppled over. There was a biggish stone I hadn't noticed. I rested the butt end on it and it nearly overbalanced. I remember thinking that if it had fallen the noise would probably have scared the kingfisher away."

"Well, let's see if we can find a biggish stone under a tree," Bobby suggested, and, moving in a direct line towards the tall birch, they soon found one, underneath a sturdy young oak, the only oak apparently anywhere near. "You see," Bobby explained, "there's been a suggestion that someone may have found the body, and instead of reporting it have stolen the gun. If you left the gun here, some distance away both from the murder scene and the path, that doesn't seem very likely."

Lord Adour blinked as if he did not quite follow this argument. More did Bobby, for that matter. But he had wanted to say something. He was feeling a good deal worried. Jane Felgate, if she had been near, might have seen her uncle, have seen him put down his gun and run off towards the house. There was a vision in his mind of the strong, calm face of Jane, tense with resolve, of the loaded gun ready to her hand, close by the man who had deserted her and now was lurking near for a glimpse of his successful rival passing by.

No pleasant picture, and Bobby dismissed it from his mind. Mere phantasy, he thought and hoped.

Lord Adour wanted to know if Bobby had now seen enough. Bobby said he thought so, and they went back to the house, silent companions, for Bobby's thoughts were troubled; and his Lordship of Adour and Avon was in an extremely bad temper, resentful and contemptuous of this futile poking about and raking up of unessentials.

At the house there was still no sign of Helen Adour. Jane had left a message that she thought Helen must have gone down to the river, and she was going there to see. Bobby said it didn't matter. He would wait another opportunity another day. For one thing, he reflected, Miss Adour's absence, intentional or accidental, would give him an excuse to call again at Kindles, as he thought he might well wish to do. So he took his leave, Lord Adour showing no visible regret; and, returning to his car where he had parked it by the side of the drive, he arranged with some care a small defect that prevented it from starting. After a few minutes spent in lifting the bonnet and looking rather helplessly within and another minute or two in crawling rather vaguely under the car, Bobby went round to the back of the house.

There he found a grumpy-looking, elderly—more than elderly—man who stared at him suspiciously. Bobby explained who he was, said his car refused to start, and he wondered if he could ask for a little help. He was talking to Mr. Pearson, wasn't he? Lord Adour's chauffeur, and therefore no doubt knowing a lot more about cars than he did himself. Mr. Pearson evidently thought that was very much more than likely, and agreed, though grudgingly, to come and have a look. He was grimly amused to find that so trifling and so easily adjusted a defect had baffled the London police swell.

Bobby expressed profuse gratitude, admiration for such skill, half a crown changed hands, a cigarette was offered and accepted. The ice thus broken, and Mr. Pearson put in a good temper by such a display of superiority as never fails to please and flatter human vanity—the fundamental human characteristic Bobby went on to mention that Miss Felgate had said that Mr. Pearson believed the recent tragedy was a case of suicide, not murder. Was Mr. Pearson still of the same opinion?

Mr. Pearson emphatically was. He proceeded to expound his theory. By this time the old man was thoroughly enjoying himself. He liked teaching other people their own business, as do most of us for that matter. Often enough he had tried to put Sergeant Gregson in the right way. The sergeant had seldom shown much appreciation, but here was this London chap listening with proper attention. That showed intelligence and deserved encouragement. Bobby mentioned Miss Adour, and the old man's rugged face, lined with the years and much complaining, softened visibly.

"If it wasn't for her," he said, "I wouldn't be here—got another job long ago. There's plenty would be glad enough to know as I was looking. But there"—the hard, wrinkled, old face, the sharp, suspicious eyes, softened even further—"but there, when she passes by it lightens all the day. You just stand and watch like as you do at times when the sun comes up at dawn."

Bobby remarked that he hoped to meet Miss Adour soon. Pearson said he had just missed her. A few minutes ago, she had gone through the yard, on her way to the river probably. She liked to sit there, quiet like, watching the water go by. Just by herself without being bothered by people buzzing round as if they were wasps and her a pot of honey. Bobby remarked that he had, however, met Miss

Felgate, who seemed a very pleasant young lady. Pearson agreed, though a trifle grudgingly, as if reluctant to admit that anyone or anything could be pleasant in this thoroughly unsatisfactory world. For one thing, she wasn't such a "know-all" as most young people nowadays, who didn't want to listen to them as knew a thing or two before they were born. She would make a good wife, would Miss Jane, and Itter Bain had been a fool to throw her over, especially when he knew very well that Miss Helen wouldn't even ever so much as look at him. Not likely. She wasn't for the likes of Itter Bain. She kept herself to herself, did Miss Helen. But Miss Jane took it bitter hard. Not that she showed her feelings. She wasn't one for that, not her. But he knew. You couldn't fool old Pearson. He knew all right. He saw her look the way Betty Haines looked the day she heard she had been jilted and went down to the sea to drown herself. But then Miss Jane wasn't one to take it that way, and when Bobby drove off he was still wondering whether she was one to take it another way.

That night Bobby wrote, among other things:

"Of course, Olive, you see from what I've told you that I have been given one clear hint to the murderer's identity. It may be a misleading hint, and it does seem to suggest the guilt of a person whom the other evidence shows equally clearly can have had nothing to do with it. A contradiction I don't for the moment see my way to get round. Possibly the hint in question means nothing though it's glaring enough. It'll all need a lot of checking up, and at present I feel it'll be a lot easier to know the truth than to prove it. But then knowledge that can't show itself in action is sterile knowledge, the knowledge of the dry-as-dust scholar who keeps all his learning to himself, the miser of wisdom.

"One thing I shall have to do is to check up Seers's dossier pretty carefully. There is nothing in it about Jane Felgate's engagement to Itter Bain. Seers probably thought it irrelevant. Lord knows what else he may not have left out because he thought it irrelevant.

"I haven't met Helen Adour yet, though it seems to the other results produced by her merely passing by you have to add that of keeping crabby old Pearson in his job. I gather Lord Adour wants to get rid of him—a cantankerous old boy, I expect—and he wants to go, but he won't because he can't make up his mind to miss the chance of sometimes seeing her!

"I'm not sure I shouldn't call that the most remarkable of all the results she seems able to achieve.

"Incidentally, what do you make of this story of her liking to go down to the riverside and 'watch the water' flowing by? Would psychoanalysts deduce a Narcissus complex? Does it mean that she is in love with no one because she is in love with her own beauty? The vanity of Lilith?"

The rest of the letter is of a personal nature and would not interest the reader.

CHAPTER XIII

MEDITATIONS

BOBBY SPENT MOST of the rest of the day in a careful re-examination of the dossier compiled by Commander Seers. In the light obtained during the last day or two by personal contacts, it seemed to Bobby even more inadequate and incomplete than he had previously believed.

Not to be wondered at, perhaps, that there was no mention of the motor launch or its sale. Bobby himself was by no means sure that that was in any way relevant. But more and more clearly did it appear that Commander Seers had carried out the investigation under the strong influence of preconceived ideas.

One was the assumption that in any crime committed in the neighbourhood, one of the newcomers, the workmen in dock or factory drawn by the promise of high wartime wages, must certainly be involved. That was where the Commander had started his search and there it had almost automatically remained. Another was the axiom that people in Lord Adour's position did not commit crimes of violence, and, of course, they seldom need to. If proof were shown, naturally the Commander would know and do his duty, but the proof would have to be fairly obvious before he recognized it. Again, he was quite clearly under the influence of the simple belief that it was the first duty of everyone worthy of the name of English gentleman to protect any woman from "talk" or "scandal," these being regarded as much the same. This dogma applied especially if the woman in question came under the technical description of "young lady." Jane Felgate, for instance, was never mentioned. From Helen Adour no statement had been taken and the references to her were vague and incidental. Those made by her father or by Wing Commander Martin Winstanley had been thought sufficient.

In this way Winstanley's evidence that he had accompanied her through the spinney on her way home had been accepted as proof of innocence, nor had the possibility that she had returned later been taken into account. True, there was the evidence of the Kindles maidservant that on her return with her eggs she had gone direct to the kitchen, but there was nothing to show that she continued there. The cakes and other dishes she used the eggs for might have been prepared later. Nor indeed was there anything very conclusive to show that the death of Itter Bain had not occurred before her arrival at the River Farm, though other considerations did make this seem unlikely.

There was again nothing to show that any real attempt had been made to confirm that Prescott Bain had been in the company of the two bank officials during the whole of the fatal afternoon. Apparently Seers had been content to ring up the bank and get confirmation of the fact that there had really been such an interview. The important question of the actual hours covered had not been gone into at all thoroughly.

"Slipshod," Bobby pronounced severely. "There may be a loophole there as big as a barn door. I shall have to go along and see the bank blokes myself."

Finally, at the end of the dossier, came a brief record dealing with Mr. Harry Haile, not at all flattering in tone, and hinting that he was lying when he denied having been in the district before his appearance there as a reporter in the employ of the *Seashire Herald*. However, no attempt had been made to follow this up, no motive for supposing he was implicated in the murder was suggested. All that really emerged was a fairly strong suggestion that any excuse for arresting Mr. Haile or otherwise dealing with him would be warmly welcomed and any such action strongly supported.

"Me, too," said Bobby, who also had acquired some dislike for the activities of Mr. Haile, even apart from the instinctive disapproval of all professionals for all busy amateurs.

The theory, however, that the murder had been committed by some tramp or other casual passer-by who had seen Lord Adour's gun, apparently forgotten, had recognized its value, had decided to appropriate it, but had been seen and checked by Itter Bain, who then had been shot in a subsequent scuffle, was a theory that had to be considered very carefully. If it were true, a speedy and successful solution to the case would become even more unlikely. The unpremeditated murder, no known connection between culprit and victim, is always the one that presents the greatest difficulty.

"It'll have to be gone into," Bobby decided, shaking a gloomy head. "Only how did it happen that Itter Bain was there? Pure coincidence?" and at pure coincidence Bobby shook a still more doubtful head, for pure coincidence was a thing he much disliked and still more distrusted, all the more because he knew well that sometimes it happened.

At this point in his meditations he was interrupted by the appearance of Mrs. Gregson with his tea. She brought it in on a tray with a plateful of hot scones on which the poor lady had lavished nearly the whole of the week's ration of butter for herself and the sergeant. Bobby was both severe and pathetic. What had he done, he asked, that he was to be condemned to eat his meals in solitary confinement? And why had he been put permanently in the sergeant's bad books by this raid upon a whole week's supply of butter?

Would, therefore, Mrs. Gregson please take the tea and scones —for which his mouth was already watering—into the kitchen he supposed they had now to use as their sitting-room since he and his papers were occupying this one? Moreover, tea was never what you could really call tea unless a lady poured it out, and was Mrs. Gregson going to refuse him that kindly office?

Slightly flustered, Mrs. Gregson retired. A little unnerving to pour out tea for one so high in the police hierarchy, one on a special mission from almost legendary Scotland Yard. But this feeling grew less as the meal proceeded, and by the time it was over Mrs. Gregson had heard all about Olive, knew that Olive, like herself, had a light hand with pastry, but was inclined to be a little envious on hearing that Olive could turn dried eggs into admirable omelettes. But then omelettes for Mrs. Gregson had always been a doubtful and unexplored territory into which she had never dared to venture. Bobby, for his part, had heard all about Mrs. Gregson's boy in Burma and how there he had become very pally with an American boy—after two or three black eyes given and exchanged to decide the burning question of whether London or New York was the bigger, better, brighter town. Mrs. Gregson only wished she had them both there to give them a real good talking-to. Also Bobby heard about Mrs. Gregson's girl, Gwen, in the A.T.S., and how she had been given a "mention" for returning to carry on with her 'phone after bomb blast had blown her twenty feet away. In Mrs. Gregson's opinion —and in Bobby's, too—Gwen deserved a medal, let alone a "mention," but Gwen said that if they gave medals in the "Ats" for things like that, almost every girl would have one, and what would be the good?

Incidentally, Bobby gathered a good deal of useful local information supplied by Mrs. Gregson in what it would be unkind to call a general gossip. It seemed clear, for instance, that the engagement between Jane and Itter had either never been generally known or else entirely forgotten. No hint appeared in Mrs. Gregson's chatter of any sign of strong friendship or feeling between them having ever been apparent. Bobby also gathered that Commander Seers's unconcealed belief that one of the dock or factory workers must be guilty, had caused a good deal of resentment.

The sergeant, Mrs. Gregson made it plain, had had to exercise tact, and plenty of it, in making the inquiries ordered by Seers. The dock workers, of course, were not "casual" labourers, but skilled "directed" men, not in any way recruited from such an irresponsible floating vagabond population as Seers imagined, and could not be persuaded otherwise. The same was true of the men employed by Bain Products. Besides, Itter, if undoubtedly a bit of a bully, was a good deal admired by most of the men for his boxing abilities, since, in their illogical British way, they were inclined to associate a "straight lead" with a "straight deal." And Bobby soon realized that both the Gregsons shared the general impression in the neighbourhood that Lord Adour was guilty, but that, as it was assumed he was protecting his daughter from unwelcome attentions, a good deal of sympathy was felt for him.

"Any decent man would do the same," declared Mrs. Gregson, and was not much impressed by Bobby's remark that to kill was always to kill, and a thing no man must ever do on his own responsibility.

Quite an interesting talk, and, by the time tea had been cleared away, Bobby and his hostess were on the best of terms, and she a little inclined to assert over Bobby the strict authority she wielded over the sergeant. Because, of course, as every man knows, give a woman an inch and she takes an ell or two. Bobby was lucky to get off with no more than a sharp reminder to wrap up well if he went near the sea after dark, the sea air being notoriously treacherous. Mrs. Gregson, indeed, had a very poor opinion of the moral qualities of the atmosphere. In her view it was always lying in wait to get in some stab in the back or another.

However, it was to the harbour that Bobby now took his way, in spite of all lurking dangers from the sea air. Various small craft were lying there, and he asked one of the men on the jetty to point out the launch formerly belonging to Lord Adour. He explained he had heard it was for sale. He was shown where it lay alongside the jetty, but was told that the engine was out of action. Mr. Itter Bain, on his return from his last trip, had in part dismantled the engine, though whether with the idea of introducing some new gadget to increase power or improve running, or simply because one part or another needed renewing, no one seemed to know.

Bobby also learned that the launch could be taken out under sail, but it would require skilled seamanship to handle her. She had the reputation of being awkward under sail. The cabin was locked of course, and Mr. Mauley Bain had the key. Naturally a watch was kept on the launch, as on all the other boats in the harbour. They paid their dues and no unauthorized person would be allowed the use of any of them.

From the harbour Bobby went back into the town and there he met Jane, he was not sure whether by accident or design. There seemed no very obvious reason why she should be in this part of the little town now that night was falling and all the shops closed, and he thought there was about her a certain suggestion of waiting for someone or something, though whether for himself or another it was impossible to guess.

However, greeting her, he stopped to make a few vague remarks, so that she might have an opportunity to speak if she wished to do so. She seemed nervous, replied in kind to his one or two commonplace observations and then said:

"Helen was by the river. I told her you had wanted her.

"Oh, yes. What did she say?" Bobby asked.

"Mr. Mauley Bain was there, too," Jane said without answering his question. "I mean, close by, I mean he was sitting there just in the same way."

"Mauley Bain?" Bobby repeated, and possibly a certain subtle uneasiness in his voice communicated itself to her.

She spoke a little more freely as she said:

"He frightens me. I don't know why. He never did before, but now he does. He always seems to be watching, just as if he were waiting, always waiting. And he keeps out of your way. You see him and then he isn't there and he never speaks. By the river this afternoon, it was just as if he were watching Helen. Men always do stare whenever she is there, but this was different, and besides he couldn't see her. I mean, not really see her, because she was sitting under some trees and they hid her nearly. I expect you think I'm silly?"

"No," Bobby said. "No. Anything but. Did you tell Miss Helen?"

"Yes."

"What did she say?"

"Nothing. She doesn't. I mean, she never takes much notice. She makes you feel sometimes as if she felt her beauty were enough. As if nothing else were real. Perhaps it isn't. Is it?"

"I see," Bobby said thoughtfully. "It's a complication. It's only since his brother's death you've felt like this about Mauley?" She nodded, did not speak for a moment or two and then said slowly:

"It may be only that he's brooding. He's always seemed rather sulky and silent and bad-tempered, and I suppose what's happened may have made him worse. Uncle has noticed it, too. I mean, Lord Adour. He's not my uncle really, I'm a sort of cousin, but I've always called him uncle. Uncle says he saw Mauley in the spinney this afternoon, and he has seen him near the house, too, after dark, but he never speaks."

"I'll try to get a talk with him," Bobby said, really disturbed, and decided it would be wise to ask Commander Seers to post a man to watch Kindles and to challenge Mauley if he were seen near. Loitering or trespassing, it could be called, Bobby supposed. He went on: "Did Mauley know you saw him?"

"I don't know. Another man came up and spoke to him and they went away together. It was Mr. Haile. He called at Kindles once and I saw him. He is a reporter for the *Seashire Herald*, and he wanted to ask a lot of questions. I had to tell him to go away."

"Yes. I've heard of him," Bobby said. "Reporters can be a help, but they can be a nuisance, too. Getting a story is all they think about. I take it you knew Mauley well when you and his brother were engaged?"

"It was such a short engagement," Jane answered, smiling a little, and without any trace of embarrassment. "I don't think I ever met Mauley while it lasted. It was funny. Poor Itter quite swept me off my feet, just like the cave man in the films. But then I began to recover, and so did he, and then he met Helen and that ended it. We were both very glad to break it off."

"You remained perfectly good friends, then?"

"Oh, yes. Why not? I think we were both grateful to each other for not wanting to go on. I don't think I could possibly have gone through with it and I'm sure he didn't want to, especially not after meeting Helen," and Jane gave her rich, low, bubbling laugh in which at least there sounded no trace of resentment or regret. Her laughter stopped. Bobby looked at her. She said apologetically: "I'm so sorry. I must be getting nervy. I thought I saw someone in the shadows there."

She pointed. Bobby flashed his torch. No one was there, no sign that anyone had been there. He said:

"I'll walk back to Kindles with you."

She thanked him, a trifle tremulously.

"I don't know what's the matter with me," she said. "I've never been like this before."

"It's natural," Bobby consoled her. "There's never been a murder here before."

"It'll never be the same again," she said in a low voice, "till we know who did it," and Bobby wondered if he were right in thinking that in her voice as she spoke was a subtle hint that she thought perhaps she knew already.

CHAPTER XIV

WAYLING TRANSFORMATION SCENE

Next morning, Bobby starting on his way to Drinks for his interview with the manager of the Drinks branch of the London and Coastal Bank, received one of the greatest shocks of his young life.

For there, outside the "Good Haul," was Mr. Alexander Wayling, in his shirt sleeves, polishing the big brass door plates and handles till they shone like the sun at noon in the desert, or even like the buttons on the tunic of a guardsman on parade.

Bobby halted his car and stared. He even shut his eyes for a moment, but when he opened them again Mr. Wayling was still there, still polishing away. Never, never had Bobby thought that one day he would see Wayling busy at an honest job of work and doing it well. Wayling, pausing for a moment in his labours, became aware of Bobby's presence and waved a cheery greeting.

"Doesn't look too bad, does it?" he said, surveying the result of his labours with pride.

"What on earth ... ?" began Bobby and stopped, speech failing him.

"Oh, about that five pounds you lent me, and very kind of you too," said Wayling.

"Did I lend you five pounds?" asked Bobby, still slightly dazed, but still able to lay a certain stress on the word "lend."

"Forgotten it?" demanded Wayling smilingly. "Lucky for you I've a better memory. But I never forget a temporary loan, however small," His tone suggested that a loan of five pounds was so small it was as easy to forget it as creditable to remember it. He produced a small note-book. "I always jot everything down," he said, "so as to be sure." He regarded his little book with affectionate pride, for indeed it had always seemed to him, and quite sincerely, that to make a note of a liability was much the same as discharging it. "Now I've got a good steady job at a fat screw," he went on, "I'm arranging a kind of sinking fund so as to clear up everything at once. I think that's much fairer than handing out driblets of cash one at a time, don't you?"

"Well," Bobby answered cautiously, "speaking for myself, I shouldn't mind the driblet of cash here and now."

"Ah," declared Wayling with a distinctly patronizing air, "you don't appreciate the magic of compound interest."

"Probably not," agreed Bobby. "Do you mean you've taken on a regular job here?"

"Assistant manager," Wayling explained. "I'm a bit of a novice, of course, so I lend a hand everywhere to get the hang of things before taking over, as I'm told they'll want me to before long. Mornings I help straighten things up. Afternoons, the business end—interviews, letters, correspondence, accounts, all that. Evenings, I superintend the bars."

"Oh," said Bobby, quite overwhelmed, and Wayling waved a farewell and bustled inside.

Wonderingly, Bobby drove on to Drinks, arriving soon after the bank opened its doors for business. By the manager, who was expecting him, he was received with a polite but wary firmness. Bobby had been prepared for that. His idea of the meeting of the irresistible force and the immovable object was that of the meeting between a policeman armed with the authority and prestige of the law and a bank official armed with the prestige and authority of high finance. The manager made the expected opening move by declaring with great emphasis that banks regarded the private affairs of their customers as sacrosanct. Bobby managed to get in at last a remark that he didn't care two hoots about any one's private affairs. All he wanted to know was whether the managed could swear, if necessary in court, that he had been in the company of Mauley and Prescott Bain during the whole afternoon of the day of Itter Bain's murder. He did not care, Bobby repeated, what they had been talking about. It might be the most likely winner of the two-thirty, for all that mattered to him. But had they all been in each other's sight and company the whole time.

The manager, looking shocked, said with some severity that it was not the habit of responsible officials of the London and Coastal Bank to discuss the—er—hypothetical winner of the—er— two-thirty, was it?—during business hours. He and Mr. Jameson—one of the Bank's inspectors—had undoubtedly spent the whole afternoon discussing somewhat—er—intricate financial arrangements with the directors of Bain Products. On their arrival there had been a brief talk at which Itter, Mauley, and Prescott had all been present. Itter Bain had then said that his cousin, Prescott Bain, had full authority to speak for him and he would support whatever arrangements were agreed to. Itter

Bain had then withdrawn and they had not seen him again. This was before lunch. The discussions had then begun. They had necessarily taken considerable time. Once or twice, the two bank men had been left alone. This was so that they might talk over between themselves the suggestions made, the difficulties raised, and also to compare and check the figures submitted. Such intervals had never been prolonged. Probably they had never occupied at one time more than half an hour at the outside. Prescott Bain had taken the leading part in presenting the Bain Products case. His was the financial mind. Mauley Bain had seemed sulky, uninformed, almost uninterested, easily confused by figures. He had plainly welcomed any interruption calling him away to attend to details of factory management. If it had been necessary to consult him or obtain information about the staff or production, or about the progress of contracts in hand, then Prescott had called him up and consulted him over the private factory exchange. The bank manager confessed that both he and Mr. Jameson were relieved when Mauley was absent. His comments had often been—er—unhelpful, uninstructed.

That seemed about as much information as Bobby could collect, and he retired accordingly. In a dissatisfied mood. The alibi was by no means as watertight as Commander Seers's reports had suggested. But still strong. Even the more strong for not being too suspiciously complete. Difficult to suppose, for example, that anyone could leave an important business conference, commit a murder, and then come back as though nothing much had happened. Unfortunately, the two bank officials, precise as they might be over pounds and pence, seemed as woolly-minded as anyone else when it came to hours and minutes. They did not think Prescott Bain had ever been absent from the conference room for more than twenty minutes or half an hour at once. But they had paid no special attention to the time, and Bobby supposed that time could pass with unexpected speed when you were discussing the best way to get hold of a good going concern in temporary difficulties owing to the changeover from war to peace. For that, Bobby felt fairly certain, was the object the two bankers had in view. Mauley Bain, too, had apparently always been in touch over the factory private 'phone exchange, and had been frequently consulted thereon.

Bobby got himself some lunch and then smoked a reflective cigarette over a cup of coffee that made him think yearningly of the coffee he got at home. Then he drove to Kindles, where he found that Lord Adour and Avon was in town, attending a business conference; Jane out, visiting a neighbour; and Helen lying down with one of the bad headaches to which it seemed she was subject.

A journey for nothing and Helen still invisible. Nothing to do but drive away again, but soon he met Haile on his motor cycle. Bobby stopped his car, Haile dismounted and greeted Bobby smilingly, quite oblivious apparently of Bobby's somewhat stern and official manner.

"On my way to Kindles," Haile explained. "I thought I would try to get another talk with the divine Helen. Have you fallen in love with her? It is the common fate of all, you know."

"I haven't seen Miss Adour yet," Bobby told him. "I want to talk to you. Have you been giving people the idea that you are connected with the police?"

"Not me," declared Haile with every appearance of extreme indignation. "Why, it would be felony or misdemeanour or something, wouldn't it? High treason probably. Give me the name of anyone who has told you that and I'll start an action for libel."

"A good many people seem to have the idea," Bobby said. "I hope you'll contradict it, and I do suggest it would be wise for you to be careful."

"Now, now, old man," Haile said in his most persuasive manner, "don't let's get in each other's hair. Do us no good, either of us. I've my job. You've yours. If I get anything I'll turn it over to you, pronto. You can trust me." (Bobby didn't.) "I'm just a harmless reporter on the staff of the *Seashire Herald*. A most influential paper in all this district."

There was a hint of a threat in these last words that Bobby ignored.

"A reporter with a retaining fee from the gentleman who calls himself Jack Cade Junior, busy just at present, I believe, trying to bring off another unofficial strike somewhere, isn't he?"

"I don't know, and I don't care either," retorted Haile with some appearance of sincerity. "I'm trying to bring off a journalistic scoop, and if it puts the new Government in a hole, a fat lot I care. I'm not interested in bringing pressure on any government unless it means getting me a better job. No jolly old ideology complex about this lad. By the way, thinking of going in for yachting?"

"Why?"

"Well, there does seem a certain sudden interest in Itter Bain's launch he bought from old Adour the other day. You don't think Itter was killed in the launch, do you?"

"Do you?"

"Ain't saying nuffen? Downy bird, aren't you? Rather points to his lordship, though, if the launch is the locus. Mr. Jack Cade Junior might be interested if I told him. Any objections?"

"You are responsible for what you say or do," Bobby answered. "Don't try to quote me."

"Why can't we be a bit more friendly?" Haile sighed. "Open-hearted friendship, that's me. Have you heard about Old Ugly?"

"Old Ugly?" repeated Bobby, puzzled for the moment. "Oh, you mean Wayling? Is that it? What about him?"

"Do you know he is the new potman at the 'Good Haul'?"

"Well, he called it assistant manager when I was talking to him," Bobby remarked.

"Oh, he would," Haile said, though evidently a little disappointed that Bobby already knew of the Wayling transformation scene. "Why do you think he took the job?"

"Most likely," suggested Bobby, unable to keep a touch of bitterness out of his voice, "most likely to get a chance to touch the manager—and the customers as well. The barmaids, too, probably."

"Wrong," said Haile with decision. "That'll happen, of course, but only by the way. What he is really after is a chance to hang around and get a glimpse of Helen Adour now and then." Haile paused and then said: "He has hopes," and in his voice was a kind of incredulous and wondering doubt as if he asked himself whether this hope were as completely absurd as it might seem.

"If he has, it's his affair," Bobby said. "But not necessary to become a potman in a pub for that, is it?"

"Only way to get a bed," Haile explained. "Not one unoccupied for miles around. You're all right. Been wished on a brother cop, haven't you? I sleep on a sofa in a brother reporter's dining-room, and his wife will probably be suing for a divorce before long. Oh, not what you think," added Haile with a snigger. "I've told her my heart's breaking for the divine Helen, and she can't imagine what men see in her. Dowdy, she says, which means that Helen doesn't bother about the beauty aids that beauty itself doesn't need."

There was an odd note in these last words that made Bobby wonder if there was not more in Haile's flippant talk about his "breaking heart" than he wished to appear. Then, too, Bobby was growing a little worried by so much talk of a beauty about which he had not yet had a chance to form his own opinion.

"I must get a talk with her to-morrow," he observed.

"You know the River Farm bloke?" Haile asked; and when Bobby nodded, and said he had had a chat with him, Haile added: "Did you know he was meeting Helen Adour every night?" and this time did succeed in bringing off a surprise.

"Are you sure?" Bobby asked, gravely disturbed.

"Saw 'em both," Haile said. "Plain as you like in the moonlight. Bright as day it was nearly. They were saying goodbye." Very slowly, in an odd, far off tone, he said: "It was the moon, that was all."

"What was?" Bobby asked, but Haile did not answer.

Instead he said:

"We were a churchy family when I was a kid. My mother. She laid it on too thick, I suppose. But I took it all right then. You wouldn't think it now, but I did. I took it bad."

"Took what bad?" asked Bobby, frankly bewildered. "What do you happen to be talking about?"

"About being a kid, and wanting to be a parson, and all that. It was what mother wanted. Good job she died when she did. And being alone in church one night with the moon shining in on the altar. It all came back to me last night. The moon, you know. That was it. Just the moon being so bright, and that's why I could see the girl the way I did."

Bobby gave it up. He thought perhaps Haile had been drinking, and yet it did not seem quite like that. Except perhaps for the odd look in his eyes. That might be alcohol, Bobby supposed, or it might be something else. He didn't know. He said:

"Did you speak to them?"

But Haile's mind still seemed far away. Back perhaps in those queer, adolescent days when he had watched the altar in the solitary moonlit church and dreamed of being good. Or back perhaps in the hours of the previous night when he had lain and watched the parting between Winstanley and Helen.

"It was the first time I had seen her," Haile was saying. "I mean to say—seen her. I had before, but not like this time, if you know what I mean. It was the way she stood with the moon shining round her. Like a silver fire. What was that you were saying? Did I speak to her? Good lord, no." He paused and looked at Bobby with the same queer manner he had shown before, and then he began to laugh. "I'm getting batty," he said. "It must be that last drink I had at the 'Good Haul.'" His manner was more normal now, his laugh more natural. He went on: "No, I didn't speak. They mightn't have liked it if I had, and Winstanley had his gun with him. I didn't want to give you another job. I stopped where I was and watched them go. I think she had come out to meet him. She hadn't a hat on, only a shawl. I don't know if it matters, but I suppose I ought to tell you, as pal to pal."

"Yes, thanks," Bobby said; and then was immediately annoyed at himself, for he felt this was too much like accepting the "pal to pal" attitude he suspected Haile of wishing to establish, that might even be at the root of his queer sort of lost manner at the beginning of their talk, but that now he seemed to have dropped completely, to be even half ashamed of. Bobby's voice had a sharper edge to it as he asked: "Where did all this happen?"

"In the spinney, on the path to Kindles from Toad-in-Hole, not so far from where Itter Bain had his." Anticipating Bobby's next question, Haile added: "I was having a cool off after a few drinks at the 'Good Haul' before riding home. I prefer a good clear head when I'm on a motor bike."

"Quite right," approved Bobby, though reflecting that only a head already fairly clear would entertain that preference.

"I should keep an eye on the Winstanley bloke if I were you," Haile added.

"A good tip," approved Bobby again. "You gave me another about Mauley Bain, I remember. Seen anything of him at night near Kindles?"

"No," answered Haile slowly. "No. But Mauley's not so easily seen if he doesn't want to be. Better tell the man you're putting on guard there to keep his eyes skinned. Or maybe you'll find the poor beggar laid out one morning."

This was another shock to Bobby. Had Haile already heard of the proposed watch to be instituted for Haile's own special benefit?

"What do you mean?" Bobby asked sourly. "Who's been telling you there's to be anyone there?"

"Oh, Wayling," Haile answered. "Why? Supposed to be confidential? Sorry. Thought it was just routine. Wayling always knows things. You ought to give him a job. Probably your bloke grumbled to his wife about fresh night duty, and she grumbled to a neighbour, and the neighbour had a drink at the 'Good Haul' and told everyone. Quite simple."

"Quite simple," agreed Bobby, more sourly even than before. If that constable had been one of his own men, he would have had something to say to him. The mischief was done, though, and no good complaining. He said abruptly, and with meaning, for by now Haile was looking altogether too perky, too self satisfied: "How was it Mr. Sammy Robinson Jack Cade Junior hit on you for this job of his?"

"My dear man," protested Haile, deeply offended. "Mr. Deputy Chief Constable the Honourable Robert Owen—"

"I'm not," interrupted Bobby, this time not so much sourly as furiously. "I'm no more an 'honourable' than you are."

"—nephew," pursued Haile inexorably, "of a peer of ancient lineage—"

"That's a lie," snapped Bobby. "The blasted title only goes back to the eighteenth century—a Walpole creation, one man's price probably."

"—is not," Haile continued, totally ignoring Bobby's interruptions, "the only pebble on the beach. My work in the secret service at M.I.5—if you know what that is?"

"London's best-known landmark," said Bobby, vicious now. "When you had to direct a stranger, you said: 'You know the hush-hush place they call M.I.5? Well, starting from there, it's so-and-so, as the case might be. You were in charge of a room where some of the circulars were typed, weren't you? You and two A.T.S. girls. Confidential, of course, but just like any other office job."

"You are entirely misinformed," Haile declared with dignity. "Entirely. That typing job was camouflage. That's all. I can't go into details. It's still jolly secret and probably always will be. Some stories can't be told. But it's because of my M.I.5 work that Sammy came to me."

"Doesn't explain, though," Bobby remarked, "why you were in the district before Itter Bain was murdered?"

"I wasn't. That's a lie. Who told you that?" demanded Haile, and he looked both startled and alarmed. "Nonsense."

"There seems fairly strong evidence," Bobby told him, "that you were seen both in Drinks and in Toad-in-Hole before the murder."

"I wasn't. Pack of lies," Haile repeated, and stared challengingly at Bobby. "Or mistaken identity. Or just a police dodge. Fishing. I've tried that game myself before now. To see what you get. Nothing this time, because I wasn't anywhere near the place. If you mean to try any of those tricks with me, they won't come off. I know too much."

"I'm sure you do," Bobby said; and it almost seemed as if Haile read a double meaning into that reply, for he looked more startled, more angry, more afraid than ever as he remounted and rode away.

CHAPTER XV

NOCTURNAL EXCURSION

THIS AFTERNOON Sergeant Gregson, his tour of duty done, was there to help with Mrs. Gregson's admirable scones—alas! no butter this time, and not much margarine, as there had been some delay over Bobby's food cards. The sergeant was much preoccupied with news of a drifting mine that had been sighted, bobbing up and down in the direct line of approach to the harbour. A bomb-disposal squad had been sent for, but would not arrive till morning. Many mines had been loosened from their moorings by a recent gale, and the bomb disposal squad had its hands full. So Commander Seers and the Harbour-master rowed out and attached a buoy with a red light burning on it to the mine, hoping so to guard against the risk of collision with any vessel returning to harbour. Sergeant Gregson was, however, inclined to take a gloomy view of possibilities.

"Touch and go with them things," he said. "Bump against a bit of driftwood and up she goes and us, too. I said to Commander, I said: 'Oughtn't we to evacuate, same as in 1940 when we thought Jerry was landing and parson and his missis rang the church bells all on their own.' Lummy! I shan't forget that night and them bells and old Willie Wright, what had rung them fifty year, man and boy, sobbing like a baby over the jingle jangle. He's joined the methody now. But Commander says, no, not unless mine drifts nearer and he'll watch her till the squad gets here. He says he calculates she'll likely drift west, and then," said the sergeant comfortably, "it won't be us."

Bobby said that after tea he would go down and have a look and Mrs. Gregson disapproved. Why go looking for trouble when trouble was always looking for you? If Mr. Owen wanted to see a mine, there would be plenty more. Troubles never came singly, they came in threes; if one child got measles, two were sure to have whooping cough; and Mr. Owen could take it from her that two more mines were sure to follow this one.

The sergeant observed with an air of surprise that for once his old woman was talking sense. Commander Seers had said he thought it likely that others might have broken loose, and, if so, would probably follow the same line of drift.

Bobby said that, anyhow, he would like a stroll after this excellent tea so as to be sure of a good appetite for the still more excellent supper of which he could already detect certain savoury preliminary smells. He went on to ask a few questions about tides and currents, about ease of access to the harbour, and how long it would take, for example, Lord Adour's launch, *Seagull*, Itter Bain had bought shortly before his death, to reach the French coast.

Probably his questions showed no great knowledge of the sea. But they did show knowledge of the French coast, directly across from Toad-in-Hole. A remark of his that he had spent holidays there in pre-war days made Gregson ask if Mr. Owen knew French.

"Would have been handy to have someone who could speak the lingo," Gregson remarked, "when we were trying to get sense out of that Frenchy chap the other day."

Bobby asked who that was, as, Mrs. Gregson permitting smoking, he passed his cigarette case round. He was told that a Frenchman had recently appeared in Toad-in-Hole, and no one could find out who he was or where he came from or what he wanted. His papers had been demanded, had been perfectly in order, had given a name and address in Hull. But Hull, inquired of later, knew nothing of him. He had been asked to go to the local police station for further inquiry, but, not being carefully watched, since no special suspicions were entertained, had taken an opportunity to walk out again. Nor had anything more been seen of him. He had vanished as mysteriously as he had appeared. A very tall, thin man, middle-aged, with a black, strong-growing beard, the sergeant described him; and, though of so striking an appearance, so certain to attract attention, it had been impossible to find out either how he had reached Toad-in-Hole or how he had left again. The railway people knew nothing of him. No bus had been running at that time, no one had seen a strange car or cycle. No one answering his description had been seen on the roads entering or leaving the town. He had just materialized there and then vanished again, and Gregson was plainly still a little puzzled and uneasy.

"Hope he's not been murdered, too," said the sergeant, laughing at his own joke.

Bobby said he hoped not, and Mrs. Gregson told her husband not to talk so foolish. The cigarettes finished, Bobby said he would stroll down to the harbour and see how they were getting on. He would like another look at the *Seagull*, too, while he was there. The sergeant, slightly surprised at this, said he believed the launch had been moved from its moorings in the harbour. One of the Bain company barges, engaged in transporting raw material to, and the finished product from, the Bain factory, had this morning taken the launch in tow in order to convey it up river to the factory, where the engine was to be taken down, cleaned, and put in good running order again.

Bobby said it was of no great importance. All the same, he wondered privately if this was merely coincidence, or a result of the interest he had shown earlier in the launch and the questions he had asked.

On his way to the harbour he went into a 'phone call-box he had noticed previously. After the manner in which the fact that a man was to be stationed at night at Kindles had leaked out, he had thought it as well not to use the Gregson instrument. He need not have troubled. The answer he received when he got through to Mauley Bain's address in Drinks was that Mr. Bain was in London and not expected back for a day or two.

So Bobby proceeded on his way to the harbour, where he found Commander Seers far too interested in the mine bobbing up and down off shore to have time or thought to spare for Bobby or Bobby's activities. He thought the danger to the town was nearly over, as the tides and currents should now be taking the mine out to sea again. Bobby asked a question or two about Sergeant Gregson's mysterious Frenchman and his unexplained appearance and disappearance, but Seers was not interested. Plenty of foreigners knocking about and control not enforced very strictly now the war was over. Anyhow, it could have nothing to do with Itter Bain's murder, since that had only happened two or three days later. As the Commander was evidently in no mood to answer questions, Bobby asked no more; but remained for some time, watching the bobbing up and down of the tiny light that showed where such great forces of destruction lay, all ready to break loose at a touch.

"Rather risky sort of job, fixing that light to the thing, wasn't it?" Bobby asked.

"Why? Because it might have gone off?" the Commander asked, slightly surprised. "Oh, that wasn't likely. I would rather handle a dozen mines than cross Piccadilly once. Mines are all right if you know how to go to work. The only real danger is that they may drift in at night, or in fog, without being noticed and explode as soon as they touch shore. But it's quite all right if you know they are there."

To Bobby this attitude seemed somewhat optimistic. For his own part, he felt he would rather know that they weren't there. He thought also that Seers was evidently a good deal more at home handling a few hundred pounds of high explosive, liable to go off at any moment, than he was with criminal investigation. So he went back to the Gregsons' for a rest, since he had decided that after supper he would do a prowl round the Kindles territory. An intruder might be prepared and ready to avoid the one watcher he knew would be on guard and, having done so, be all the more likely to expose himself to another, unexpected and unprepared for. A little afraid of further leakage, Bobby took the precaution of warning the Gregsons that he did not wish anyone to know he would be out part of the night. The Sergeant, fortunately, was not going on duty again. He was already yawning, ready for bed. If any neighbours did come in for any reason, they were to be told that Bobby, also, had retired for the night.

Declining with many thanks an offer from Mrs. Gregson to put him up a packet of sandwiches and a thermos flask of tea, Bobby started out. The constable told off for the Kindles duty was a man named Jackson, and Bobby lay and shivered in the shelter of a hedge by the

Kindles road till presently Jackson appeared, on his way to take up his post. Bobby introduced himself, warned Jackson to keep his eyes and ears well open, reminded him that it might be a murderer they would meet, instructed him to come out into the open field that lay between the Kindles garden and the Coldstone spinney and flash his light skywards if he needed help or saw or heard anything unusual. Bobby added that he would do the same if he needed Jackson's help. So both must be on the look out for such a signal, and, of course, in case of necessity, police whistles must be used.

Jackson was plainly both puzzled and alarmed by these instructions that seemed to put in a very different light what he had been inclined to regard as a routine duty slightly more boring than usual. Distinctly disturbing, this casual observation about the possibility of meeting a murderer in the darkness of the spinney, in the silence of the garden, now that darkness and silence, spinney and garden, had become invested by those few whispered words with so sinister and threatening a background. Give him, reflected Jackson gloomily, lighted streets and tackling a drunken dock worker with no malice on either side, and he was all right. You knew where you were. But possible assassins lurking unseen were a bit thick, a bit too thick. Still, duty was duty, so he squared his shoulders and marched bravely on; and no doubt any psychoanalyst would have been able to explain why, somehow or another, though he tried to pick his steps with care, he yet managed to step on every twig, to kick against every stone, that lay in his path.

"The march of the law," Bobby reflected, listening; "oh, well, anyone dodging him and finding it easy will be all the more likely to get careless."

He had already selected a strategic position from which he could watch both the approaches to Kindles from the main road and most of the southern fringe of trees bordering the Kindles garden, as well as much of the northern edge of the spinney where were the openings of the other paths crossing it. At least he hoped that would be so after the rising of the moon, for as yet, until the moon did rise, the darkness was profound. Once or twice he thought he heard footsteps, but it was only leaves rustling in the slow night breeze. He could hear, too, an occasional rabbit scuttling by, one of those for whose benefit presumably Lord Adour had brought out his gun on the day of the murder. Indeed, Bobby had occasion again to wonder at the multiplicity, at the variety, of the sounds that, taken all together, make up the tremendous and majestic silence of the night, a silence that is in itself in some strange way a part of the universal harmony. It was cold there in the undergrowth, it was damp and uncomfortable, and it was still dark, though the tiniest hint of coming light on the horizon showed where the moon was beginning to rise, when Bobby saw a light flashed skywards from the field that lay between garden and spinney.

CHAPTER XVI
HIDE AND SEEK

Bobby was wearing light, rubber-soled shoes he had brought with him for any such emergency as this. Now he raced on silent feet across the open field towards where he had seen a light flash out and vanish. Through the dark night he sped, and when he reached what he judged must be somewhere near the spot whence that signal had been flashed into the sky he whistled softly and shone his torch downwards to the ground and waited for response. None came. He whistled softly and still there was no reply. He tried again, whistling once more and flashing his light downward. Then, since there was still no answer, he crouched down, hoping he might be able to distinguish something or some one silhouetted against the horizon, against the faint, almost imperceptible glow that told where the moon was about to rise, though herself yet hidden. At first he saw nothing, and then across his field of vision, shown against that faint and distant glow on the horizon, there passed a silent, swiftly moving figure, direct and purposeful and evil in the night, running towards the belt of trees that lay at the foot of the Kindles garden. It passed, it was gone, it had vanished among these trees before Bobby had had time to do more than scramble to his feet again, and why that momentary apparition had left upon his mind an apprehension so acute, a premonition of danger so near at hand, he himself could not have told. But it was as though an inner voice warned him to beware, and when this time he flashed his light skyward, in the hope that now his signal might be seen and answered, he thought he heard a voice calling softly from among the trees, a woman's voice, he thought, and yet he was not sure nor even whether it was in fact a voice that he had heard.

He began to run, angry that his signal had not been answered and yet afraid that there might be for that, good reason. He reached the trees; and as he did so he heard someone laugh, a laugh that had in it no pleasant sound, either of mirth or of joy.

"Who's there?" he called and plunged forward among the bordering trees, but it was from behind that there came an answer, an answer in a loud, cracked voice, evidently disguised, that said:

"Go home, go home, little man. You've nothing to do here."

Bobby made no answer, but ran fast, or as fast as conditions permitted, in the direction whence the voice had come. But now he heard a rustling and what he thought were footsteps in front again, and so he dashed forward, only to be brought up abruptly by collision with a strong wire fence running through this belt of trees and undergrowth that served as a windscreen to the Kindles garden and as a boundary between it and the fields belonging to Martin Winstanley's River Farm. Though only some ten or twenty yards deep, it, together with the unchecked undergrowth that had grown up during the war, formed a considerable obstacle, complicated by this wire fence, strong, high, and barbed that ran through it. Indeed, previously it had played its part in the scheme of defence laid down for this district when invasion seemed inevitable—inevitable, at least, till the battle of the skies and the rain of German planes falling from the clouds, brought relief, as rain in season brings relief where famine has been feared.

Now Bobby flashed his light again to judge better of this obstacle that had checked him so abruptly. Doing so, he saw a figure flit between the trees on the other side of the fence, not running now, creeping rather, and yet still with that same air of dark and secret purpose, so silently it went, so purposely, so indifferent to the light that held it plain for a moment, so indifferent to Bobby's sharp call to it to stay.

He could not tell who it was, and now the trees hid it again. A cap drawn down over the eyes had met, or nearly met, the scarf that muffled most of the lower part of the face. A long, dark coat covered all the body, and the stooping position adopted, to avoid overhanging boughs, made it impossible to judge the height. He was not even sure it had been a man, though he thought so. But it might have been a woman. He could not be certain. And he had seen, too, that the hands were gloved, and that one of them held what seemed like some kind of club or bludgeon.

"Stop or I'll fire," Bobby shouted, though he had no weapon on him wherewith to implement his threat; and all the answer that he got was the scuffle of a rabbit running by and the faint murmur of the night breeze through the trees, as though they laughed together.

He flashed his torch again and found a convenient tree with overhanging branches. With its aid he swung himself across the wire fencing and hurried in the direction in which he had seen vanish the dark and ominous figure he pursued or sought. Without success, for both pursuit and search seemed more difficult, more baffling still, now that level rays of light from the risen moon threw long shadows from the trees and made alternate lanes of light with deep pools of darkness at the roots of the trees and where the thick bushes grew.

Abruptly there fell on him a bright strong ray from not far away, a ray from a powerful electric torch. He felt himself oddly revealed, uncovered. The light was like a pointing finger and he had to resist an impulse to run behind a tree to avoid it.

"Who is that?" he shouted angrily and ran towards it, only to be checked once more, and almost at once, by that same strong wire fence.

If it was the same person he had seen a moment or two before, then the fence must have been crossed again in the other direction. Not difficult, if you knew where to find the right spots, or possibly where there was a gate. A game of hide and seek that might go on long enough, he supposed, and now the ray that had been focused on him was suddenly switched off. A game of hide and seek, of whose purpose and of whose object he had no knowledge. Not much use trying, on this confusing chequer board of moonlight and shadow, to follow a fugitive who it seemed could always be on the other side of the fence, so making swift pursuit impossible. But all that might be easier, more practicable, when the light grew stronger and these long shadows and dark pools of night among the bushes less baffling and mysterious.

"All right. All right," he called into the darkness and in his voice was all the helpless and indignant anger that he felt. "You've been warned."

"Warned yourself," came the same snarling, high-pitched voice, plainly disguised, he had heard before, and there flew by, within a few inches of his head, some heavy object thrown with force and fierce intention.

It smashed heavily against a tree trunk near, with a thud that told what the result would have been had it hit instead of missed. Bobby dashed in the direction whence it came, but tripped and nearly fell as his foot caught in an entangling bramble. A momentary delay, but sufficient, for when he recovered his balance and could hurry on, there was nothing.

"Two of them," he thought, "one on each side of that damn fence and they're just playing with me. I mustn't get excited," he thought; for he felt within himself such a buzzing of frustrated, storming rage as made him want to make blind rushes to and fro in the hope of finding someone or something. But there was always the fence between, the fence across which, knowing the appropriate places, others could slip with an ease and speed denied to him. "They hold all the trumps," he told himself. Then he thought: "All right. I'll throw the lead."

He remained standing quietly and very still in the deep shadow of a tree near by, waiting and listening with every faculty stretched at its full. At the back of his mind was an uneasy wonder as to what had happened to the constable on duty who should have been there to help, who it was presumably who had sent out that message of the flashing skyward light to which he had responded, but never found the sender. Had he done so, had he had someone to help, then there could have been one of them on each side of the dividing, baffling fence and that would have made all the difference. It would have made impossible the game now being played of dodging to and fro. Now the best chance seemed to be to remain silent, watchful and hidden, in the hope that whoever might be here would presently betray himself or his position. If he did so, then, Bobby told himself with emphasis, for by this time he was very much annoyed indeed, he would know what to do—and how he would do it. A nice thing, he thought gloomily, for a Deputy Chief Constable of Wychshire, for a just faintly possible future Deputy Assistant Commissioner at Scotland Yard, to be played with like this.

For a time, strain his hearing and his sight as he might, he heard, saw nothing. Nothing that is to suggest that any other living, moving human being was anywhere within this belt of trees. Yet now he was beginning to think there must have been two others—the one who had thrown at him, with intent to end his activities for the night, that heavy object which had missed him only by inches, and the one whose bright electric torch had picked him out from the further side of the fence. Or, again, there was the secret and silent figure he had seen passing by as though intent upon some pressing mischief. With that figure he identified in his mind the high, cracked, certainly disguised voice that had bidden him go home. But did that mean there were three—three others besides himself within the narrow compass and shelter of this windscreen of trees? If so, what was their business here so late and so secret, and who were they?

Questions to which as yet there seemed no answer—no answer at least to which he could relate what else had happened hereabouts.

He stiffened to even closer attention. There came to him the sound of low, murmuring voices, distant and indistinct, yet recognizable as coming from two who were talking to each other. Did this mean that the two unknowns of whose presence he had had evidence, had now come together in consultation or in greeting? As silently as cautiously as he might, Bobby made his way in the direction whence those murmuring voices came. They ceased, but now instead he thought he could hear footsteps. He hurried, he almost ran, though still with caution, for he felt that any sound he made might well cause those he sought to vanish once again. The light was stronger now as the moon rose higher, and her less level, stronger rays threw shorter, lighter shadows. He could still hear retreating footsteps. Terrifyingly in that still moonlit night rang out a scream, a fearful scream, a woman's scream.

There was in it, such urgency, such need and such appeal, that Bobby forgot his caution and ran. Once more there closed upon the night an uttermost silence. Challenged and broken for the instant by that one loud, dreadful cry, instantly it came together again and now was as it had been before.

Bobby shouted. He flashed his torch hither and thither and shouted again, and still he had no answer, and still there seemed to echo in his ear that cry of one in most deadly fear and peril.

CHAPTER XVII

A TWEED CAP

IT WAS FROM the Kindles garden, on the north side of the tree belt, that this loud and dreadful cry had seemed to come; and in that direction Bobby now ran, breaking, not without relief, from among the dark and treacherous shadows beneath the trees to the flower beds and lawns and paths where the uninterrupted moonbeams gave a stronger and a clearer light. He called out as he ran. He came to a broad, straight, gravel path, and there at once he saw at a little distance a white patch on the path, clearly visible in the white light of the moon. He ran towards it and saw that it covered in part a crumpled human body. Nearer still, he saw it was the white swansdown cape he remembered he had seen in Lord Adour's study and that Jane Felgate had claimed as the property of her cousin, Helen. So still lay that huddled form he thought death must be there before him. It came into his mind that only in death, and only perhaps when it had passed away, was he to see the strange beauty which had seemed to have on so many others such powerful effect. But when he knelt by the side of that still figure it stirred, it moved, it raised itself, and Bobby recognized Jane Felgate.

She was looking at him a little wildly from startled and fearful eyes. Her body was shaken by strong tremors so that even her teeth chattered. She put out her hand and clutched at his coat, but when she tried to speak words would not come. Bobby put to her lips the small brandy flask he always carried.

"Drink this," he said.

She drank obediently. The strong spirit set her spluttering and gasping, but evidently did her good. The tremors ceased and when he felt her pulse it was stronger and she seemed less cold. For a moment Bobby thought of leaving her and starting in pursuit of her assailant, since evidently she had been attacked. He gave up the idea at once. Pursuit so far had been no great success, nor was Jane in any condition to be left. He said to her: "Feeling better? It's all right now. Quite all right. Are you hurt?" Then he saw there was a trickle of blood on her cheek from a slight cut above one eye. He flashed his torch to see it more clearly and made sure it was only superficial. He said: "What happened?"

"He was going to kill me," she said fearfully. "Don't let him."

"Rather not," declared Bobby heartily. "You're quite safe now. Who was it?"

"He meant to kill me," she repeated, and now in her voice there was a note of surprise. "I don't know who it was. I couldn't see." With sudden fear, she said: "He's coming back. Listen." In fact, Bobby could hear rapidly approaching footsteps, those of a man, he supposed, as they sounded heavy. "Let's run," Jane panted, and tried to get to her feet.

"That's all right," Bobby said, restraining her gently. "This chap's making too much noise to mean mischief. Mischief goes silently. No such luck," he added regretfully, "as the bloke who went for you coming back. I only wish he would."

Jane did not seem much inclined to share this pious aspiration. The approaching figure came nearer, plainly visible now in the clear moonlight. A man certainly. He called:

"What is it? What's happened? I heard someone—"

"It's Martin," Jane said with relief in her tone, and Bobby, also recognizing the newcomer, said:

"Mr. Winstanley, isn't it?"

Winstanley came up to them. He was carrying a double-barrelled gun and had an air of being very ready to use it.

"What's up?" he asked. "Jane, was it you called out?" He paused and glared suspiciously at Bobby. "Has this chap—?"

"Shut up," Bobby interrupted rudely. "Miss Felgate, what did happen?"

"A man jumped at me," she said and her voice was not very steady as she remembered that moment of fear. "I didn't hear him. I thought it was Martin come back, but he jumped at me, and I fell down. I knew he meant to kill me. I couldn't speak or move or anything. He had a great club in his hand. I knew he was going to kill me and he wanted to. I don't know how I knew, but I did, and I knew nothing could stop him. I couldn't stir or move or cry out or anything. It was like being dead already, only for still knowing things. I saw the great club coming and I jerked my head and it missed somehow. I heard how it went thud on the ground so close I felt a sort of jerk. I thought if that had been my head it would have smashed like an egg. I thought of Helen breaking eggs for an omelette, and then I don't know what happened, but the man wasn't there any more, and it was Mr. Owen instead."

A strange story; and Bobby might have been inclined to doubt it, but that he could both see and feel where some tremendous blow had smashed the surface of the gravel path. Easy to guess what would have been the result had any human head endured the force of that savage blow.

"What was he like?" Bobby asked.

Jane had got to her feet now. She had taken her hand from Bobby's coat and was holding Winstanley's arm instead. She said: "I don't know. I couldn't see his face. It was all hidden. I only remember that great club thing he had. I knew he was going to kill me. I knew he wanted to." There was again a note of surprise and wonder in her voice as she repeated: "He wanted to. I just lay and waited. I couldn't speak or move or cry out or anything." Bobby felt this last remark wasn't very accurate. If she hadn't moved her head at the last moment, almost certainly it would have been no pleasant sight that he would have found there waiting for him. Evidently, too, she had no knowledge or memory of that great and dreadful cry that she had uttered at the last as she had seen what had seemed like death descending, and that had brought him running to her aid. Winstanley said:

"We must find him." He looked angrily at Bobby: "Why aren't you doing something?" he demanded.

"First things first," Bobby said. "We'll do our best, but for the moment I would like to know what you are doing here? Had you and Miss Felgate arranged to meet each other?"

"No. We hadn't," Winstanley retorted, still angry.

"Please, can I go?" Jane said. "I ... I feel so dizzy somehow."

Winstanley was all concern at once.

"Can you walk?" he asked. "Shall I carry you?"

He put down his gun in preparation for this task. Bobby took the opportunity to glance at the gun's butt end. Clean, polished, unscratched, it had certainly not been used to strike that blow of which the gravel path showed so clear an impression. Bobby said: "There's someone coming."

Hurrying footsteps were now in fact plainly audible, and soon Lord Adour could be recognized.

"What's going on here?" he called authoritatively.

"As far as I can make out," Bobby said, "Mr. Winstanley and Miss Felgate had been meeting. When they separated, someone made an attack on Miss Felgate, apparently with intent to murder. She doesn't seem to know who or why."

"Tried to—what?" Lord Adour said. "Nonsense. Impossible." But he did not pronounce these last two words very confidently. Bobby noticed that he was wearing a scarf round his neck, a cap pulled down low over his eyes, and that he had on gloves. "Why should anyone ...?" he began and left it at that. He turned sharply on Bobby: "Why are you here?"

"I'm a policeman," Bobby explained, "and it's the business of the police to be as much on the spot as possible. I see you have been out, too. A little late for taking a stroll, isn't it?"

"That's Helen's cape," Lord Adour said, without answering Bobby. "Where's Helen? Is she here?"

"She's at home," Jane answered. "She went up to bed early. I borrowed her cape to come out. I'm sorry I—" She paused and would have fallen had not Winstanley supported her. "It's my head," she said. "It goes funny. Please, can't I go?"

"Your cheek's bleeding," Bobby said. "Let me look."

"I felt something," Jane said. "I think it didn't quite miss me, only nearly."

Bobby assured himself again the wound was only slight. He assured her, too, when she asked a little anxiously, that it would not even leave a mark. He thought that probably the very great violence with which the gravel path had been struck, had thrown up a splinter or fragment of stone with force sufficient to inflict this small injury. Proof of what would have been the effect had the blow been better aimed. Winstanley and Jane began to move away towards the house, the girl leaning heavily on Winstanley's arm. Lord Adour was about to follow them. Bobby stopped him and said:

"Did you know Mr. Winstanley and Miss Felgate were meeting here to-night? Did you object in any way?"

"I had no idea anything of the sort was likely," Lord Adour answered. "Quite the reverse. If I had known, I shouldn't have objected. Why should I? It's not so late as all that and Miss Felgate isn't a child."

"No. No," agreed Bobby. "I see you've been out. Do you mind telling me where?"

"What do you mean, out? I've not been out all evening. I've been at home."

"Oh, sorry," said Bobby. "I noticed you had on your coat."

"I heard something," Lord Adour answered and his tone was not pleased. "Someone calling. I wondered who it was, so I put on my hat and coat and came out to see. Why?"

"There has been an attempted murder apparently," Bobby answered, thinking, but not saying, that though hat and coat were natural enough, even for someone in a hurry, gloves were not so easy to explain. Odd, perhaps, that gloves have become so suspicious and so sinister an article of attire. Bobby went on: "As an officer of police, I have to try to establish—"

"Good God, man," interrupted Lord Adour, nearly shouting. "You aren't trying to make out I attacked Jane?"

"Of course not," Bobby protested, "but the very first thing necessary in these cases is to try to establish the whereabouts—"

"I consider—" interrupted Lord Adour again and stopped.

"In my opinion—" he began. He paused, stuttering with anger. He said: "Oh, this is too absurd—" and started to walk away.

"Please, please," protested Bobby pathetically. "If only your lordship would allow me to finish what I was saying. It is important— most important to make sure if possible where everybody was at the time. Suppose you say you were on such a road at such a time, and a suspect's alibi depends on his being there at the same moment, then if you can say he was or he wasn't, surely you see what a tremendous help that would be."

"I've told you already I wasn't out," Lord Adour retorted, though in a slightly mollified voice, as if he found this explanation plausible, but only half believed it. "I was at home all evening."

"In your study?" Bobby persisted.

"Really, this is too absurd," Lord Adour repeated. "No, I wasn't. Not all the time. I had my dinner, for instance. If you really want a full time-table of my movements to-night— ridiculous—you can come and see me to-morrow. Now you must excuse me. I must get back. I'm responsible in a way for Jane. I must see what's being done. Good night."

With that he marched away, and Bobby, looking after him, wondered if his reluctance to answer questions precisely was merely resentment at any fresh hint of suspicion, or whether it hid something he had good reason to keep concealed.

"It's those gloves," Bobby thought. "Why gloves?"

He turned to retrace his steps through the trees, and he had not gone more than a few steps before he saw a light flashing skyward, from the further side of the belt of trees where the pasture fields lay.

Thinking that this might mean perhaps that the missing constable might have returned to duty, Bobby hurried on, following the gravel path that led, as he had hoped it would, through the trees to a gate in the wire fence. If those others he had pursued so uselessly, so ineffectively, had known of it, then they would have had no difficulty in slipping from one side to the other, while he had been obliged to swing himself across by the aid of convenient, overhanging boughs. It crossed his mind that Lord Adour, for one, would certainly have known the exact position of the gate. So would Winstanley, for that matter.

Through the gate, beyond the trees, Bobby hurried to where the light from the torch was still being flashed with monotonous regularity into the skies. Halfway across the field Bobby found his missing assistant, bareheaded, seated on the ground, switching his torch on and off with a kind of puzzled and mechanical regularity.

"That'll do. That's enough," Bobby said to him. "Where have you been?"

"I thought I was at home in bed," the man answered, "but I'm not. I'm here." This fact, undoubted as it was, seemed to puzzle him, and he looked round with a dazed expression as if to make quite sure. He stared up at Bobby. "You're the London bloke," he said accusingly. "The guv'nor don't like it, not half he don't." He tried to get to his feet, but only succeeded by Bobby's help. "Damn meddling bounder," he muttered, "but the guv'nor didn't know as sergeant heard him." He seemed to pull himself together. "Beg pardon, sir," he said, "I think something hit me and I've lost my helmet."

"So you have," agreed Bobby, and to supplement the moonlight, at the moment obscured somewhat by a drifting cloud, he flashed his torch. At a little distance lay the helmet, badly dented and broken. It had evidently received a blow of very considerable force. Near by lay another object that interested Bobby even more. It was a tweed cap. Bobby, giving the battered helmet back to its almost equally battered owner, examined the cap with considerable interest. Well worn, of common make and pattern, it would have offered small hope of any possible identification, but for one thing. It was size 7, and Bobby wondered how many in the neighbourhood wore caps of that size. But he thought Wayling did. Only it smelt very strongly of hair oil, and Bobby was sure Wayling used no such extraneous aids. He was probably of the opinion that ugliness unadorned fascinated more.

Bobby wrote home that evening:

"So you see from all this that an exciting time was had by all and a highly baffling time by me.

"Why did the attack on Jane Felgate, with every appearance about it of a determined and ruthless resolve to kill, end in the anti-climax of a bash on a gravel path? Did the assailant's heart fail at the last moment and did he turn his blow aside, overwhelmed by the horror and enormity of his own purpose? You would not think so if you had glimpsed as I did for a moment that figure running beneath the trees, between the moonlight and the shadows—murder incarnate. Yet, if it wasn't that, what was it? If the first blow had missed merely through haste, or because Miss Jane moved in the nick of time, easy enough to strike again.

"Obviously, as you will see at once, the failure to carry out what seemed so evident a purpose, may possibly indicate who it was killed Itter Bain.

"There is a sort of tagging, worrying notion trying to get itself free in my at present highly confused and doubtful mind which does seem to suggest as much. But I can't see how. I feel it may be that way, but as yet I don't know, and a feeling is no earthly good without proof.

"You may be sure that when I die, the words 'No proof' will be found engraved on my heart.

"Was Helen Adour there? If she was, was she there secretly or was her presence known to any of the others? Haile says he saw her and Winstanley together the night before. But this time it was Jane. Does Winstanley meet the two girls on alternate nights and do they suspect and watch each other to be sure? Is Jane telling the truth when she says she borrowed Helen's swansdown cape for

the occasion, or does the cape mean that Helen herself was there? I suppose girls do occasionally borrow each other's things, or, for that matter, borrow them without their being lent.

"Winstanley was on the spot—that means, identity of time and place established, but I don't think he had anything to do with the attack on Jane. Can't be sure, of course. He didn't use his gun, anyhow, for I took a look at the butt and it wasn't damaged, or even scratched, as it must have been had it given that tremendous whack on the gravel path. Moreover, he was wearing fairly heavy shoes, and, if he had come back, Jane would have heard him and known who it was attacked her. There is the possibility perhaps that he ran back on tip toe on the grass edging the path, and that she didn't hear him, but I don't think it likely. Besides, she had a glimpse of whoever it was 'jumped at her,' as she puts it, and she would have recognized him.

"Then there's Lord Adour. Identity established again, for he, too, was on the spot. And why gloves? That worries me, though it may mean nothing. If you hear a cry one evening after dark and go out to see what it was, you may stop to button up your coat and wrap a scarf round your neck and you may happen to pull your cap down over your eyes. But would you stop to put on gloves? Or would you, knowing all about dabs, as everyone does in these days, when, as good old Payne used to be fond of saying, no five-year-old goes to the pantry to steal mummy's jam without first putting on gloves? Adorn does in a way resemble that figure of murder incarnate I had a glimpse of under the trees, but only a general resemblance. No proof there, either.

"Haile was on the spot the night before. Was he there again? I can't make up my mind what to think about Haile. He warned me against Mauley Bain, the dead man's brother, but that may have been to divert suspicion from himself. Is there any chance that the attack on Jane was stage thunder, meant to cover something else he is up to? If he can manage to produce evidence to suggest that the case against Lord Adour was not pressed because of social position and connection with 'big business,' then apparently the political consequences may be serious. There seems to be an idea that it would strengthen very considerably the people who want this present Government to go ahead full speed, all brakes off, to produce an ideal world made up of men and women who themselves are so very far from being ideal.

"Mauley Bain mustn't be forgotten either. But he is said to be in London and, if he was, that's a sound alibi. Only what is it worth in these days of cars and motor-bikes? I shall try to check up, but even if he can say what hotel he stayed at, there's always the bare possibility of slipping in and out again unseen, unnoticed. Not likely, but a possibility to be remembered.

"Then again, who knocked out the man Seers posted to the job of watching Kindles? Not a very highly intelligent specimen of the local constabulary, and am I being merely spiteful in entertaining a faint, unworthy suspicion that Seers picked out the most dunderheaded man available? I suppose it's only bad temper and disappointment and a general sense of failure, that allows so improper a thought to pop into my mind. It must pop out again.

"What does Wayling's cap mean? I'm sure it is Wayling's, for I'm sure there's no one else here with a head that size. It certainly wasn't Wayling I saw, though it may have been Wayling who shone the light of his torch on me. Anyhow, I'm also sure Wayling wouldn't knock anyone on the head. He's a disreputable, dishonest little scamp you couldn't trust with either a sixpence or a woman, but I don't believe he would ever hurt a fly. You can't trust him with money because he always sees himself as a prospective millionaire about to hand you a wad of bank-notes in return for your sixpenny loan. You can't trust him with women because—well, because he and women are both like that. All the same, I don't suppose he has ever deliberately, of 'malice aforethought,' injured or meant to injure any living soul. Besides, he was probably on duty at the pub where he got himself a job, 'Superintending the bars,' as he said—in other words, and in the cold light of a less luxuriant imagination— washing up the beer glasses and sweeping the floors.

"As soon as I got back I rang up Seers to tell him what had happened. Unluckily, he was in bed and very sound asleep—also very, very grumpy at being rung up. Probably he made a few remarks like the one it seems he didn't know the sergeant heard. You can't wonder after his mine-spotting activities. He blew up another to-day, Gregson says, by potting at it with a rifle. It was far enough out at sea for that to be done safely. I'm glad I work in the retail line, not in the wholesale slaughter department—section, mines. I shouldn't much care for the job of tacking a light on to a thing that any bump or mishandling may send up in a whirl of general destruction. All the same, poor old Seers was very grumpy indeed, and much too sleepy to get it all straight, though not too much so to prevent his getting very fierce indeed when he heard Adour mentioned. Seers is getting what I suppose nowadays is called a 'complex' about Adour—a sort of Adour persecution complex with Commander Seers as the noble, single-handed defender against my wicked machinations.

"I expect you're saying, 'Bad temper again.' Very likely. The fact is, I'm worried. What happened to-night is disturbing. Disturbing, because significant, and all the more so because I've no answer to the question, significant of what?

"By the way, the Seagull launch has been removed from the harbour and taken upriver to the Bain works for the engine to be repaired. Is that merely routine or is it part of a pattern not yet clear? I am coming to think that probably I was mistaken in believing I knew the whereabouts of Lord Adour's missing gun, supposed to be the murder weapon. Supposed, for there is again no proof another gun may have been used. Any number of shot-guns in the district. Winstanley has one, for example, and so has every other farmer; others as well. If my first idea that I know where it is turns out to be correct, of course there will be no chance of my being able to get hold of it. But if I'm wrong about that, and it's somewhere else, there may be a chance still. One never knows."

The letter continues with matters of purely private interest.

CHAPTER XVIII
NINE THOUSAND POUNDS

FIRST LIGHT, THEN, to adopt the Army phrase, saw Bobby out and hard at work, examining with minute care the scene of the incidents of the preceding night. To help, there had been sent him by a sergeant, deeply thankful that seniority protected him from duty at such unearthly hours, two of the local constabulary, sleepy, sad, and disgruntled men, mournfully remembering the warm beds they had been forced to leave.

Nor had the search any great success. Bobby himself discovered, thrown among some bushes, a pick handle, badly splintered and broken at, one end. A comparison with the damaged surface of the gravel path showed it was the instrument used and induced one of the constables to remark that he was glad his head hadn't been in the way of that descending pick handle.

Bobby, remarking that he felt the same way, packed the pick handle carefully, ready for dispatch for examination by experts. Not that he thought anything useful would result, but there was always the chance, and everything has to be tried once. The cap he had picked up would have to go, too, though first he meant to show it to Wayling to see if he acknowledged ownership and could give any explanation of its appearance where Bobby had found it.

The search completed without further result, Bobby dismissed his two assistants, as full of hate for him, both of them, as they were both empty of breakfast, and himself returned to Mrs. Gregson's and his own breakfast. He made a hasty meal, for he had much to do, and went off to the "Good Haul," where he found Wayling hard at work, polishing the "Good Haul" brass work, though, or so Bobby thought, with a slight relaxation of the zeal and appreciation with which he had at first tackled the job. He was bare-headed, and his rough and unbrushed hair showed no sign of the use of any kind of hair oil.

"This yours?" Bobby asked, after greeting him, and Wayling looked very surprised when he saw the cap Bobby was holding out.

"How did you get hold of it?" he inquired. "Someone pinched it last night."

"Do you know who?"

"No. No idea. Why? There was a bit of a scuffle last night. Fellow making a nuisance of himself in the bar. Six-footer and thought he could get away with it. Had a drop too much. They had to send for me, and, as he wouldn't be sensible, I had to take him by the scruff of the neck and throw him out. Lost my cap in the process. I expect one of his pals pocketed it as a kind of revenge. Thanks for bringing it back." He held out his hand and looked surprised again when he saw Bobby carefully putting the cap away in the small dispatch case he had brought it in. "What's the big idea?" Wayling asked. "That's my cap."

"Yes, I know," Bobby said. "Sorry and all that, but I've got to hang on to it for the present."

"You've no right," Wayling protested. "My property, isn't it? I shall have to get another. That'll mean five bob at least for a new one."

"Oh, that's all right," Bobby said happily, for he had seen suddenly a chance to get a little of his own back. "It wouldn't do to put it on the expense sheet, but I'll stand the five bob myself."

"Very good of you," said Wayling with appreciation.

"You can deduct it from that five pounds you owe me," Bobby explained, "and we'll call it four pounds fifteen now."

Wayling looked at him with grave reproach.

"Do you think," he asked, "that that is quite playing the game? Quite what one expects between people who call themselves gentlefolk?"

Before Bobby had time to answer a door opened and one of the "Good Haul" staff, a good-looking girl, put her head out. She did not notice Bobby, who was standing to one side. She said softly:

"Mr. Wayling, there's a nice bit of bacon I saved for you from the boss's ration he thinks he finished yesterday. Don't be long. It's nearly ready."

"Thanks, Bessie," Wayling said. "I'll be in in a jiffy." The head disappeared. Wayling said with appreciation: "Nice girl, that."

"Well, don't get her into trouble," Bobby said, and Wayling looked deeply hurt and offended.

"I consider that remark most offensive, most uncalled-for," he declared coldly. "If you don't mind, I'll be getting on with my work."

He turned his back and began again to polish, now with renewed zest. Bobby, though reluctantly, produced two half-crowns. It was probably worth that to keep on good terms with Wayling, and, after all, what's the good of being senior if you can't stretch expense sheets just a trifle now and then?

"Well, of course, if you feel you really ought to have the cash," he said, and handed over the two coins to an always easily placated Wayling. "By the way," Bobby added, this financial transaction safely concluded, "you know Harry Haile, don't you? He's a *Seashire Herald* reporter now. Was he in here last night?"

"Yes. So he was," Wayling answered after a moment's hesitation. "I noticed him keeping out of the way while the little affair I told you about was going on. I think he was afraid he might be next to go out on his ear, but he was being quiet enough, so I took no notice. Do you think he pinched my cap?"

"Oh, no. I was just wondering," Bobby answered, said goodbye, and was moving away when Wayling called him back, anxious to give good value for that very handy five shillings he had so unexpectedly received.

"There was one of the office staff at Bain's in last night," he said. "He got a bit tight. Celebrating, he said."

"Celebrating what?" Bobby asked.

"Oh, he had been expecting to have to look for another job," Wayling explained. "If the bank took over, that is. If they did, they would be sure to close down here and amalgamate Bain's with Tomlinson's in London. Rationalization, you know, that sort of thing, and the extra staff out on their ear. But it's the bank that's out instead. Prescott turned up yesterday with nine thousand pounds in cash and cleared the overdraft."

"Did he, though?" said Bobby, interested. "I wonder how he managed that? Is that what Mauley Bain has been in town for?"

"It doesn't look as if Mauley had anything to do with it. He's still away, unless he got back last night. Prescott just turned up with a couple of suitcases stuffed with banknotes, got this bloke who was in here last night to help him count them, and then bunged it all in at the bank. Funny when you come to think of it. If he got finance from someone, why not a cheque? Why pound notes packed in suitcases?"

"Does seem unusual," Bobby agreed and looked thoughtful. "Hadn't the man who told you about it any suggestion to make?"

"What he said was that now his job was safe and he didn't give a damn for anything else. Prescott might have pinched the lot for all he cared."

"Oh, well," Bobby said, not wishing to start more talk. "Not our business, I suppose. Probably whoever found the money didn't want his name known."

Wayling thought in that case the transaction would generally have been carried out through a solicitor, and Bobby agreed that would have been more usual, but no doubt there were good reasons.

Anyhow, Bain Products seemed to be on the map again, and that was all to the good. When Bobby nodded farewell and strolled away, while Wayling, having finished his polishing, departed in search of the rasher of bacon the manager of the "Good Haul" would never know had once been his. Nevertheless, though Bobby had not wished Wayling, for whose tongue he had equal respect and dread, to think so, he was a good deal disturbed and worried by this news.

Whence indeed had so large a sum, packed in two suitcases, so suddenly emerged? Was there connection with Itter Bain's murder? Was the vulgarity of money, and not the strange disturbing influence of a woman's beauty, the secret cause and hidden motive of what had happened? It did appear there had been quarrelling and ill will among the three partners. Probably, as so often happens when things begin to go wrong, each blaming the others, each thinking the others responsible. If so, where did the previous night's events fit in? Profoundly disturbing, those, with their dark suggestion that the climax of events had not yet been reached.

Greed for money, the sex urge, are two strong motives, and what part had each or both or either played in the tragedy of Itter Bain? What part had they still to play in what was yet to come?

Bobby went back to where his car was garaged and got it out. First, he drove to the Bain factory. But, as it was a Sunday and war work no longer pressed with such clamorous need, the place was closed. After some trouble, Bobby discovered an old watchman, who evidently bitterly resented being disturbed in his peaceful routine, and was either the district's champion imbecile or else giving a very good imitation thereof. He knew nothing of any launch, this wasn't a yachting club, and he wasn't going to let anyone go poking round his factory, not without orders, so he wasn't. That was that, and Bobby had to retire defeated. Not that he supposed "poking" round the factory would be much good. If the *Seagull* had been removed purposely to avoid a police examination, then it was probably well hidden. If not, and its removal had been innocent and purely for the purpose of effecting required repairs, then there was no hurry and to-morrow would do as well.

Bobby knew Haile's address, and thither he drove next. When he knocked his summons was answered by a lady who regarded him with no favourable eye when he asked if Mr. Haile was in.

"In, and snoring still in my drawing-room or what used to be my drawing-room before he planted himself here," she told him.

"Too bad," said Bobby sympathetically. "Do you think you could wake him? It's rather important."

"It's no good knocking. He takes no notice," the lady answered. "And the door's locked or I would have had him out long ago. How can I get through my work," she demanded bitterly, "with him upsetting everything?"

Bobby said he couldn't imagine. It must make things very difficult. And was there a window? He was, he explained, like Field-Marshal Montgomery, a great believer in the flank attack, and windows sometimes offered such opportunities. The suggestion was received with surprise, but not with disfavour. There was a window, it appeared, and Bobby could certainly be shown it. He expressed gratitude, and, when he had promised faithfully not to scratch the paint, it was pointed out to him. Fortunately, it was easy of access, and Haile was sufficiently a believer in fresh air to have left it slightly open. So, while the lady of the house looked on with a certain grim approval, Bobby pushed up the sash, thrust the curtains aside, placed carefully on the floor a really magnificent aspidistra, climbed in, and roused the startled Mr. Haile from profound slumber by jerking off the coverings from his extemporized bed of a couch and two chairs.

CHAPTER XIX

BEAUTY UNDER THE MOON

THUS UNKINDLY ROUSED from his peaceful slumbers, Haile sat up and stared around. Clutching his pyjamas to him, he blinked at Bobby. Slowly recognition came.

"What the devil ... ?" he began and paused.

"Not at all," protested Bobby, his feelings slightly hurt. "Far from it. It's only me."

Haile swung his legs off the bed and sat staring at Bobby, and once again Bobby saw fear leap into his eyes, fear that drove all sleep instantly away.

"What do you want? How did you get in?" he asked, and, when Bobby nodded at the open window, he said: "You had no right. Police have no right to enter private property without a search warrant. You're trespassing. I can order you out."

"Not at all," Bobby explained blandly. "I have the householder's permission. Hadn't you better get dressed? You'll be catching cold like that. I'll shut the window, shall I?

He did so. Slowly Haile began to dress, and, as he did so, still watched Bobby warily.

"What's it all about?" he asked.

"Oh, I just wanted a bit of a chat," Bobby answered. He wandered over to the mantelpiece, where, incongruous amidst a medley of fiddling china ornaments stood a shaving brush, a safety razor, and other toilet articles, among them a small bottle of a well-advertised brand of hair oil. "This stuff any good?" Bobby asked, picking up the bottle and showing it to Haile.

"Why? What do you want to know for?" Haile retorted. "What are you trying to get at? I know you," he said bitterly. "You ask questions."

"Well, it's the only way, isn't it, if you want to get answers?" Bobby protested. He put the bottle down and went to sit by a small occasional table on which he had noticed a brush and comb. "I expect," he remarked meditatively, "lots of people use the stuff. I might try it myself, only I know my wife would kick up a row—pillow cases and all that sort of thing. Of course, you're a bachelor, so you're all right."

Haile grew suddenly angry.

"What the hell's it got to do with you if I'm a bachelor?" he almost shouted. "What are you up to? What do you want? If you've anything to say, say it. If you haven't, get out and leave me alone."

Bobby opened the small dispatch case he had with him and showed Wayling's cap.

"See this?" he asked.

"What about it?"

"Do you know whose it is?"

"Looks like Wayling's."

"Correct," said Bobby. "Wayling says he lost it last night. There seems to have been some sort of row or another at the 'Good Haul.' Wayling says you were there. Can you tell me anything?"

"Not much. Nothing much to it. A put-up job if you ask me. There's a girl there the cellarman is sweet on. Bessie, I think they call her. Wayling's been making the pace with her. Automatic with him. Women fall for him just as they fall for a lost kitten with a lame leg. Automatic with them. They don't know Wayling has claws. Not that he means it. It just happens, just as a kitten can scratch without meaning it. All the same the cellarman got ratty, and he fixed it up with a pal to make a bit of a fuss in the private bar and got Wayling sent in to see to it. Wayling bustled in all set to do his stuff and the cellarman's pal took the poor little devil by the scruff of his neck and threw him out on his ear. The big idea was to show up Wayling. The result was to make Miss Bessie more sorry for Wayling than ever, more maternal than ever. If she doesn't look out, he'll have her maternal in good earnest."

"He told me about that," Bobby said. He had turned in his chair slightly and was fidgeting with the brush and comb on the small occasional table just behind where he sat. He said: "Wayling's version wasn't quite the same, though."

"It wouldn't be," agreed Haile, grinning, and then suddenly grew angry again, and frightened, too. "What are you doing?" he cried. "You leave my brush alone."

"Only a souvenir," Bobby explained. "A lock of your hair." He had collected a few stray hairs from the brush and comb. "You don't mind, do you?"

"Yes, I do," Haile said. He was nearly dressed now and his tone was low and menacing. He came angrily and threateningly towards Bobby, his fists clenched and ready. "Hand that over," he said, and repeated: "Hand that over."

"Can't be done," Bobby answered. He looked up at Haile. He didn't move or try to rise from his chair. He said quietly: "I wouldn't try that if I were you, Haile. You ought to have more sense."

Haile went back to his makeshift bed and sat down heavily. He was still very pale, there was still that same frightened look in his eyes. In a low, muttering voice, he said:

"You devil."

"No," Bobby said gravely. "Only a plain man doing his duty as best he can, so that other plain men can go their ways in peace and safety." He was silent as he busied himself replacing carefully Wayling's cap in his dispatch case, equally carefully putting in an envelope the few hairs he had collected from Haile's brush and comb. Haile watched him moodily, fearfully. Bobby said: "Murder. That's a thing apart. Killing, 'Whoso sheddeth man's blood.' ... You remember? That's still valid, even if we don't bother much nowadays about the Book it comes from." He closed his dispatch case and stood up. "Nothing you would like to say?" he asked.

"It doesn't mean a thing," Haile said, "if you do find a few of my hairs in that cap. And you said yourself there's plenty use that hair oil. You're only wasting your time fooling about."

"Now, look here," Bobby protested, "you have seen something of Intelligence work, which must be a bit like detection, though much simpler, of course, and you must know quite well that ninety per cent, of it is always just fooling about. Well, I'll be going. Think it over. You know where to find me any time you want me. If you've anything you care to say. We may be cops,' but all the same we are, or at least we try to be, friends and helpers to all decent people. It's only the others who need say, 'You devil.'"

He nodded, and, opening the drawing-room door, went out, and back to his car. That Haile was disturbed, frightened, was clear enough. Less clear, Bobby thought, was the reason. Now it would be necessary to go more carefully into the story that Haile had been seen in the neighbourhood before the murder took place. Yet what motive could he have had? Bobby shook his head dolefully as he reflected that the problem seemed only to grow more complicated, the more he discovered. This cap of Wayling's, for instance, and the sudden production by Prescott Bain of so much money in the form of bank-notes stuffed into suitcases. It all seemed to cut clean across the provisional theory that had been beginning to take form and shape in his mind.

So ran his thoughts as he drove back to Kindles, where, however, he found only Jane to receive him. She explained that Lord Adour and Helen lunched invariably on every alternate Sunday with an aged great-aunt, who exacted—and received—much deference by reason of her age. She was over ninety, still as brisk as ever and even more authoritative, one might even say totalitarian. Also she was a rich woman and had entire control of her property, together with a tendency to change her will every now and again. So this fortnightly lunch was not lightly to be forgone and Lord Adour and his daughter had left in good time, since unpunctuality and a new will were apt to be closely associated in the great-aunt's mind. All this Jane explained, and Bobby said regretfully that he seemed somehow to have bad luck in trying to meet Miss Helen. Jane said it was a pity this Sunday happened to be great-aunt lunch Sunday, and Bobby asked how she felt after her terrifying experience of the previous night.

Jane said she was all right, but she tried not to think of it, and, though she had been pale enough before, she grew paler still as she spoke. She admitted she had never managed to get to sleep all night, or, rather, if she did manage to close her eyes, immediately she saw again that dark and strange figure leaping at her from out of the nighty Her uncle had insisted on her seeing their doctor, and he had given her some medicine for her nerves and to take before she went to bed. If Mr. Owen wished to ask her any more questions, she felt quite able to try to answer them. But she didn't think there was anything she could tell him beyond what he knew already. It had all happened so suddenly, almost simultaneously. The dark form leaping at her, the sure conviction that intention to kill was resolute and purposed, the descending blow that crashed so near, missing by only the fraction of an inch and yet leaving her unhurt except for the tiny wound that was now almost completely healed. Nor could she offer any explanation why a blow so resolute and purposed, so deliberate, so full of deadly intent, had been allowed to fail in its aim.

"Difficult to understand why," Bobby reflected aloud. "Or why, if he really meant it, why he did not try again?"

"I thought perhaps he heard you coming and that frightened him away," Jane suggested, but Bobby shook his head.

"I knew nothing about it," he explained, "till I heard you cry out. Nor apparently did Mr. Winstanley, and Lord Adour says the same. It might be your own cry for help frightened him off. Not very likely. He could very easily have struck again before he ran. The main thing is that he didn't and that you are safe. There are one or two other points I wanted to ask Miss Helen about, but perhaps you could clear them up for me as she isn't here. My information is that Miss Helen met Martin Winstanley in the same place the night before. Do you know if that is so?"

Jane looked startled and uneasy and it was a minute or two before she replied. Then she said:

"Well, yes. How did you know?"

"But it was you who met him last night," Bobby continued, ignoring this question. "Gould you explain how that came about?"

Jane, still very startled and uneasy, did not answer. Leaving that for the moment, Bobby went on: "You had on Miss Helen's swansdown cape. Miss Helen quite possibly wore it the previous night. Do you think it may be that you were attacked in place of Miss Helen, mistaken for her, and that the blow aimed at you was diverted at the last moment when it was seen who you really were? It might be that your voice was recognized when you called out."

"I did wonder," Jane admitted. "I don't know.'

"If that was it," Bobby continued, "do you think that was why a club was used—a pick handle, in point of fact?"

"Oh, no," Jane cried and shuddered as she spoke. "Oh, no," she repeated. "I know what you mean," she said. After another pause she said: "Helen is so lovely, you think she must belong to another world."

"There may be an explanation there if only we could think it out," Bobby said slowly.

"I don't know what that means," Jane said in a troubled voice.

"So far it's all guessing, groping in the dark," Bobby went on, without attempting to explain. "You haven't told me yet why you took Miss Helen's place last night—that is, if you did, and if she wasn't there as well."

"Oh, she wasn't," Jane said. "I'm sure she wasn't. How could she be?"

"Why not?" Bobby asked. "There's nothing to show that, even if she went up to her room, she stayed there."

"Oh, well," Jane said, and again she had a troubled and a doubtful air. Then her expression changed. "Oh, yes, she was there all the time," she exclaimed. "I asked her and she said so." This seemed a trifle less decisive to Bobby than apparently it did to Jane, to whom evidently the possibility that Helen had not told the whole truth had not occurred. Bobby went on:

"What is in my mind is whether there is anything between Miss Helen and Martin Winstanley? Are they in any way in love with each other?"

"Oh, no," Jane exclaimed immediately, and seemed amused at the idea. "Of course, Martin is. I mean in love with her. All men fall in love with Helen when they see her," and Bobby heard as it were a small and gentle sigh that fluttered between the words, as she added: "Martin, too."

"But not Miss Helen with Mr. Winstanley?" he asked.

"Oh, no," Jane answered. "Helen is in love with no one."

"Are you sure?"

"Quite sure." Jane answered at once. "Helen loves her own beauty far too much ever to think of sharing it with anyone else." Bobby thought over this in silence for some moments. He did not feel he understood. He was not sure that he believed. He was sure Jane did. His impression of her was that she simply did not know how to lie. Presently he said:

"You know, I don't follow that. It's strange."

"Beauty like Helen's must be, I think," Jane said. "Very strange and a little dreadful, too."

"If it's like that," Bobby asked, "why did she go out to meet Mr. Winstanley?"

"I don't think she did," Jane explained. "I'm sure she didn't. It was Martin. I expect he was hoping he would see her. I suppose he knew."

"Knew what?"

"It's the moon," Jane said.

"The moon?" Bobby repeated, completely puzzled.

"I think it's that. I think Helen knows she is never so lovely, that her beauty never seems so much like something that doesn't quite belong to this world, as when she walks by herself in the moonlight. It's quite true. I've seen her. I'm a woman, too, but I held my breath as I watched. You never know how lovely and apart she is till you have seen her like that. Somehow it makes you think of all the beauty that there is in this world or the next, and you feel you wish it was all like that."

"Well, you know," Bobby said, and there was a distinct touch of exasperation in his voice, "all this makes it very difficult. If everyone goes looney whenever they come near the girl, how are you to work out any reasonable pattern of behaviour?" He sank into gloomy and resentful silence. He asked crossly: "Was that why you were there as well, simply to stare at a young woman mooning about—literally mooning about apparently?"

"Oh, no," Jane answered. "It was Helen. She asked me to make sure there wasn't anyone. It was Martin she meant. If he was there, I was to ask him please to go away, and I did and he promised. It was when he had gone that that—that it happened."

"Lord Adour was there, too," Bobby remarked. "He said he came when he heard your cry. I noticed he was fully dressed for outdoors, late as it was."

"I don't remember. I don't think I noticed," Jane said. "He is always uneasy about it, when Helen slips out like that. He doesn't like it. I think he feels it isn't respectable. I told him once such loveliness as Helen's couldn't be respectable and he was awfully cross. Sometimes he goes out to find her and bring her back. Perhaps he was going to last night."

Bobby supposed this was an explanation that might be accepted. Plausible certainly, but not necessarily the whole and complete truth in this household where all seemed bewitched by a girl's good looks.

"Have you any idea," he asked as he rose to go, "when Lord Adour and Miss Helen will be back?"

"It depends on how old Miss Adour is feeling," Jane answered. "Sometimes she wants them to stay and then they have to." She smiled faintly. "Poor uncle's dreadfully hard up. It'll be all right in time, he says, when things are more settled on the Continent. Some of the people he was in business with in France got mixed up with the Germans, and he can't get in touch with them. So he tries to keep on good terms with Great-aunt and then perhaps she'll lend him the nine or ten thousand pounds he wants to keep things going. It's an awful lot of money."

"So it is," agreed Bobby. "I'm rather anxious to meet Miss Helen, but somehow I always seem to miss her. Gould you make an appointment for me?"

Jane shook her head and smiled again.

"Helen is like a queen," she said. "She expects others to wait on her, not the other way."

"Well, I shall have to try," Bobby grumbled. "There's such a lot to see to, it's not easy to find time."

"It won't be any help," Jane said seriously, "if you do see her. You'll only be like everyone else and fall in love."

"Oh, I'm a policeman," Bobby told her laughingly. "That's different. Duty, you know, and all that. I must judge for myself." Jane shook her head, as if to say it wasn't different at all, but very much the same; and as by now it was lunchtime and past, he took a hasty leave and departed for Mrs. Gregson's, hoping she would have something nice waiting for him.

She had. Sole, fresh caught that morning, with all the fresh savour of the sea still intact, and where's the chef who can compose a sauce one hundredth part as good as that?

CHAPTER XX
UNTIDY WORLD

LUNCHEON OVER, Mrs. Gregson, a little shyly, a little proudly, served coffee, for she knew that was the stylish thing to do. Alas! She had made it by the simple rule of one teaspoonful for each person and one for the pot, then fill up with boiling water.

But Bobby could show himself at times of heroic mould and he sipped the stuff without blenching as he chatted amiably with them both; at first about nothing in particular, and then in a casual manner, for he had no wish to let it be guessed that what he had to say was of any great importance, he asked about the fisher-folk of the little village and if they were honest and trustworthy.

"As for that," said the sergeant firmly, "there isn't one of them I would trust any further than I could see 'em."

"The price they have the face to ask for any bit of fish ..." said Mrs. Gregson.

"I don't hold with summer visitors myself," said the sergeant, "but there are limits ... a pound a night for bed and breakfast!"

"They're human, too, said Mrs. Gregson, "even summer visitors."

"Us, being official like," said the sergeant, "the Commander holds as we didn't ought. So we don't."

"A scandalizing set," said Mrs. Gregson, "that's them hereabouts."

"As for Saturday night," said the sergeant, "you wouldn't believe it—drinking and fighting."

"An orgy," said Mrs. Gregson firmly.

"It's fair breaking Vicar's heart," said the sergeant, "the way the kids don't go to Sunday school any more."

"Most of them not speaking, though neighbours, not living in amity, same as Vicar says all ought," said Mrs. Gregson.

"Well, well," said Bobby. "Sounds bad."

"Of course," admitted the sergeant, "I don't say but, if there's need, they won't share their last crumb, even if going hungry themselves."

"That's different," said Mrs. Gregson, waving it aside. "Natural like, if a neighbour's ill or there's kiddies to see to and suchlike, they'll stop up all night if they have to, so as to do the work after they've done their own."

"I wouldn't say there's one of 'em what you might call outright dishonest, not even for summer visitors," said the sergeant. "There was that lady left her bag on the beach with jewellery in it and twenty pounds in notes. Handed in the same night."

"Three of them's got Humane Society medals for saving life," said Mrs. Gregson.

"One was only a summer visitor," the sergeant reminded her. "It counts just the same ..." said Mrs. Gregson.

"Well, well," said Bobby. "Sounds good."

"It's the way you look at it," said Mrs. Gregson.

"What I mean is," said Bobby, "could you find one of them you could trust to keep a promise if he made it?"

"There isn't any of 'em," said the sergeant, "if he made a promise, wouldn't keep it, low tide, high tide, come wind, come calm. What do you expect?" said the sergeant, and looked rather offended.

"Good," said Bobby. "What I'm after is to try to find out what has happened to the *Seagull* launch Itter Bain bought just before his death from Lord Adour. I don't want to ask you to put one of your own men on the job, because it's important there shouldn't be any talk. I simply want to know where it is. I thought perhaps Mrs. Gregson might help if she could tell us if there's any talk about it going on. Spontaneous talk, I mean. I don't want any questions asked. Just to know if there is any talk about the way it's gone from where it lay in the harbour."

"Well, sir, as far as that goes," Gregson said, though much puzzled by this sudden exhibition of interest in the *Seagull*, "I did hear as Mr. Mauley Bain sent for it to the factory for overhaul."

"It doesn't seem to have got there," Bobby remarked.

He went on to repeat that what he wanted was some trustworthy man who would try to find out what had become of the launch, but without giving any occasion for gossip. It was important, Bobby insisted, that no one should know he was taking an interest in the launch. He added that it would be useful, too, if he could be given the names of the men who had towed the boat away.

The Gregsons assured him they understood and would do their best. Mrs. Gregson reminded her husband that young Soper, one of the men at the harbour, was a steady young fellow with more sense than most young people seemed to have nowadays. The sergeant agreed and Mrs. Gregson began to clear the table. Bobby remarked that, Sunday or no Sunday, he must be getting on the job again, and by the way, there was the *Seashire Herald* reporter who was hanging about, trying to write up the Itter Bain case. Haile was his name, Harry Haile. Was anything known about him? Was he a newcomer or had he been seen in the district before?

"Wasn't it him," Mrs. Gregson said to her husband, "as you saw talking to Mrs. Mack's last young woman?"

"So it was," agreed the sergeant, "but that was a week or more before all this started."

"Who is Mrs. Mack and why her last young woman?" Bobby asked.

"It's Miss Lambert, sir," the sergeant explained. "Maybe you remember? She's the young woman who lost her fur. She was telling me how glad she was to get it back that first night you were here when you asked me about Mr. Mauley Bain and who he was?"

"Oh, yes," Bobby said. "I remember. Who is Mrs. Mack?"

The sergeant and his wife exchanged looks. The sergeant said:

"It's a nursing home. Leastways, that's what Mrs. Mack calls it. For old people mostly. Some of them die a bit quick like, but the relatives don't complain. An old body's often best out of the way, and dying quick, anyhow, and so what's a day more or less, and a mercy being took?"

"There's some that call it—now what's the word?" said Mrs. Gregson.

"Euthanasia," suggested Bobby.

"That's right," agreed Mrs. Gregson. "Dr. Norris here, he don't much like attending at Mrs. Mack's, but he has to, there being none other till there's more back from the war."

"You can't call it murdering or such like," Gregson said, "not putting a poor old soul out of pain and misery, and nothing to be done about it, even if it's true, as none know, except Mrs. Mack and no one else."

"Vicar says," observed Mrs. Gregson hesitatingly, "God knows."

"Parson's talk," commented Gregson, and waved it aside. "Parson's talk," he repeated.

"What about Miss Lambert?" Bobby asked. "She's not old."

"That's the other side to it," said the sergeant. "Miss Lambert's one of the young uns. They come, too. Girls at times, not much out of their teens, if as much. Older ones, too. You wonder a bit why they've come when you see them, because of their looking well enough. Then they're took bad, and Dr. Norris isn't asked, but their own doctor comes down from Town, and he goes again, and presently the young lady's up and about, and says she's better now. Then she leaves, and that's all there's to it, till another comes, and it's the same thing over again."

"That isn't murder, either," Mrs. Gregson said. "You can't end what's never begun. Can you?" she asked doubtfully.

"A very nice lady, Mrs. Mack," said the sergeant, "and always willing to do you a good turn. Them as have had friends there or been there themselves say how kind and attentive she is and how no one could ever have been more attentive or thoughtful. There's many round here think well of her."

"And some as don't," said Mrs. Gregson, "and say as they wouldn't like to be her come Judgment Day."

"That's a long way off," said the sergeant comfortably.

"Probably," agreed Bobby, "though you never know, and then there's always the atomic bomb that may provide a short cut. Do you mean Haile brought Miss Lambert to this place of Mrs. Mack's?"

"Nothing to show," Gregson answered. "I did wonder when I saw her talking to Mr. Haile same as old friends."

"I think I should like to have known all this before," Bobby said in a voice so soft and gentle and meditative that those who knew him better than did the Gregsons would have guessed at once how angry and dismayed he was. "I wonder why I wasn't told?"

"Well, sir, I did put it in report," Gregson answered, "but Commander said to take it out. Keep to what matters, he said. No business of ours, Commander said, even if it was him had got the young lady into trouble and Mrs. Mack had nothing to do with Mr. Itter Bain, and her place outside our district, so she's not our concern either."

"I see," said Bobby gloomily. "Perhaps Commander Seers was right," he admitted; and it says a lot for his sense of discipline and his complete acceptance of the sacred official dogma that a superior must never be blamed or criticized before one of inferior rank that he managed to utter this last sentence almost as if he meant it.

But to himself he was thinking viciously that he would like to put in his report he would have to make to the Home Office that Commander Seers was stupid, narrow, incompetent, utterly unfit for his job, his head full of nothing but old-fashioned prejudices, and should have been thrown out of his position long ago.

"I'm not so sorry myself," Gregson said, "that it isn't for us to say about Mrs. Mack and what goes on at her place, such being what no one knows," and he spoke a little uneasily, vaguely aware that Bobby was upset about something, though unable to guess what that something might be.

"I shall have to see Commander Seers," Bobby remarked.

"Oh, hadn't you heard, sir?" Gregson asked. "He was blown up this morning."

"Blown up?" repeated Bobby.

"Yes, sir. I always said as it was sure to happen, and so I told him, fiddling about with them drifting mines the way he did, but all he said was for me to shut up. They were trying to tow another of the things offshore into the westways current and they heard it beginning to tick over. Commander sent the boat off while he sat on the mine to get the tow rope right and then he would swim back. Which he did, and started to swim, but then the mine went off, and Commander, first he went up and then he went down. But he come up again and they got him in the boat and now he's in hospital, but he says as it'll take more than doctors, or even matron her own self to keep him there, and as how if they try to play tricks hiding his trousers, then he'll walk home same as when born, which he will, if put to it, as we know, having experience of what Commander's like when set on his own way."

Bobby decided that he wouldn't say anything in his report about Commander Seers being unfit for his job. But why, he wondered, was this such a contradictory muddled sort of a world, in which an obstinate, pig-headed old man, years behind the times, should also be of true heroic stature, ready to sacrifice his life to save others?

Not at all a tidy world, by no means a card-index, neatly ticketed sort of world. Yet every business man knows that a card index is the first principle of order, and order has been said to be Heaven's first law. Then he reflected that though God has been described in many ways—artist, mathematician, the Absolute, the First Cause, unwitting will, player of games, tyrant, Man vital, life force, what not, no one has ever thought of describing him as a business man. That might mean something, Bobby supposed, but, anyhow, even if it did, he had neither time nor capacity to think it out. He asked for the address of Mrs. Mack's nursing home and how to get there, since it might be useful to have more evidence of Haile's presence in the neighbourhood at the time of Itter Bain's murder. On the way, too, he could call at the River Farm, to have a chat with Martin Winstanley.

But that he was not destined to accomplish this afternoon, for when he reached the River Farm, he found that, though it was Sunday, Mr. Winstanley was out somewhere on the farm with his head foreman, a disgruntled man summoned specially from a comfortable Sunday afternoon nap. Mr. Winstanley had decided apparently on a new schedule of work, to be put in hand without delay. Bobby wondered what could be the reason for this sudden outburst of energy; and then, before he could do anything, and before Winstanley and his head foreman could be found, Bobby was urgently recalled by a 'phone call from the senior superintendent, who acted as Seers's deputy. A confession of guilt had been received from a man describing himself as a discharged worker from the Bain Products factory. Bobby knew these confessions. Hardly a murder gets into the papers but some weak-minded person comes forward to confess. However, all such confessions have to be tested and what truth they contain sorted out. It took till after nightfall to make it quite clear that this time there was no atom of truth, not the remotest approach to fact, in this particular story, and by that time it was too late for further activity. Though Bobby did make sure that another officer had been placed on guard at Kindles, and had been warned to remember that what happened to his predecessor would probably happen to him if he did not keep his eyes open. Bobby also secured from a superintendent worried to death to provide for all necessary duties that another constable should be stationed inside the house, if permission could be obtained. He did not learn till next day that this permission was firmly refused, Lord Adour pronouncing such a precaution to be uncalled for and entirely unnecessary.

Bobby wrote that night:

"This case is beginning to get me down. Every new fact I manage to unearth seems to point in an entirely new and different direction. It is like following a path continually branching off in new ways, so that you never know for certain where you are going except that it is somewhere fresh. Of one thing, though, I am beginning to grow convinced, and that is that the truth of what did happen that day in the Coldstone Spinney near Kindles will never be established by direct evidence. The only chance is to construct a pattern of events so clear and definite that only so, and in no other way, can what happened have come about. That once established, and the chances are not too good, there may be some hope of obtaining the kind of factual evidence that a jury always requires, very rightly, as a reinforcement of the logical deductions every British jury instinctively distrusts. Naturally, since, than logic, there is nothing more deceptive and misleading. Except perhaps facts. To trust to logic in this illogical world is to trust to the guidance of a blind man in a place where he has never been.

"The most important new fact that has come up is this story of Prescott Bain's sudden production of such a large sum as £9,000, so rescuing his firm from the clutches of a bank preparing to rationalize it out of existence. Where did that money come from? And why was it all in one pound notes? Why not a cheque? Generally a large payment made in small notes means there is a very good reason indeed for trying to conceal its origin? If that is so this time, what reason, what origin? And is there any connection with Itter Bain's death?

"The most disturbing new fact is the attack on Jane Felgate that does so much look like an intended attack on Helen Adour. Is that going to be repeated? If so, on which of the two of them? And how is it to be prevented? A determined assassin must always win in the end, if he is resolute and patient and watchful enough. The initiative is his.

"It is a responsibility and I am going to ask permission to sleep at Kindles, somewhere in a corridor as near the rooms of the two girls as possible. But I am not sure that permission will be given. If not, I shall have to sit under their windows all night, I suppose. A policeman's lot is indeed not a happy one, as has been said before with the most profound wisdom and insight.

"The most puzzling new fact is the apparent complete disappearance of the Seagull launch. It left its harbour anchorage in the tow of one of the Bain Products barges and seems to have vanished into thin air.

"The most surprising new fact is the emergence of Haile from troublesome and annoying rival detective into a suspect. I always felt sure he was afraid of something, but I had no idea what and there was nothing to connect him with the murder. But now I wonder, for why has he never said he was in this neighbourhood about that time? Is it possible we have been on a wrong track and the motive behind the murder was neither any rivalry or quarrel about this present-day Helen who seems to have such a power of standing people on their heads, nor anything to do with money, but something between Haile, Itter Bain, and the girl at Mrs. Mack's? Have Mrs. Mack and Miss Lambert speaking parts or are they merely supers?

"The most troublesome new fact is the blowing up of Seers and his subsequent retirement into hospital, where I expect he will have to stay, in spite of all protests. Not that any lack of trousers would be likely to keep him there, but lack of ability to stand upright or of strength to get out of bed might be harder to get over. While he was about, I could at least talk to him and get some help. But now I shall have to deal with a deputy scared out of his life of doing anything the Commander mightn't approve of. As I am afraid he doesn't approve of me. He is a pig-headed old boy and possesses what is called personality, i.e. supreme, unshakable belief in self. But you have to respect a man who, in order to get a tow rope fixed, can go on sitting on a mine that has begun to tick over. I can imagine seats where one would be more at one's ease."

The letter concludes on a more personal note.

CHAPTER XXI
CHANGE OF HEART

THE FIRST VISIT Bobby paid in the morning was to the Bain Products factory. To the gatekeeper he explained that he wished to see Mr.

Mauley Bain. He added that he could find his own way to the offices as he had been before. But out of the gatekeeper's sight—and mind— he turned off towards the wharf where were loaded and unloaded the barges plying between the factory and Toad-in-Hole Harbour.

A few men were busy there. Bobby did not speak to them, nor did they to him. He stood watching for a few minutes and then walked away; having made sure again that nowhere was there any sign of the missing launch. Now and again he was conscious of cautious movements behind him, and once he heard a cough.

When he turned sharply he had a glimpse of someone slipping swiftly away behind the corner of a shed.

He did not attempt to follow. He went back to where the group of workmen were busy and said to one of them:

"Have you seen Mr. Mauley Bain? I think he is about somewhere, isn't he?"

"I didn't know he had got back," the man answered. "Hi, Jim," he called to another man. "Seen Mr. Mauley? This gentleman is looking for him."

"Mr. Mauley? I don't think he's back yet," came the answer. "Better ask at the office."

Bobby said he would, thanked them, and moved away. Another of the men called:

"The office is t'other way, to your left."

But Bobby once again had thought he saw someone moving cautiously and furtively amidst the tangle of lorries, discarded machinery, piles of scrap, packing cases, and so on that lay around. He called softly, but got no response, and the silence that followed his summons seemed now to convey a sense of warning and of threat. Someone, he felt sure, who wished to see but not be seen. He turned away and then turned back sharply. This time he was aware beyond all doubt of a hot and angry eye staring at him through the crack of a half-open door. Bobby moved briskly towards it. The door banged suddenly. Bobby shrugged his shoulders and went away. He had no wish nor time to indulge in games of hide-and-seek. But, if the watcher had been Mauley Bain, of which he was by no means sure, then it was as well to know that Mauley wished to avoid him, but yet was interested in his movements.

Bobby walked on thoughtfully to the office, but there got no information. No one knew if Mr. Mauley Bain had returned from London or not. Mr. Prescott Bain was somewhere about the factory, and most likely he would know, but no one could say exactly where he was. No doubt he could be found if Mr. Owen cared to wait a little. It was remarked with a touch of surprise that Mr. Owen's was the second inquiry for Mr. Mauley made that morning. Bobby asked who had made the first inquiry and was told it was Wayling, the new potman at the "Good Haul." He had been so pressing and so sure that Mr. Mauley had said he would be back first thing this morning that to get rid of him he had been told to go and look for himself. He had gone off accordingly in the direction of the wharves.

So possibly, Bobby supposed, it had not been Mauley Bain who had been watching him, but Wayling. Only why should Wayling do that and why should he be so anxious to meet Mauley? Did that mean there was something between them? Yet another by-path, then, it might be necessary to explore? One of the office staff who had just come back from some errand caught Wayling's name.

"The 'Good Haul' potman?" he asked. "Has he been here? I wish I had seen him. He owes me ten bob. I can't think," he added moodily, "how the little blighter got it out of me. I had only had one glass of the nearly near-beer they give you at the 'Good Haul.'"

Bobby went away. No good wasting more time with so much to do. There was the River Farm to visit, as well as Mrs. Mack's nursing home. The River Farm first, though, as it was the nearer of the two, and there Bobby had to wait while a messenger was sent to find Winstanley, who, it appeared, either was or had been busy lending a hand "spreading muck" on one of the more distant fields.

"It's not what the master should be doing and him with his leg and all," said disapprovingly the housekeeper Bobby had seen on his previous visit. "Master's eye is better muck than any he can go help to spread. But what can you expect when there's chits of girls doing field work and glad to get them?"

When Martin did appear he certainly brought with him an aroma that provided circumstantial and convincing proof of his recent activities. He sent a message in to Bobby to say he was waiting outside, and when Bobby joined him, suggested adjournment to the stable for their talk.

"Hope you don't mind," he said, "but my housekeeper wouldn't let me indoors like this." He laughed pleasantly and Bobby thought he looked much brighter and more cheerful than before. He led the way into the stable and produced a couple of buckets to serve as seats. "I can't offer you a cigarette," he said. "Sacking matter to smoke in any of the outbuildings—at least, it would be if I dared even say 'Boo' to any of them for fear they took offence and cleared out." He laughed again. "A good crowd on the whole," he said, "though sometimes the land-girls will try to do more than their strength is up to. Well, you know, I had half a mind to come along to see you, only there's such a lot of work on hand, and then I rather expected you would be turning up. As a matter of fact, I expected you yesterday."

"I did call," Bobby said, "but you were out and I couldn't wait."

"I know," Martin said. "It was dark before I got in. My foreman and I were having a row. He thinks I'm heading straight for ruin. When I rang you up, you had gone out, so I went to bed. You have to turn in early if you mean to be up at first light."

Bobby looked at him curiously.

"You must be working long hours," he remarked. "A lot busier than when I saw you before. Rush orders or something? The Agricultural Committee at you again?"

"No, no," Martin answered and flushed a little. "Turning over a new leaf, I suppose. I had got a bit slack. Bad on a farm. If you're fighting Nature, you have to watch her the way you watch a fighter on your tail. I don't suppose you came to talk farming, though. It's about what happened the other night, I suppose? Are you on anything yet?"

"All sorts of things," Bobby answered gloomily, "but all pointing different ways. I am wondering if you can help. My information is that you have met Miss Adour on other nights at the same spot. Is that so?"

"Not met exactly," Martin answered. "You can't call it 'met.' I knew she sometimes went out for a stroll before bed—especially when it was moonlight. I didn't think it was altogether safe after what's happened. I thought I would just go and see if she was all right."

"Was that all?" Bobby asked.

"How do you mean all?" Martin demanded, and then he flushed again and more deeply. "Well, no, it wasn't all. It was partly just to look at her. I know it sounds damn silly. I suppose it is. All the same, to stand and look at her with the moonlight all around her and the darkness beyond—well, it's an experience. I suppose cops are a hard-boiled lot, but you try it and see."

Bobby let this last remark pass. He said:

"Did Miss Helen expect you?"

"Lord, no," Martin said and laughed. "Not likely. I suppose I ought to say, 'No such luck.' I didn't even mean to speak to her. Just to watch. Just to stand and stare and you may think me as big a fool as you like."

"Oh, I dare say I might be moonstruck, too, if I saw the young lady," Bobby answered smilingly, though to himself he was thinking, "Not me," and then he thought of Olive and smiled again. "What I'm wondering is, was anyone else hanging around for the same reason?"

"For the same fool reason, you mean," Martin suggested. "Don't trouble to spare my feelings. No one was around as far as I know."

"You say you didn't mean to speak to her. Did you in fact, the first night?"

"I said I didn't mean to speak to her, or to let her see me for that matter, the second time," Martin said. "The first night I pretended to be out looking for rabbits, I think I said. Rather thin. Of course, she knew better. I told her it wasn't safe for her to be out alone so late. She didn't take any notice. I think she knows too well the power of her beauty for her to have any fear."

"She didn't say anything?"

"No. Nothing much. Only good night. She went back towards the house. I watched till she was home safe."

"And the second time?" Bobby asked.

"It was just the same. There is something so strange about her loveliness you can't help feeling you must look again. At least, that's how I felt. Not so much now. Jane was there, though, not Helen. She told me Helen thought I might be dodging around and she wanted to be alone, so Jane had come to say would I please get out and stay out, and, of course, I said I would. She made me promise and promise not to sneak back, and I did. Then I cleared off and then I heard Jane cry out—you know as much after that as I do."

"Were you and Miss Jane talking for any length of time?"

"Oh, well, perhaps. I don't know exactly. Jane told me she knew just how I felt. She's an understanding sort of person. I told her exactly how it was. Funny thing. After I had told her how I felt, I didn't feel that way any longer. Jane's so—so restful. You can tell her anything, I want you to understand. What I mean is, I'm through playing the fool over Helen. That's finished. Helen had me standing on my head, but Jane's put me straight again. And if I could lay my hands on the swine who attacked her last night, I would wring his neck with pleasure."

"Please don't," Bobby said. "I've enough on my hands already. Do you think it possible Miss Jane was mistaken for Miss Helen, and that the attack was really intended to be on Miss Helen?"

"Well, I did think of that," Winstanley said. "Of course, Jane was wearing that cape thing. I went to Kindles this morning and made her promise never to wear it again. She rather laughed at me. There does seem no reason why anyone should want to attack either of them. Jane says it's impossible anyone in their senses should want to hurt Helen. It's not as if Helen had ever given anyone any sort of encouragement. She simply doesn't know you exist. Perhaps she doesn't really know that anything exists except her own loveliness. She's sort of withdrawn into her own beauty. That's what Jane says. If there really is anyone so crazy as to want to kill Helen to pay her out for being such a beauty, that's no reason for Jane to run her head into danger."

"No," agreed Bobby. "No proof it's that, though, and it hardly seems credible. I never heard of anyone wanting to kill beauty simply for being beautiful. An odd world, but surely not so odd as that. And no proof there's any connection with the Itter Bain murder, which is the job I have on hand."

They talked a little longer and then Bobby drove away. As he did so he remembered with some surprise that though Martin said he had gone out at night simply to stand and stare, himself unseen, at Helen's beauty, now it was Jane's safety he seemed chiefly concerned about.

"An odd world," repeated Bobby thoughtfully.

CHAPTER XXII
NURSING HOME

MRS. MACK'S NURSING establishment was situated about halfway between Toad-in-Hole and the Seashire county town, though it was still known as the Toad-in-Hole Nursing Home, since it was in

Toad-in-Hole it had been started. It stood, facing due south, on the edge of a low cliff overhanging a rocky and dangerous shore. On the west the line of cliff rose towards Toad-in-Hole, where it dipped abruptly to the valley of the Adour River. On the east the cliff sloped more gently to a small, pleasant and sandy cove where in happier days there had been a cluster of small holiday bungalows, one of those summer resorts so angrily denounced by some who in general can exercise a freer choice less hampered by considerations of cost and time. Now these bungalows presented a sad spectacle of the waste of war, though war itself had passed them by. They lay waste, desolate and destroyed in a nightmare wilderness of rusting wire, of huge, broken concrete blocks, of trailing iron barricades, of sudden pits; defences against a landing for which this small cove had been thought to offer opportunities.

Scattered on the slope leading up the cliff where the nursing home stood were a few still-occupied houses and shops; the shops serving also a small scattered population further inland. There was, too, a summer hotel, now almost as busy turning away wouldbe guests as in attending to those who had been graciously granted accommodation—at a price.

Bobby noticed that the hotel was open to the south, but well protected, both by trees and the lie of the land, from the north and east. The Mack nursing home lay higher, fully exposed in both directions. It did just cross Bobby's mind that a strong north or east wind and an open window might prove a combination well calculated to release from their sufferings the aged and the senile whose too-prolonged life had become no more than a burden to themselves— and even to their relatives.

Bobby set such thoughts aside. He had lunched on sandwiches put up by Mrs. Gregson, and, though it was still early, he decided to get a cup of tea at one of the shops near. Tea-shop waitresses are, of course, not in the same class as barmaids. Where barmaids know it all, waitresses hear only a modicum of local gossip, so much more effective is alcohol than tannin as a promoter of chat. All the same, in these small places waitresses often have a good idea of the standing and character of local residents, and Bobby was anxious to know what her neighbours thought of Mrs. Mack.

He left his car therefore in a convenient spot nearby and was strolling towards the smaller and less attractive of the two establishments announcing "Teas," for he thought that on the whole there was a chance it might be less concerned with visitors and more with the permanent residents. As he approached, the door of the shop opened and there emerged a buxom, jolly-looking, middle-aged woman, half leading, half carrying one so small and old and frail it seemed as if even the light breeze coming across the sea might have blown her away had she not been held in such warm and comfortable arms. An invalid chair stood nearby. In it the younger woman settled carefully her charge, apparently joking as she did so, for Bobby heard distinctly her jolly laugh and the cackle of the other's ancient merriment.

When they had gone Bobby entered the shop and asked for tea. He was soon chatting with the waitress, asking her about the district, the climate, the amenities. Then he asked if that was Mrs. Mack of the Toad-in-Hole nursing home, he had seen going away with an invalid lady.

"Mrs. Mack and old Mrs. Orchard," said the waitress. "Poor old soul. You can't help thinking it would be a mercy if she were took like others. So she would have been long ago only the way Mrs. Mack looks after her—like a daughter to her."

"You could depend on Mrs. Mack taking good care," Bobby asked, "of anyone who needed more attention than can be given in an ordinary way?"

"Oh, yes," agreed the waitress, "but she is thinking of giving up. Poor old Mrs. Orchard was very upset when Mrs. Mack told her. She says only Mrs. Mack keeps her going and it won't be the same anywhere else, even if Mrs. Mack does take her with her. Mrs. Mack is so conscientious. She doesn't feel as if she wants to carry on here."

"Why should Mrs. Mack's being conscientious make her give up?" Bobby asked.

"Well, you see," the waitress explained, "what she feels is that her doctor made a mistake. He's a London gentleman and he attends nobility and royalty, Mrs. Mack says, and he got Mrs. Mack to come down here because he thinks ozone from the sea is what you want more than anything when you're old. Mrs. Mack says he ought to know, and it may be what science says, but she thinks it's too strong for some, and it's quite true old people do seem to die off quick like after they get here. Not but that it's a happy release for the poor old souls. But Mrs. Mack is that conscientious doing her duty to her patients she's worried like, and she thinks she'll close down. She says if she does the doctor gentleman won't ever forgive her, and she'll have to do without him. But she'll try to manage somehow."

Bobby said it was fine to think Mrs. Mack thought first of those in her charge. The waitress agreed enthusiastically. She said it made you feel better to know there were people like Mrs. Mack in the world. Bobby agreed in his turn, and asked if Mrs. Mack only accepted aged people. The waitress said, Oh, no. Ladies came quite often. The strong sea air seemed to suit them better, and they seldom stayed long. But then, of course, they were young. The Waitress seemed less willing to talk now or to pursue the subject of these transitory patients. It was with evident relief that she went off to attend to a large party who had just entered the shop.

Bobby paid his bill and departed, leaving a generous tip to reward talkativeness, a quality he much approved—in other people.

A well-worn path led up the slope of the cliff and along it, past the nursing home. No doubt a favourite stroll for visitors, affording as it did a fine view over the sea and plenty of fresh air. Bobby strolled on, and then left the path to approach nearer the edge of the cliff. He stood there for a moment or two, watching the incoming tide foaming angrily on the formidable rocks below. Not much chance, he thought, of anything thrown down there ever being found again. He turned back again to the nursing home. It stood in a rather bleak garden, separated from the open cliff by a brick wall. In the garden were two or three shelters, open to the sea, where in fine and sunny weather it would evidently be pleasant for an invalid or a convalescent to sit for a time. One of these was occupied now by a young woman well wrapped up and as good-looking as any young woman needs to be. Bobby knew her at once for the Miss Lambert he had seen before; and if he stood where the corner of the wall provided a little shelter and watched her, it was not because of her looks, but because, as she sat there so quietly, hardly moving, she seemed somehow to convey a most strange impression of an inner radiance, a hidden but intense content and joy. It was as though in some way she had become a joy incarnate, as if all about her were a golden dream. Bobby found himself wondering how it was she could spread around this, as it were, aura of delight; and then he discovered he was being oddly reminded of Helen, who walked alone and aloof in beauty as this other sat and communed with herself in joy. His own business in life was grim enough and led him into grim surroundings, and it came to him that he would always be glad to remember that in this investigation at least he had seen joy and seen beauty both made manifest on earth.

There came quietly and quickly round the corner of the shelter the plump, comfortable figure of Mrs. Mack.

"My dear girl," she said scoldingly, "you know you oughtn't to be sitting there like that. What would Mr. Haile say? You'll be catching cold."

"I'm quite warm, really I am, Mrs. Mack," Miss Lambert said, getting to her feet.

"You can't be too careful," declared Mrs. Mack, still severe, "till baby comes."

"Have you made up your mind yet?" the girl asked while Mrs. Mack fussed to see she had all her belongings and was properly wrapped up.

"Yes. I'm giving up. I've told the agent so," Mrs. Mack answered. "But not till I've seen you and baby comfy together. I haven't told Mrs. Orchard I've decided, but I'll take her with me if she likes, poor old soul."

They moved away together towards the house and Bobby watched thoughtfully till they vanished indoors.

Even more thoughtfully he asked himself how he was to reconcile this care for Miss Lambert, this thoughtfulness for old Mrs. Orchard with the dark and ugly hints he had been given.

A contradictory world, he told himself. He hoped very much he was following a false trail and that all this had no connection with the Itter Bain murder. But of that it was his duty to assure himself, no matter what the cost, or to whom.

CHAPTER XXIII

AN ENGAGEMENT

WHEN HE KNOCKED, Mrs. Mack came to the door. He asked if he could have a few words with her and she hesitated, plainly both doubtful and suspicious.

"What's it about?" she asked. "I saw you outside. You looked as if you were after something, listening. If it's to take anyone in, I'm leaving."

"Yes, I heard you say so," Bobby agreed. "Not that I was listening, but I couldn't help hearing what you said." He produced his official card. "I thought you might be able to help," he said.

She took the card and read it and gave it back to him in silence. But she had changed as she read, changed oddly and suddenly. The smiling, good-tempered face became alert and wary; the mouth grew hard, too, hard and tight-lipped; the eyes were hostile and angry now, the eyes of one ready for attack, ready to attack in turn. A formidable and dangerous personality had leapt into sudden being from behind the façade of the stout, comfortable, motherly matron. She said in a slow and careful voice:

"All right. Come in if you must. I've nothing to hide. I've been expecting this."

"Why?" asked Bobby.

"Because fools talk," she answered. She led the way into a comfortable, conventional sitting-room, such as could be matched anywhere in any suburb of any town in England. Even the engravings on the wall were familiar, and so were the spindly occasional tables, the china ornaments, the framed photographs on the piano lid, the flowery pattern of the wallpaper. Bobby followed her. She turned to face him, without either seating herself or offering him a chair. She was still silent, but when Bobby, too, was silent, she said:

"There's never been a death in this house that wasn't properly certified. Ask Dr. Norris. He knows, though none too civil about it either, and always paid on the dot. Was it him sent you?"

"No," said Bobby.

"Well, then," she said, and watched him as a boxer fresh into the ring watches his opponent for the first blow.

"I'm told old people have a way of dying here rather quickly," Bobby said. "I don't know if that is true or not. I have no authority to ask. There have been no complaints."

"There's been no call for any," Mrs. Mack retorted swiftly, but at the same time with such an air of quick, unconscious relief as Bobby felt must be the measure of the apprehension she had felt. "Nothing's ever done here but what was wished by all and for the best."

"Well, then, if that's so, that's all right, isn't it?" Bobby said.

She nodded in assent and then sat down, first pushing forward a chair for him. But she still seemed to feel a need to justify herself. She said:

"If it was only what the relatives called incurable, even if there was doctor's word for it, I never took the case. Because incurable— well, you never know, not even doctors. But old age—well, there's no cure for that, is there?"

"No," agreed Bobby. "None."

"Lingering," she said. She went on: "You could see plain there was nothing left, only suffering, and being a burden to all. Lingering," she repeated as if it were a word she found comfortable, soothing. "Just lingering. Nothing left except wait, just lying there, groaning and suffering, and why should young strong lives with all before them be sacrificed for a few weeks or months of nothingness but pain? The children's education, too, as likely as not."

"I haven't come to talk about that," Bobby interposed, but Mrs. Mack went on unheedingly:

"It's not like that with old Mrs. Orchard. She's lively enough, even if fretful as a baby at times, and enjoys her cup of tea and the wireless you can always turn on to send her to sleep, and no one can say there's not been good care taken of her ever since I had her, and that's two years or near."

"Yes, I know," Bobby said. "So I've been told."

Mrs. Mack gave him a quick, half-defiant, half suspicious look, as if asking what else he had been told and why it was he had been told anything at all. She went on talking, a little quickly, a little nervously.

"Her daughter has a job in a London store," she said. "Five guineas a week and she sends me half as regular as clockwork, which isn't my regular terms or anything like, but the other half's not much to live on and look respectable the way things are today and like to be for long enough. No chance to go out and meet people and maybe find a man for herself. Well, if old Mrs. Orchard were like some and no life left in her but sleep and suffering, if you can call it life, wouldn't it be best for it to end, so that others could have their chance of life as they've a right to? Instead of two lives going on and neither to be called rightly a life at all? What do you say?"

"No one has made me a judge in such things," Bobby answered gravely. "People must take their own decisions—and the consequences. Some people might call a girl a fool if she gives up her own life for an old woman's sake. A matter of opinion. I suppose other people have sometimes given up their own lives for the sake of others, though in different ways. Shall we talk about something else? I understand you are leaving here?"

"That's right," said Mrs. Mack, but the urge, the half unconscious urge to justify herself was still strong upon her. She said: "Mostly they were willing enough to go, willing and glad, tired out, so tired they only stayed for lack of strength to do else. Lingering," she said once more. She went towards a small book-case inconspicuous in one corner of the room. As she fumbled in it, she said over her shoulder, almost as if the words were dragged from her against her will: "There were a few who didn't." She turned round with a pamphlet in her hand and said: "But often only conscious half the time or less and the money not there, not unless others were to suffer for it, and they children very like. Don't the children with their lives before them count for more than those that have had their time?" She offered him the pamphlet she had found and said: "You can read about it here. They want to make it legal and for the incurables, too, and so they ought. It's only right. Read this."

"No, thank you," Bobby said.

Mrs. Mack put the pamphlet down.

"Oh, well," she said, "if people won't hear reason." More briskly and in a more satisfied tone, as if pleased with the defence she had not been asked to make, she continued: "I told the agent this afternoon I was giving up, but it isn't about that you've come, is it?"

"No," said Bobby. "The young lady you were talking to is a Miss Lambert, isn't she?"

"What about her?" demanded Mrs. Mack, and once again was alert, on guard, formidable, no longer on the defensive as she had been just recently, but ready to attack if need be. "She'll have her baby soon, and when she does I'll see she gets every care, and they'll be married first as well."

"Married?" Bobby repeated quickly, for that was something he had not expected. "You mean Miss Lambert and Mr. Haile are getting married?"

"That's right. He gave the notice in this morning."

"Did he?" Bobby said. "Good. It was Mr. Haile brought Miss Lambert here, wasn't it? Can you tell me the date?"

"Let me see now," Mrs. Mack said. She gave the date after reference to a book she produced, and it was the day of the murder of Itter Bain. "Mr. Haile came with her by the early train," she remarked as she put her book away.

"Did he stay long?"

"No. He went off almost at once. He had an engagement. What do you want to know for?"

"It is only a question of fitting in times and dates and so on," Bobby explained. "Very useful sometimes in checking what you hear, very helpful indeed. If times fit and everything, then it's pretty sure to be true. If they don't, there's generally something wrong. Are they keeping their engagement private? Mr. Haile didn't say anything to me when I saw him last. Not that there's any reason why he should."

"Nothing private about it that I know of," Mrs. Mack said. "No reason why there should be. It's only just been settled, this morning."

"Oh-h," said Bobby, understanding, and smiled as he remembered how the girl had looked, sitting there in the shelter facing the sea, as if lost in a kind of golden dream. "I thought she was looking rather happy," he said.

"So would you look happy," Mrs. Mack told him sharply, "if you were a girl and you thought you wouldn't have either a husband or a home or a baby, or a name, and something to hide all your life, and then all at once you knew you were going to get 'em all and nothing to keep hidden from all the others. You're a man," she added with a touch of pity in her voice. "You couldn't understand."

"I expect not," Bobby said. "I'm glad Haile has made up his mind. I wonder what made him?"

"Helen Adour," said Mrs. Mack.

"What on earth has she got to do with it?" Bobby demanded, astonished.

"It was seeing her go by," Mrs. Mack said. "Watching her pass. It makes you feel like that somehow. It's a sort of loveliness she has that's frightening in a way, like the stars some nights when their shining makes you want to run away, only you can't, because there isn't anywhere to go. Have you seen her?"

"No," said Bobby. "I must as soon as I can. Somehow I've always missed her till now."

"You'll be like all the others when you do," Mrs. Mack told him. "Every man falls in love with her at once. Or else it's not with her, but only with her beauty."

"Are they different?" Bobby asked.

"The warmth of the sun is not the sun," Mrs. Mack answered. "Mr. Haile said that this morning. I thought at first he had been drinking when he got here, he was so wrought up. But it wasn't drink, it was Miss Adour's beauty working on him. Gone to his head like spirits. He said when some could show such loveliness he wouldn't spoil it by doing the dirty on Emmy—that's Miss Lambert. When he went, I said to him Emmy was that happy it was worth Miss Adour's loveliness ten times over—and he had done it, so it was up to him to keep it so. He said he would. But all worked up he was, and you can't tell."

"We can hope for the best," Bobby said. "I shall be more keen than ever on getting to see Miss Helen."

"Better mind," Mrs. Mack said, and laughed. "There's never any knowing what she won't do to you. In a way, it was my seeing her while I was hanging about near the agent's office and not knowing whether to go in or not that made me decide. She went by at the top of the street and all the street seemed to light up, and before I knew there I was in the agent's office, giving notice to end my tenancy, and glad they were to have it, too, with a long list of clients all waiting and ready to pay any price. So that's settled. Can't be undone now, but I don't know if I should have if I hadn't seen her just at that moment."

"Well, I'm glad you have," Bobby said. "You can tell me it's no business of mine if you like, but I'm sure it's better so in every way. I must be getting on now, so I'll say goodbye and thank you."

"What for?" Mrs. Mack asked with a sudden return to her former attitude of doubt and suspicion. "I don't know what you wanted, but I haven't told you anything, have I?"

"Oh, no," agreed Bobby. "Except about you leaving and Mr. Haile and Miss Lambert getting married and all that."

"Everybody's welcome to know," Mrs. Mack said, but still a little doubtfully.

"Well, why not?" Bobby agreed.

"If it wasn't about the old people you came," Mrs. Mack said, "was it about ... the other thing?"

"What's that?" Bobby asked.

"You know," she said, watching him steadily. "If it was, though you've never said, you ought to have heard how the girls thanked me and how grateful they were with a chance to start their lives all fresh and new. Men don't know what it is to have a baby without a father."

"It's a pity, don't you think?" Bobby said, "that some girls don't think of that a little sooner. But I've no authority there either, and it's not for me to say. Goodbye and thank you very much. I hope I shan't have to trouble you again. Take good care of Miss Lambert—I mean, Mrs. Haile—when her baby arrives."

"Trust me," said Mrs. Mack. "There's been too many babies never born here for me to miss the chance of one that may be."

CHAPTER XXIV
LAUNCH LOST

BOBBY DROVE AWAY from the Toad-in-Hole Nursing Home in a very troubled frame of mind. It was not that he was thinking of what had been happening there, or of how there the deepest questions of life and death seemed to have been dealt with on an irresponsible basis of private judgment and convenience. All that was for the law of the land to deal with, the law and public opinion of which the law can only be the formal expression. But it was as though as he drove on there floated by his side the smiling, glowing features of one to whom had come a joy as great as unexpected. It might be his duty, he knew, to take such action as would wipe away that joy for ever, to turn that happiness into the ultimate despair.

He hoped it would not come to that, but he did not know, and, strive as he would, he could not banish from his mind memory of that great contentment he had seen and that now hung in such peril. Nor was it any avail for him to remind himself that in this world joy is the most fragile, the most ephemeral of all that ever the human spirit knows.

When he arrived back he found waiting for him a young harbour man named Soper. He was the man who had been engaged by Sergeant Gregson to search the river for any sign of what had become of the *Seagull*. His report was emphatic. He had covered the whole length of the river to and beyond the Bain Products factory, to, in fact, the point where the river branched into its two main constituent parts, both too shallow for the *Seagull*. He had seen nothing of it and was quite certain that nowhere could it be concealed along the river banks. A conclusive report and Bobby thanked the man and dismissed him thinking to himself as he did so that anyhow that was that. No *Seagull*, and so what had become of it?

There was also a message for him left with Mrs. Gregson to say that Mauley Bain had rung up and was anxious for an interview. Would Mr. Owen ring up and make an appointment? Bobby did so, but was told that Mr. Mauley hadn't yet returned from Toad-in-Hole. He was probably still there in the hope of seeing Mr. Owen as soon as possible. This was interesting, but no great help, as nothing was known of where in Toad-in-Hole Mauley might be. On that point the 'phone had no suggestion to offer. A vague suggestion about the harbour side was made, but, as it had now begun to rain heavily, that did not seem a spot where anyone was likely to be lingering. Bobby went out, though, on the off chance of finding Mauley somewhere, but instead ran into Sergeant Gregson. Gregson promptly suggested the "Good Haul" as being a likely place to try. So he and Bobby went back to the house, where a call on the 'phone confirmed the fact and brought Mauley's reply that he would come round at once.

"There's been an upset there," Gregson confided to Bobby before resuming his tour of inspection. "About that new potman of theirs."

"Wayling?" Bobby asked. "Why? What's happened now? Has he got the sack?"

"He had a row with the manager and walked out. The manager wanted to keep back what Wayling owed him out of his wages. Wayling wouldn't have it. Quoted the Truck Act and said he wouldn't go on working for a man with loose ideas like that about money."

"Nothing," agreed Bobby, "more likely to upset and distress Wayling than any show of irregularity or looseness about money."

"Yes, sir," agreed Gregson and added: "Though, they do say there isn't no one at the 'Good Haul' staff or regulars that hasn't lent him something. But very liberal with it when he's got it. And most of the women staff are up in arms and say it's such a shame, and, as for owing the regulars, that makes them more regular still, hoping to get their money back, and now he's sacked he won't be able to pay anyone at all. And they are saying, too, it's only because of the manager being jealous."

"Jealous?" repeated Bobby. "I thought that was the cellar-man?"

"Yes, sir; it's him, too," Gregson agreed, "but the manager as well because of someone telling him Wayling was seen first thing this morning on the Kindles road."

"Was he?" exclaimed Bobby, startled. "I thought the report from your man said no one had been seen near there last night?"

"Oh, yes, sir," agreed Gregson; "that's right. Robins it was on duty; he's a good man, you can trust what he says. And it wasn't that worried the manager. Mrs. Parker lives up that way and the story is Wayling was coming out of her garden very early, soon as it was daylight."

"Who is Mrs. Parker?" Bobby asked.

"She's a widow lady with a tidy bit of property of her own, and the manager's sweet on her, so he doesn't like to hear about anyone coming out of her garden gate first thing of a morning. Wayling says it's all nonsense, he was in bed in his room at the 'Good Haul,' but the manager's not so sure."

Bobby wasn't so sure either. Gregson departed to resume his interrupted duties, but opened the door again to say that Mr. Mauley was coming.

Mauley was in fact coming down the steep narrow street with that long, slow, stealthy stride that seemed characteristic of him. Silently he came, and slowly to all appearance, and yet was at your side almost as you were thinking how deliberately he moved. It was indeed as if he did not move at all, but was simply immobile, first at one point and then immobile at another, nearer to you, without ever having traversed the intervening space, as an electron was once supposed to leave one orbit round its nucleus and to appear immediately in another without ever passing between. Bobby remembered well those deep-set, burning eyes, the angry mouth, the sullen, brooding expression he had seen before, all now intensified if anything. Bobby had gone to the open door on hearing what Gregson said. Mauley, coming up, said without preliminary, in those low, careful tones of his that still conveyed that odd impression of other words kept back, but struggling for release:

"My launch has been stolen. I thought I had better let you know."

"You mean the *Seagull*?" Bobby asked. "Come inside, won't you?"

Mauley followed him into the small Gregson parlour. He took no notice of Bobby's offer of a chair. He said again:

"The launch has been stolen. I thought I would let you know."

"Can you give me any details?" Bobby asked.

"No," said Mauley, and stared at Bobby with his great burning eyes. "Have you found out who killed my brother?" Without waiting for a reply, he said: "All I know is, it's gone—stolen."

"When did you find out?"

"This morning, after I got back from Town. I told one of our barge men to bring it up. It wanted an overhaul. He tied it up at the wharf and left it there. Next morning it had gone. He didn't pay any attention—thought it was being seen to somewhere. It wasn't. No sign of it to be found. No trace. No one knows anything about it. I've asked everywhere. It's been stolen."

"Why?" Bobby asked. "What for?"

"Good lord," exclaimed Mauley impatiently. "It's worth a couple of thousand, isn't it? That's what was paid for it and cheap, too. Look at the advertisements in the papers."

"Mr. Prescott Bain offered it me for one thousand," Bobby remarked.

"More fool he," retorted Mauley. "Besides, he had no right. It doesn't belong to him. Nor to the firm. Itter bought it on his own."

"It will be part of his estate, then. Is it mentioned in his will?"

"There's no will," Mauley said.

He went and stood by the mantelpiece. Bobby had seated himself, but Mauley was still ignoring the chair Bobby had pushed forward. Bobby was always willing to give anyone he was questioning the supposed advantage of looking down on the other party to the interview. It seemed to give confidence, and he had found by experience that a sudden question flashed upwards had often the same disconcerting effect as an upward blow that gets under a guard. He remarked now:

"I suppose then you'll act as next of kin? You are sure there's no will?"

"Why should there be?" Mauley asked. "Itter did not think he would die so soon. Nor did I." Then he said again: "Nor did I."

"If it's been stolen," Bobby said, "how could it have been moved? I thought the engine was out of action?"

"It had mast and sails," Mauley answered. "Or it could have been rowed downstream, or towed. No difficulty going down-stream. The current's pretty strong. And now it isn't anywhere, either in the river or in the harbour. I've made sure of that."

"Well, it must be somewhere," Bobby observed. "Could it have been taken out of the harbour without being seen?"

"I don't know. I should think so. Anyhow, a five-pound note would close the eyes of any of those harbour fellows."

"Tried it?" Bobby asked sharply; and was rewarded by a stare even darker, angrier than before, but one in which there seemed now to mingle a certain sudden uneasiness.

"No," Mauley said then, and gave Bobby an odd impression that this was true. "No. I don't give people bribes. They do what I tell them, and if they don't—then it's up to both to see who gets his way." He said this with all the strange hidden force of his dominating personality, as though he knew that generally it was his way that was followed. "I don't give bribes," he repeated, "but I've heard enough about them. Ask anyone, if you don't believe me."

Bobby saw no reason to disbelieve, but he knew also that there is a measure in all things, and that the same men who would see no great harm in shutting an eye to a boat slipping out on some smuggling or similar trip would act very differently in the case of serious crime. He changed the subject.

"When I asked," he remarked, "about Mr. Itter's will, I think I was wondering if that was how Mr. Prescott had been able to pay off the bank. I hear that's been done. Or was it to raise the funds the firm wanted that you went to Town?"

"No, it wasn't. Who told you the bank had been paid off?"

"Common report. Isn't it true?'

"I expect so. Prescott did it on his own. I know nothing about it. He's responsible for the finance. He wouldn't have come in if he hadn't had full control of that side. He put up most of the capital. He's smart enough. Anyhow, the firm's on its legs again and that's all that matters. I don't see what it has to do with you."

"I don't either," agreed Bobby. "Only rather a lot of curious things are happening and I am a little afraid sometimes they may go on happening. Whether paying out the bank comes under the heading of curious, I don't know. One has to check on everything. I was only wondering. Can you tell me where you stayed in London?"

Mauley, still standing by the fireplace, stared down at him from those strangely burning eyes of his. They made Bobby think of Blake's lines: "Tiger, Tiger, burning bright, in the jungles of the night." So burned Mauley's eyes against the dark pallor of his countenance. He did not speak for a little. Then abruptly he threw himself into the chair he had hitherto ignored. He laughed harshly and said:

"Is this a check?"

"If you like to call it one," Bobby said.

"You think I'm lying and never went to Town at all? Why should I?"

"I don't know," Bobby said. "I'm always having to tell people I wouldn't ask questions if I knew the answers. I don't think you're lying. I don't know. A detective has to keep a perfectly open mind. Not easy. I try. Well? Where did you stay?"

"I don't know," Mauley said.

"Don't know?"

"No."

"I said just now," Bobby remarked, "that there were a lot of curious things happening. It's rather curious, isn't it, not to know where you stayed on a visit to London?"

"Not a bit of it," Mauley retorted. "Quite simple. I take it you can hold your tongue?"

"I can," Bobby answered, "and I always do, except when it's a police duty to speak."

"Well, I dare say I shall shock your police-regulated mind, but I may as well tell you the truth."

"Just as well," agreed Bobby. "Unhappily, it's not so easy to shock police as I wish it was. Yes?"

"I tried hotels," Mauley said. "They were all full up. Most of them seemed to think it a good joke that anyone who hadn't booked a room should expect to get one. I began to think I should have to sleep on the Embankment. It was starting to rain, too. Then I met a woman in St. James's Street. I went home with her. A squalid place. But there was a bed and it was shelter. I gave her her money and cleared out early and I've no idea where it was, except that it was somewhere behind Leicester Square. I got away as quickly as I could. I didn't want any of her bullies turning up and I never looked back or looked where it was. I never wanted to see the place again or the woman either."

"Do you know her name?"

"I never asked," Mauley said and laughed harshly. "I don't suppose she would have told me the truth if I had. I didn't tell her my name either. I didn't want to run any risk of blackmail. You might be able to find her if you did a broadcast or something, and described me. But I hope you won't and I dare say it wouldn't be much good. Women of her sort aren't too fond of the police."

"No," agreed Bobby thoughtfully. "They aren't, are they?" He reflected that this story might well be true. True or not, it had to be accepted, for there was no way to prove it false. Except, of course, by direct evidence of Mauley's presence elsewhere. "There's nothing more you can tell me?"

"I thought detectives told you," observed Mauley with a perceptible sneer.

"Well, we have to be told first, you know," Bobby said good humouredly. "We aren't clairvoyants. There seems to have been a rather mysterious Frenchman turned up here shortly before your brother's murder and then vanished again. Do you know anything about him?"

"A Frenchman?" Mauley repeated and looked puzzled. "First I've heard of it. A Frenchman?" he repeated and now looked not so much puzzled as startled. "Before Itter ..." he began and stopped. "No, I don't know anything about it," he said firmly. "Never heard anything about any Frenchman. Where does he come in, anyhow? You don't suppose he stole the launch, do you?"

"No, but perhaps he came over in it," Bobby said, and saw at once that this was exactly what Mauley, too, had been thinking.

"Well, I don't know anything about it; never heard of it before," Mauley repeated; and Bobby was inclined to believe him, but was also more than inclined to believe that some train of thought, some fresh idea had been suggested to him, but one that he had no intention of revealing.

"Do you think the theft of the launch can have any connection with your brother's murder?" Bobby asked next.

"How could it?" Mauley asked in return. "That wasn't in the launch or anywhere near where it could be." Then he said: "Have you found out anything new?" When Bobby did not answer at once, Mauley added: "You never will, because you do not understand."

"Understand what?" Bobby asked, but Mauley only replied by a vague and sweeping gesture. "Understand what?" Bobby repeated, but still got no answer. Indeed, it was almost as if Mauley had not even heard, so deeply now did he seem sunk in his own thoughts. Bobby said: "I think there is much you could tell me if you would."

"Nothing," Mauley answered now, but with an effort, as though it had been difficult for him to rouse himself from his abstraction. "Nothing that I can tell you. Nothing that you would understand— or believe."

"Tell me what it is. Belief is unimportant."

"I might as well tell you my dreams."

"Dreams are important," Bobby said. Mauley was silent. "I must ask you this—what are you keeping back?"

"I have told you," Mauley answered. "My dreams—and you will never know them, and, if you did, they would mean nothing to you. Is it true there's been an attack on Helen Adour?"

"Yes. Who told you?"

"It's common talk. You don't know who it was?"

"No. The assailant escaped."

"Was Lord Adour anywhere near?"

"You don't want me to suspect her father, do you?"

"Your affair whom you suspect. This is different, altogether different. You'll never understand. No policeman could. Or anyone perhaps. I know I don't. Lord Adour told me once Helen's beauty was a fatal thing. It was after dinner. He was talking about Itter—Itter and Helen. He said beauty like Helen's was like a high explosive and no way of stopping it. You think what's happened has been a murder just like any sordid affair in the East End or anywhere. Well, it isn't."

"What is it, then?" Bobby asked.

But Mauley only stared at him with a strange and tortured expression, and once more Bobby felt that the other had sunk into a maze of dark and complicated memories and fears and thoughts where he could not be followed, where indeed he was himself lost and wandering. Mauley said abruptly:

"I must go."

"Listen to me," Bobby said, and he spoke sternly. "You are brooding on what you call your dreams. Are they only dreams?" Again there was no answer, only an abstracted stare and a movement towards the door. "This can't be left as it is," Bobby said. "You must tell me what is in your mind."

"You talk like a fool," Mauley retorted with unexpected violence. "I couldn't even if I tried, for I do not know myself." He had had the door half open. Now he banged it to again. He still spoke with a new vehemence and he was still staring intently, even violently, at Bobby, but almost as if he no longer saw him. "Murder?" he muttered. "They call it that, but it may be it was something that had to be. Something that happened because it was there to happen."

"What's that mean?" Bobby asked sharply; but Mauley opened the door again and was gone, nor was there any way of stopping him except by force, nor any way at all of getting him to speak more plainly while he remained in his present mood.

"This isn't a murder case," Bobby reflected grimly; "it's just a psychological problem where none of the ordinary principles apply. And how the dickens am I going to find the answer?"

Bobby wrote that evening to Olive:

"So you see that once again a new factor emerges. When I asked Mauley Bain if he knew anything of this supposed visitor from France Oregson told me about, it was merely on my part a shot in the dark. But now I am certain that the question suggested to him a new, and rather startling and, I think, disturbing line of thought.

"I only wish it suggested anything at all to me—except a blank wall.

"Though there is the possibility that whatever it was may have some connection with Prescott Bain's sudden production of the money necessary to square the bank.

"If so, that might mean that this money is the underlying motive and ultimate cause of Itter Bain's death. Yet I find it hard to think that Helen Adour's beauty and personality which seem to upset so completely everyone who comes near her—I haven't seen her yet, but shall to-morrow—doesn't come into it somehow, is not in fact the predominating cause in all this complicated, bewildering affair. Hard enough in any case to find a way through such a maze, but worse still when the said maze is one where a girl's face seems capable of opening or closing any one of its paths.

"It makes it all jolly difficult.

"Incidentally, are you wondering what will happen when I do get my talk with her to-morrow? No need. A policeman moves in an aura of cold, impersonal officialdom and can be no respecter either of persons or faces. Not to mention that forewarned is forearmed. Or is it his legendary boots that keeps a policeman so solidly planted on the earth?

"Anyhow, it does seem to me that these new developments must of necessity mean that somehow, somewhere, sometime soon, the truth is bound to break out, just as after due period of incubation the chick is bound to emerge from the egg—whether of the domestic fowl or of the ill-omened vulture.

"Can you answer this?

"What connection, if any, between the mysterious visitor from France, the disappearance of the Seagull launch, the appearance of enough money to put Bain Products on its legs again?

"Not too difficult, that one, perhaps, only what light on the Itter Bain murder?

"That's more difficult, for does the answer to the first question give the motive for the murder or must that be sought elsewhere?

"At the moment, I am inclined to say that every chance there is of bringing the case to a satisfactory conclusion hangs on the question of what has become of the Seagull.

"I needn't explain where I think it may be, that's obvious as a possibility. But there is also the other possibility that it may have been smuggled out of the harbour. Mauley Bain may have known *something when he talked about a five-pound note being enough to manage that. If so, the launch may have been taken across to the Continent and sold there. Probably there's a black market in motor launches as in everything else. It certainly needed overhauling, but that may have been done. Then I'm told it could have been taken across under sail by a man who knew how. I got Gregson to inquire if any man capable of handling her under sail was missing. He says, none. A stranger may have been brought in, but that would make any bribery more expensive and much more difficult. The harbour men might accept something to shut their eyes to what a neighbour was up to, but refuse absolutely to do the same for any stranger—five pounds or fifty notwithstanding. Human nature has these odd little quirks, since after all a bribe remains a bribe, whether from friend or stranger. But I dare say that's a pedantic, official view.*

"As I see it, and Lord knows, I've been scratching my head hard enough and have increased the paper shortage by nearly a basket full of torn notes, memoranda, theories of one sort and another, the issue has now been narrowed down to these main possibilities.

"(A) Prescott Bain.

"Difficult to think the appearance of the large sum necessary to save Bain Products from the bank's rationalising scheme is in no way connected with Itter Bain's death. It seems clear that Prescott would have been the one of the three of the Bain partners who would have been most seriously affected. He had put up most of the capital, and it was his money and position that would have been lost if the bank's plans had been carried out. I don't know if it would have meant anything you could call ruin. But certainly a heavy financial loss, which will not happen now. Itter Bain, if he had survived, would have kept his profession and his unusual skill in it. Mauley Bain would have kept his managerial experience and the practical certainty of another job—even under the bank's new schemes—in the present scarcity of good managerial experience and ability. But Prescott would have lost his chief—only?—asset, his capital. And there is no doubt there had been a good deal of quarrelling among the three of them. But —is this decisive?—there's his alibi, supported by the unimpeachable evidence of the two bank officials. Unimpeachable, certainly, but relevant? That's more doubtful, for

there may be a flaw in the time element. In any case, an alibi only holds good till it's busted.

"(B) Mauley Bain.

"A dark, secret, puzzling character, pursuing I think his own hidden aims. What are they? Haile warned me to watch him. Yes, but little good watching when there is nothing on which you can take action. There are, of course, those two details you will remember and that may be significant, but only as indications. But what is he keeping back that came into his mind when I asked about the visitor from France seen here once and never again? What I said about Prescott's alibi seems to apply to Mauley as well. Good enough to stand up in court—till busted. He puts forward another alibi, too, for the night of the attack on Jane that may have been meant for Helen. But it's an alibi that rests entirely on his own word. It is true, for I have checked it, that he left for London by train early that morning and that he returned by train, but there's only his own word for how he spent the interval.

"(C) Henry Haile.

"I don't see that he can be left out. Is it only a coincidence that he got the job of trying to show Lord Adour was guilty when already he knew the persons concerned and the locality? If he is guilty, to divert suspicion elsewhere would be an obvious move. Why this sudden promise to marry the Lambert girl? Is it genuine? For her sake, I hope so. But it comes immediately after the attack that may have been aimed at Helen and he was clearly in the vicinity at the time. Is the promise to marry Miss Lambert a demonstration that he isn't interested in or affected in any way by Helen? One can't help seeing the possibility of a smoke screen. The possibility that the murder was a result of mutual jealousy between two aspirants for Helen's favour has always to be remembered.

"(D) Wayling.

"Totally unpredictable, with his own twisted ideas of what is permissible and what isn't. Never actively malicious, I think, but all the same capable of almost anything that happened to suit himself at the moment. The perfect egotist perhaps. If one could understand and follow his own private line of thought, one might I think trust him. But the difficulty is just there. One can't help noticing that he was remaining in the neighbourhood in the not very exciting job of

potman at a pub. He even held the job a few days, which I believe is more than he has ever managed with any other job. What is the idea? To watch what's going on? Why should he? Again, he was apparently seen coming first thing in the morning either from Kindles or else from this Mrs. Parker's. If Kindles, what for, what had he been up to? If Mrs. Parker's—well, no explanation needed! Wayling possesses somehow a great, an inexplicable, bewildering fascination for women. What they see in the ugly, unreliable little brute passes all under-standing. Has Helen come under this spell or charm or whatever you like to call it? Or has she in a way revenged her sex by exercising the same fascination upon him? He threatened once—and I think for the moment he meant it—that he would kill me if I laughed at his feeling for Helen. It impressed me, for somehow that moment seemed to give me a glimpse of something sincere, something very deep down in him and generally entirely overlaid. I suppose psychologists would give it some long name or another. I felt for the moment that I had had a glimpse of the essential man. Later, the thought came to me that possibly he had already killed for Helen's sake —to save her from some threat or danger or even from some inconvenience. For I am not sure he would not kill even to save her from a cut finger. That was my impression at the time. I do not think he can be left out. A grotesque little man, but it may be much love, an impossible love, has made him mad. Who was it said that men have died and worms have eaten them, but not for love? That may be true, but men have killed for love, and Wayling may be of the company.

"(E) Martin Winstanley.

"The dark horse of the case. He was on the spot both when Itter was killed and when Jane was attacked. Why the change apparent in him, the renewed interest he seemed to show in his farm, in life generally? Why did he seem to want to give the impression that it was Jane he was thinking of, not Helen? Camouflage again? Well, all I can say of him is that he is the dark horse you mustn't forget.

"(F) Lord Adour.

"Two motives seem possible in his case—the father protecting his daughter idea, the association with Itter Bain in some complicated transaction in which Itter Bain and Lord Adour, Prescott Bain, £9,000, the Seagull, the visitor from France, all played a part, and

that led finally to some quarrel or danger that had to be met by, or that led to, the killing. I think this aspect of the case is so far advanced that I can now tackle Lord Adour and ask for explanations. If he refuses them or if they are not satisfactory, I shall have grounds for going further.

"(G) Helen.

"She has to be included. A bit startling, but necessary all the same. I know she seems so much a thing apart, so solitary and aloof, so far removed by her strange gift of beauty from all ordinary life, that it is difficult to connect her with the thought of action—especially violent action. She again was certainly on the spot—identity of time and place once more established. She and Martin alibi each other. Is that conclusive? Wouldn't they in any case? Suppose her father overtook her as he was hurrying back to the house for his camera and told her about the kingfisher? If so, she may have turned back to see for herself. If so again, she may have come across Itter Bain. If so, once more, did he 'molest' her, as we say in the witness-box? And was there then perhaps a fatal outcome, with the gun left standing by the oak ready for her to snatch up and fire, though very likely more with the idea of frightening than of killing. It has to be considered. I hope I shall be able to form a better opinion after seeing her to-morrow, as I shall insist I must. I know such violent action is against all one has been told of her goddess-like attitude of aloof indifference to all but her own loveliness. But why is she so careful to avoid me? My failure so far to get a talk with her is due to her own deliberate action, I feel certain.

"Finally—

"(H) [or should it be (X)?]

"The unknown visitor from France, or at any rate from the Continent.

"There's no proof he was in fact a Frenchman, except that he spoke in French, and did not seem to know English well. Not conclusive. Many from many lands speak French well and English badly. I can't say much about him for the very good reason that I know nothing about him—except that there is a possibility that he was somehow mixed up in the queer Itter Bain-Lord Adour-Seagull transaction and there may have been quarrelling or ill-

feeling, or even threats of blackmail or denunciation whereto a gunshot seemed the only answer.

"Shall I, should I, add one more, a possible addition after my 'finally'? I will, if you won't think me quite mad. After all, you have to consider every possibility, even the most unlikely. Well then:

"(J) Commander Seers.

"I suppose that gives you a bit of a shock; and I know as well as you do that there is not so much as a hint of evidence on which to found a ghost of a suspicion.

"All the same, you didn't see, and I did, how he went what Collier called all 'goo-goo' at the mere mention of Helen's name. Not much, I think, the strange fascination of her beauty would not make him willing to do for her. I can imagine circumstances—but I won't, for imagination is no help. I do know he was out all that afternoon, on a motor-trip in a high-powered car. I have not tried to check up at all. I have not felt justified and I shall not unless something turns up to give some kind of substantial foundation to what at present is no more than a vague possibility.

"Well, there's the list of my candidates—though 'J,' I think, is less a candidate than a possibility of becoming a candidate some day. I don't think I should know which would be my favourite, except for those two trifling indications you will remember—one of them does seem as if it might mean something even if the other is almost too trifling for serious consideration.

"What is really bedevilling the whole issue is the effect of Helen's looks on all who come near her, so that it is difficult to form any opinion or any estimate of how anyone is likely to behave after that apparently upsetting experience. All who see her seem to become straightway moon-stricken, lunatics of love.

"Makes it difficulty especially in a case like this where every clue and indication seems psychological, and there is nothing solid and material—no 'dabs,' no shreds of cloth, no direct evidence, nothing on which a case must rest for convincing evidence.

"By the way, Gregson has told me that Commander Seers is still in hospital—malgre lui (excuse the French). It seems to have been a case of the irresistible force (the Commander) meeting the immovable object (the Matron). The immovable object won. But only by promising that if there's another gale—and the Air Ministry

is forecasting the break-up of the recent dead calm spell and lots of
gales due in a hurry—and if more of these drifting mines appear off
the harbour, then Seers is to be allowed out. I suppose the irresistible
force would acquire priority then."

(Note: The letter concludes with remarks of no public interest.)

CHAPTER XXV

FRESH INFORMATION

WHEN HE AWOKE next morning, Bobby decided that the first thing
to do was to pay a visit to Kindles. But as he was starting to get out
his car, immediately after breakfast, Haile came up. Bobby nodded a
greeting. Haile mumbled some sort of response and stood watching
with an uneasy and a troubled air, half sullen, half doubtful, wholly
apprehensive. Bobby said something about the weather. It had been
a rough and stormy night, but now the wind was beginning to drop.
Haile took no notice of the remark, and Bobby went to get a spare can
of petrol. When he came back Haile said gloomily:

"You were nosing round the Toad-in-Hole Nursing Home
yesterday."

"So I was," agreed Bobby. "Have to do a lot of that sort of thing on
this sort of job. As ex-intelligence men ought to know."

"Asking questions," said Haile, still more gloomily.

"Best way," explained Bobby, "to get answers. By the way,
they told me you and Miss Lambert are getting married soon.
Congratulations."

"Emmy's a good sort," Haile said, a little defiantly, a little as if
challenging Bobby to deny it.

"Emmy?—oh, Miss Lambert. I'm sure she is," agreed Bobby
warmly. "Much too good for you probably. Normal. They generally
are."

"They know nothing up there," Haile said.

"That's what I have to be sure of," Bobby said. "That's why I went
there—to make sure."

"I take it you did?"

"No," said Bobby gravely. He turned away from the car, over
which he had been fussing, and faced Haile. "I'm not too clear in my
mind about the Toad-in-Hole Nursing Home—or about you." Haile
seemed to consider this, looking gloomier than ever. Bobby felt sure

something was coming. He got into the driving seat and made ready to drive away. Haile watched. Then he said: "There's something I could tell you if you'll promise to leave Emmy alone."

"No promises," Bobby snapped. "God knows I wish you no harm— to you or to her or to the child Mrs. Mack told me was on the way. But I may have to hurt you both pretty badly. And she is in no condition to stand any more worry than she has to. She wouldn't like to hear you had been arrested even on suspicion. If you've anything useful to tell me, your best plan is to tell it. But no conditions, no promises."

"You make it hard," Haile said.

"It's a hard world," Bobby answered. "God made it so. I don't know if He made me harder than other people. But I do know nothing's going to stop me doing what I'm paid to do. There's no room for sentiment in hunting down a murderer." He sat silent then, for he was remembering how once his wife had said to him that she thought she had married a hard man, and he knew in a sense that it was true and he wished it wasn't. At the time the words had stung. He had almost forgotten Haile. He was about to start the car in earnest when Haile said abruptly and as if making up his mind at last:

"Ever hear of anyone called Thibaut?"

"Thibaut?" repeated Bobby. "Thibaut?" The name seemed French and Haile had given it a faintly French accent. Bobby's mind flew back to the tale of the mysterious visitor from the Continent who had been seen talking to Miss Lambert. "Oh," he said, "you mean the chap who turned up here before the murder and then vanished. Is Thibaut his real name? We're trying to trace him. Can you help?"

Haile looked decidedly disconcerted. He had expected he would be giving Bobby entirely fresh information, opening up an entirely new line of inquiry, and so establish a claim to gratitude and even to some degree of co-operation in the future. Instead, here was Bobby showing no surprise, but talking as if this were no new development, but only something already being worked upon. In a disappointed tone, Haile said:

"Oh, you know about him?"

"Not as much as I would like to," Bobby said. "How did you come to hear of him?"

"I'm not telling that," Haile answered defiantly.

"I hope that won't mean," Bobby said, "our being obliged to put you in the witness box—or even Miss Lambert. Because, you know, it's a fairly good guess she told you about the stranger who spoke to her in French and she wondered who he was and what he wanted, and that you've worked on that. Another good guess might be that you've heard something from your present boss, Mr. Jack Cade Junior. Because I shouldn't be surprised if he hasn't a good many pals among the Communists in the French Resistance Movement. They could find things out for him."

"You're too damn good at guessing," Haile said sulkily.

"Easy to guess when you know a good deal already," Bobby told him.

"How much do you know?" Haile demanded.

"And I'm not telling that," Bobby retorted. "Anyhow, nothing like as much as I would like. Is Thibaut this bloke's real name?"

"I don't expect so."

"Do you know it?"

"No."

But this Bobby did not believe. He had his share of that sort of instinct by which experienced barristers, judges, police officials, claim to be able to recognize a lie when they hear one.

"A pity," he remarked. "If we knew his real name we could trace him through his visa. No good if the passport is in another name."

"No good either if he got here on the Q.T.," Haile observed. This was another hint and one that Bobby had been on the lookout for, since he had expected that if Haile knew, as was probable, that a landing had been made surreptitiously, then his tendency to show off—a weak point in all of us, and very specially weak in Haile—would make him display his knowledge.

"You mean," Bobby said thoughtfully, "that Thibaut, or whatever his name is, was smuggled across in the *Seagull* for a quiet chat with Lord Adour," and now Haile had a very disconcerted air indeed.

"Oh, well," he muttered and then again: "Oh, well." Finally, he said sulkily: "No good my telling you what you know already."

"Not a bit," agreed Bobby, "but hadn't you better tell me exactly what you do know? Supplementary information is often very useful indeed. For instance, you might tell me why you made up your mind now to tell me as much as you have. Pretty plain it wasn't just simply a pure desire to help justice—or me. And I don't think it was all because of my visit to the nursing home, though very likely that helped. Well, what was it?"

"I want to be quit of the whole thing," Haile admitted. "I've a good chance of a job in Liverpool. I want some cash to go on with. I don't want to start with Emmy on my uppers."

"More fool you," Bobby said calmly. "Haven't you sense enough to see that all the blessed girl wants is to pig in along with you, good luck, bad luck, or no luck at all? Women are like that. A queer lot. No common sense. You must have known you wouldn't get much cash from us. We don't go round handing out pound notes, making ourselves targets for every liar in the land."

"I'm so hard up even a fiver would help," Haile admitted. "I thought you might run to that."

"Never get through expenses," Bobby declared pessimistically. "I might run to it myself. As a loan, on a strict promise to repay. But more for Miss Lambert's sake than yours. She's got a tough time ahead if she is going to hitch on to a chap like you."

"That's right," Halle grumbled. "Rub it in. All very well for you to talk. You're O.K."

"You've got a girl of your own and you say you've a chance of a job," Bobby retorted. "What else do you want? All you need now is to run straight for a change. Up to you. Let's get back to business. I take it what you mean is you've tried to squeeze Lord Adour and it didn't come off."

"He wouldn't even see me," Haile admitted. "Has he told you?"

"Goodness no. But I can put two and two together when it's not too difficult. Plain you wanted money and thought you knew something worth money. Plain you would think you had a better chance of getting more out of Lord Adour than out of police. Plainer still that if he is innocent he would turn you down and that then you would try us as the only chance left."

"He isn't innocent," Haile said. "He's your man all right. But it wasn't because of Helen. He and Itter were doing a bit of black market smuggling or whatever you like to call it. Plenty to be made playing round with currency, or with gold if you can get it. Then they quarrelled."

"How do you know all this?"

"Old Sammy Robinson—Jack Cade Junior, as he calls himself — Itter and Mauley's uncle, has been hearing things from his pals in the French Resistance Movement. Just as you said. He says they've told him a lot more than I have and he's shut down on the cash. A dirty trick. Says he'll only pay on results now, blast him."

"It doesn't seem too likely," Bobby remarked, "that a man in Lord Adour's position would join in that sort of smuggling. I should want a lot of proof before I accepted that," but all the same he was remembering very clearly the chart he had found in the library at Kindles with on it marked a track leading straight to a lonely spot on the French coast.

"It didn't begin like that with him," Haile explained. "At least that's what Sammy says. If it had only been that, his Resistance Movement pals wouldn't have known about it—or cared. The smuggling began when Itter Bain found his firm was being hit pretty badly by the peace and might have to close down. He was willing to take big risks to prevent that, because there he was his own boss and could spend all the time he wanted playing round with his own inventions. When he got to know there was easy money to be made in the gold and currency racket he thought it was a chance to get the necessary."

"I suppose that is where the £9,000 came from that Prescott Bain produced so suddenly the other day?" Bobby commented.

"That's right. Trust Prescott for nosing out any cash going. He and Mauley may have suspected what was going on, but I don't think they knew. Itter must have had the cash tucked away somewhere and Prescott had a look and found it."

"It seems to fit in," Bobby agreed, "but there'll have to be a lot more to make me believe Lord Adour was taking a hand in that sort of thing. His interests are too big for it to be likely he would mix up in cross-Channel smuggling."

"I don't know about that," said Haile doubtfully. "Don't see why he would be likely to turn up his nose at an extra thousand or two. But, according to Sammy, it didn't begin like that with him. What he wanted, and wanted pretty badly, was to get in touch with his old business pals and see what he could save from the wreckage—and if he could get hold of any of the coin they had pocketed during the Occupation. Only they were mostly in quod, the French authorities knowing all about the big profits they had made, working for the

Germans. So Lord Adour decided to stay at home, in case when he got to France they might start asking him nasty questions about pre-war deals. Adour was a hot Munich supporter, you know, one of the 'there won't be any war' lot. A dead cert, he was doing deals with the Germans right up to the last moment—or beyond. But he was still desperately keen on getting in touch with his old pals. That's where Itter came in. Mutual assistance idea. Lord Adour had a launch, the *Seagull*. Itter wanted one he could slip across to France in on a calm night and not too many questions asked at the harbour here, where they all knew him. A bottle or two of brandy and a few pound notes go a long way these days. And Adour wanted one of his pals brought across on the Q.T., so he could know how things stood with his interests over there. That's where the Resistance people came in. They wouldn't have troubled their heads about the smuggling, but they're hot stuff when it comes to collaborators and ex-collaborators and their agents, like Thibaut. The sale of the launch to Itter was most likely 'phony.' Just Lord Adour covering up his tracks or trying to. The real consideration was Itter's undertaking to bring back a representative of Adour's French interests to tell him how things stood and was there any way of saving anything from the wreck. So Itter brought Thibaut back and put him ashore and then Thibaut missed his way trying to find Kindles in the dark. That's when Emmy saw him. She couldn't make out what he wanted, except that it was something about Kindles, and then a cop came along and Thibaut cleared off in a hurry for fear of being asked questions. He must have managed to find his way to Kindles in the end. Perhaps he waited till it was light."

"Yes, but," Bobby objected, "this was a day or two before Itter's murder. I'm not interested in this smuggling business, especially as it will have stopped now. What I want is evidence proving who murdered Itter Bain, and I don't see where Thibaut comes in."

"He had to get back, hadn't he?" Haile retorted. "It seems he went on to London. Lord Adour met him there. He has a flat in Town. He could put Thibaut up there and no questions asked. Then they came back here, separately, no doubt, for Itter to take Thibaut across again. That's when the quarrel occurred. My own idea is that Itter tried a spot of blackmail. He knew big money was involved and he wanted a bigger share. What is certain is that there were the three of them present and one got shot. Itter. That leaves two—Lord Adour and Thibaut. Pretty clear which of the two."

"Why?"

"Who had the gun?"

"Hardly conclusive."

"Thibaut had nothing much to fear—expulsion from this country, maybe a fine, and the French had nothing on him. Slipped over to do a business talk was all he needed to say. And Itter's death cut off his best chance of getting back to France. Sammy's information is he complains now he was robbed by swindling English fishermen of every penny he had with him before they would put him over. But Lord Adour had a lot at stake. Itter's death, apart from any quarrel, saved him from all risk of being compromised. If he thought he was being blackmailed, he may have thought there was no other way of making himself safe. Or it may have been nothing more than a quarrel, a fit of anger. I don't know. Anyhow, it's clear enough that's what happened. Nothing to do with Helen. You can leave her out. That's not because I'm in love with her. I'm not. She scares me. She always has. Not like Emmy. You know where you are with Emmy," he added comfortably.

"You were on the spot, though," Bobby remarked, "that night the attack on her was made. Why were you, if you aren't interested in her?"

"I didn't say that," Haile retorted. "She's worth looking at. I knew she went walking alone in the moonlight at times. I think in a way her own knowledge of her own beauty has made her a bit abnormal. But I saw the two of them together and I saw the girl wasn't Helen, so I cleared off. Besides, I knew you were snooping round. I saw Wayling flash a torch at you. He was there, too."

"But you left his cap?" Bobby said.

"I picked it up after he had been thrown out of the 'Good Haul,'" Haile explained. "I thought I would wear it as a sort of disguise. Everyone knows I never wear a hat, and if I were seen I thought I wouldn't be spotted so easily. I didn't want it to get round to Emmy that I had been trying for a sort of last look at Helen. All the same, in a sort of way, it's because of Helen I made up my mind about Emmy. Somehow when you look at Helen you sort of feel you don't want to do the dirty any more than you have to—anyhow, not on another girl. You can laugh if you like," he added defiantly.

"Why should I?" Bobby asked. "Beauty can be a strong wine, to make you mad or make you—different. You've nothing more to tell me?"

"No," Haile answered. He said: "I expect I'm a fool to have told you so much, but I want to get out of here with Emmy as soon as I can. Besides, you seemed to know it all, or guess it all. I don't know which."

"Neither," Bobby told him. "Not so hard when you know bits and pieces to put other bits and pieces together to make a whole. Oh, half a minute, have you any idea what's become of the *Seagull*? It has vanished from its moorings. Mauley Bain says it's been stolen."

Haile laughed, and his laughter had just a touch of malice in it.

"I'm afraid Mauley got ahead of you there," he said. "I think he knows, but he doesn't want any questions asked about that £9,000 or to have his dead brother's name brought into it. I told you before to keep an eye on him. He may try to square accounts on his own."

"Yes. I remember," Bobby said slowly. "I remember very well. Do you think he has managed to get rid of the launch?"

"I expect he took it out to sea, sank it, and swam back to shore, Haile answered. "He's in the number one plus class at swimming, you know. Anyhow, that's the talk. They all have a good idea about the smuggling that was going on. There's a story that Mauley was afraid there might be traces in the launch of earth or sand from the last load brought over that might have been identified with French coast soil."

"What's a poor detective to do," Bobby sighed, "when everyone everywhere knows all the tricks of the trade?" but when he said this, or perhaps it was because of the tone in which he said it, Haile gave him a quick and doubtful look before he turned and went his way—in his pocket Bobby's five one-pound notes and in Bobby's mind some degree of doubt whether he would ever see that £5 again.

CHAPTER XXVI

AVOIDANCE

BOBBY DROVE SLOWLY on his way to Kindles, and once at least drew up by the wayside to sit there for a time in deep thought. The case put forward by Haile was plausible, so plausible indeed that it provided justification for a charge. Details would have to be checked first, of course, and there was the possibility that it was the missing Thibaut who had in fact fired the fatal shot. But, even if it had been like that, Lord Adour, if not guilty of murder, was guilty of complicity— "accessory after the act," in the legal phrase. Bobby found himself thinking that an arrest, even on the minor charge, or preferably the threat of one, might be useful in inducing Lord Adour and Avon, to give him his full title, to be a little more frank.

A difficult decision, Bobby told himself, more especially as he knew well that there were other and equally probable—or possible— explanations that had to be considered. His mind went back to that long list he had given Olive at home in his last letter. But he also felt, and very strongly, that the time had come to take some step, even at the risk of making a blunder, in order to clear the air and so bring into the light of day many things as yet obscure. There is often a moment in difficult and complicated situations when a sudden act, an abrupt decision, may prove a catalysis, as chemists call it, and so change the appearance of facts and values as to show all things in a newer and a truer aspect. All the same, he was also very well aware that to arrest a man as prominent in social, political, business worlds as Lord Adour and Avon was a step that would require very complete, very full justification.

"If it turns out a bad bloomer," he told himself grimly, "it may be the end of me."

He drove on then, his mind not yet made up, determined only to act as seemed best from moment to moment. Arrived at Kindles, he told Jane, the first of the family to appear, that he wanted to see both her uncle and her cousin. Jane said she would let them both know, and he could not help noticing how uneasily she looked at him over her shoulder as she disappeared, leaving him sitting in the small lounge hall. Soon she returned to tell him Lord Adour would be with him in a moment or two, but that Helen had retired to her bedroom, saying that one of her headaches was coming on and she didn't feel up to talking to anyone that morning. This last message Bobby did not receive with any complacence.

"It looks to me," he said sternly, "as if Miss Adour was avoiding me on purpose. Will you please tell her that it is necessary I should see her to-day?"

"I could tell her, of course," Jane agreed with a small, half-hidden smile, "though I expect I should have to shout through the keyhole or push a note under the door. But it won't make any difference. She really is prostrate when her headaches do come on."

Bobby thought he detected in the phrasing of this last sentence a touch of doubt as to whether this time any headache had, in fact, come on. He said with emphasis:

"I shall have to ask for a doctor's certificate."

But now Jane's half-smile became broader, developed, indeed, into something like a chuckle.

"Helen could get any doctor to give her any certificate she wanted," Jane told him. "They are all men doctors near here," she added casually.

"Oh, well, if it's like that," demanded Bobby with resentment, "why doesn't she try the same game with me—try to get me to say anything she wants?"

Jane surveyed him dispassionately.

"I expect she could," she pronounced finally.

"Well, then," said Bobby.

"But I don't think she's quite sure," Jane continued, a little as if she were thinking out a problem that had often baffled her. "She never is. When people do what she wants, she thinks it's because it's the natural and proper thing to do—like passing the mustard at dinner. When they stare and stutter and go red and pale by turns, she only thinks how silly they are. She knows very well how lovely she is and she knows in a way that it makes her different from other people. In a way, she's a girl like anyone else and in a way she isn't—as hard for the rest of us to understand as I suppose it is for men and women to understand each other. I told her once she made men all upside down inside when they saw her and she thought about it a long time and then she said: 'Well, why?' She said once she had seen the sun rise over the Alps and again the sun set from St. Malo, and it was more lovely than a dream, but it didn't make anyone upside down inside, and was it like the way you felt when you eat too many cream buns?"

"Well, she's got to see me," Bobby repeated. "Tell her that—through the keyhole if you have to, but tell her. Tell her, if she persists, there are ways and means. I don't want to take drastic steps, but I may have to."

"What steps?" Jane asked.

Bobby waved the question aside. He wasn't quite sure how to answer it, for one thing. He said severely:

"Please make it plain to her I am an officer of the Law, and the Law must be obeyed."

"The Law?" Jane murmured. "Rex *v*. Beauty, the lawyers would put it, wouldn't they? I wonder?"

Bobby surveyed Jane with disfavour. Her tone seemed to show less respect for that august conception, the Law, than he felt was its proper and rightful due. He said, still in his most severe, official tone:

"Miss Adour's looks have nothing to do with it."

"Of course they have," retorted Jane. "What's the good of saying silly things like that? Helen's looks make all the difference. You feel as if they belong to everyone and everyone ought to protect them. Women are said to be cats to each other, but we all know Helen's beauty belongs to all of us, too, and we would all do anything—not for her, but for it. I know I would."

There had been a touch of almost mystical devotion in her voice as she said this. It made Bobby vaguely uneasy, disturbed him. Before he could make any comment, however, while they both stood silent, as Jane began to look slightly embarrassed as if only now were she beginning to realize what she had said, Lord Adour came bustling into the room. He seemed nervous, uneasy, but with his entrance the overstrained atmosphere became more commonplace, and when he spoke it was amiably enough.

"Sorry to keep you waiting," he said. "Come along to the study, will you? I was half expecting you. Nearly rang you up. Very disturbing business, all this." He ushered Bobby into the study, thrust forward a chair, seated himself, and said: "About this keeping your men hanging about here all night. I don't like it. It makes people talk. Gossip enough already. I don't like it. I don't want it. Seers is in hospital or I'm sure he would agree. I want it stopped."

"Well, I was going to ask you again," Bobby said, "to allow me to post a man inside the house."

Lord Adour fairly bounced in his chair.

"Most certainly not," he began, and Bobby interrupted him.

"I consider it advisable," Bobby said earnestly. "I think there is real danger, a real necessity for protection."

"Why? In what way?"

"I can't give you any specific details," Bobby said. "It is my general impression from my study of the case—"

Now it was Lord Adour's turn to interrupt.

"No," he said. "Nonsense. I know what's in your mind. I quite understand. You've been listening to some of this absurd gossip that's going on. I've consulted my solicitor and he is considering whether it is possible to take action for slander. He tells me you are protected by privilege. Others are not. We shall see. In the meantime, I have asked him to protest both to Commander Seers, as head of the police in this district, and direct to the Home Secretary. I will not have it. I have no intention of either committing suicide or of running away, and, if I had, your childish precautions wouldn't stop me."

"But I assure you—" began Bobby, only once more to be interrupted by the indignant torrent of Lord Adour's eloquence.

"I tell you I won't have it," he repeated, thumping emphatically on the table at which he was sitting. "Everyone for miles round thinks it means I am practically under arrest. Have I got to remind you that this is private property and your men are trespassers? I have every right to order them off the premises and in the future I shall do so."

"I shall greatly regret it if you do," Bobby said. "Of course, you will be within your rights if you see fit to exercise them. May I ask you to believe me when I assure you most earnestly that my only thought has been to give you protection? If any harm comes to you or any of your family—"

"I prefer to take my own precautions," said Lord Adour stiffly and disbelievingly. "I am quite capable of protecting both myself and my family against any of these imaginary dangers of yours."

"Very well," Bobby said. For a moment he contemplated using a threat he had found efficacious in other such cases—that of placing police patrols on the roads surrounding Kindles. But Kindles and its grounds occupied a space that would require a very large force to watch it with any degree of efficiency, and such a force he could neither command himself nor reasonably ask Commander Seers to supply. It would probably have needed the whole, or nearly the whole, of the local police. Also Lord Adour's attitude and his complaint to the Home Office did seem to Bobby to relieve him of responsibility. He could only hope that the danger he vaguely feared, though he could give no particulars to justify those fears, would not materialize. "Very good," he said. "I must of course respect your wishes. I shall continue, however, to ask Commander Seers to see there is always a constable on duty near at hand, should he be needed."

"Most unnecessary," declared Lord Adour, only half pacified. "I shall make a point of telling Seers so," and he spoke with such emphasis that Bobby found himself wondering, and not for the first time, whether there was anything at Kindles, any secret comings and goings, for instance, that Lord Adour preferred should not come under the notice of the authorities. Lord Adour went on: "There's another matter I wished to mention. A man named Haile called here yesterday. I didn't see him. Do you know anything about it—or him?"

"He came to see me this morning," Bobby said. "He told me he had tried to see you. As you refused, he came to me instead."

"What for?"

"Well, I'm afraid," Bobby answered, "I must regard that at the present stage of the inquiry as being confidential. I hope you won't mind my saying that so far I have not received much cooperation."

Lord Adour received this remark with a fresh and even more formidable scowl.

"The fellow seems to have been asking a lot of questions about me," he said. "About us. Can't you stop him?"

"I'm afraid not," Bobby said, and added, with a touch of malice: "If people know their rights and insist on the strict letter, we are very badly handicapped. Of course, if you can prove slander, you can always sue for damages."

"He is a tool," declared Lord Adour. "He is being used to carry out a political intrigue."

"That's entirely outside my province," Bobby answered quickly. "I've nothing to do with politics. I'm here to find out who is guilty of the murder of Itter Bain. I'm hoping to be able to make an arrest soon." He paused, but Lord Adour only looked at him blankly, and seemed quite unmoved, uninterested—too much so, in fact, Bobby thought. He went on: "I've got a lot of information together one way

and another. Some of it very disturbing, some of it even alarming."
He paused again, but Lord Adour still showed no sign of interest.
"I have," he continued, "been trying to get an opportunity to ask
Miss Adour a few questions on points on which I thought she might
know something, matters of no very great importance perhaps, but
that might help. I have not been able to see her. I have come to the
conclusion that she is deliberately avoiding me. Why?"

"Helen doesn't know anything that could possibly help you," Lord
Adour asserted with emphasis. "Absurd to suppose so. She is most
highly strung, very nervous. She has learnt to dread the intrusion of
strangers who merely want an excuse to stare. Most annoying and
embarrassing. We have even been subject to the insolence of people
actually coming in person and trying to insist on persuading her to
become what is, I believe, called a 'film star' or some such expression.
Most distasteful. I have had to show such people the door. My
daughter is not prepared to make herself a common show."

"If I may say so," Bobby said, "that is a position everyone must
respect. But I think it is hardly relevant. I need not remind you that
murder is a serious matter and that this is a murder investigation. No
private feelings can be allowed to interfere with it."

"If," Lord Adour said grudgingly, "there is anything it is really
necessary for you to ask Miss Adour, tell me what it is and I will let
you know what she says."

"I am afraid that would hardly do," Bobby explained. "I do wish I
could have a little more co-operation." He paused, but this produced
no response. He continued: "Miss Adour was on the spot at or about
the time of the murder. I understand Mr. Winstanley of the River
Farm was with her. I have questioned him and he says he heard no
shot, saw no gun, nothing in any way unusual. I must be sure that is
equally true of Miss Adour. It is possible she may be able to remember
some detail that it might be very useful for me to know. Did she know
about the kingfisher you saw? Did you tell her about it?"

"No, no," Lord Adour said quickly. "That was Jane."

CHAPTER XVII

LORD ADOUR'S STORY

BOBBY, THOUGH HE HOPED he did not show it, was considerably
startled and disturbed by this sudden introduction of Jane's name.

He remembered very clearly the explicit statement in Commander Seers's report that no one other than Martin Winstanley and Helen on their way back together to Kindles and Lord Adour himself, was known to have been in Coldstone Spinney on the afternoon of the murder. But now it seemed that Jane, too, had been in the vicinity. Either Seers had not probed deeply enough or the fact of Jane's presence had been deliberately concealed from him, or else, as was certainly quite possible, Seers had not thought it worth mentioning. With his background of social prejudice, it might well have seemed to him so inconceivable that a young lady of impeccable birth and education could be in any way concerned in crime that he had simply never considered her at all in that connection. Bobby was not so sure. There were strong depths of character in Jane, he was well assured, and he remembered with some unease the almost mystical fervour with which Jane had spoken of Helen's beauty, as in some way a general possession of all womanhood, a kind of ideal and type it was equally a general duty to defend and to protect.

"Is Miss Jane in any way friendly with Mr. Prescott Bain?" he asked abruptly, and awaited the reply with anxiety; for if she were, or ever had been, then he supposed the whole foundation on which he was trying to build up his case might be destroyed.

When the answer came—after a momentary pause and stare of blank astonishment—it came as a relief.

"Why, no, not that I know of," Lord Adour said. "She has only met him very occasionally. Why? Really a most extraordinary question."

"I'm sorry," Bobby said. "I assure you I never ask questions without reasons, though they may sometimes be very bad reasons."

"Well, you must ask Miss Felgate herself if you want details of all her friends and acquaintances," Lord Adour told him stiffly. "If there is nothing else—"

"Oh, I'm afraid quite a lot," Bobby interposed. "Can you tell me exactly what happened when you met her?"

"Happened? Nothing happened. Why should it?" retorted Lord Adour. "How do you mean? I was hurrying back for my camera. Jane was somewhere in the garden. I called to her that the kingfisher was back and I was going to try to get a snap. That's all."

"Do you know if Miss Jane went into the spinney to see if she could see for herself?"

"I've no idea. You must ask her. When I found the bird had gone, I went on to the river to see if it was there. It wasn't, and so far as I know it hasn't been seen since."

"Yes, I must ask her. I expect she'll remember," Bobby said and spoke lightly; though inwardly he was feeling more and more disturbed by this unexpected new development, and, equally, more and more convinced that Lord Adour knew more than he had told. But evidently, whatever Lord Adour knew, he was in no mood to talk. Bobby decided it would be better to change the subject, though it would certainly be necessary to return to it later. He said: "There's something else I would like to mention while I'm here. My information is that the *Seagull* launch you sold to Itter Bain has disappeared. There is no will apparently, and Mauley Bain, as next of kin took possession of the launch. I believe he has applied for letters of administration. I don't know whether they have been issued yet. He has now reported that the launch is missing."

"I heard about that," Lord Adour said. "If the thieves managed to get it across to the Continent, it would fetch a good price."

"Would that be difficult?"

"Oh, no. She's a good sea boat. The weather has been rough lately, of course. But she may quite well be somewhere along the coast, in some inlet or creek or another, waiting for a spell of good weather. I wouldn't have cared to take her out myself in these recent winds. It could be done, no doubt, but a big risk. Thieves in fear of arrest might try."

"Yes, I see. Thank you," Bobby said. "I am afraid I must put this to you. Was the sale of the yacht to Itter Bain a genuine sale?"

Lord Adour looked very angry, very disturbed, and also very uncomfortable.

"I'm not accustomed," he protested, "to being asked questions of that nature."

"I'm quite sure you aren't," Bobby answered gently, "but then, you see, this is an investigation into a murder. Outside ordinary considerations. I'm sure you understand. I suppose I ought to say that you can refuse to answer questions or you can require the presence of your solicitor. But, of course, you know that already."

Lord Adour was looking now not so much angry and disturbed as just simply frightened.

"I do refuse to answer questions that seem to me entirely unnecessary and unjustified," he declared, but not very strongly.

"Sorry," Bobby said. "It does make everything so appallingly official." Somewhat ostentatiously, he got out a fat new notebook and his fountain pen. "I'll just jot down the questions you don't care to answer," he explained. "I expect I shall have to ask you to make a statement."

"I've done so," Lord Adour told him. "To Commander Seers. He said nothing more would be necessary. Ask him to show it you."

"I should have said a supplementary statement," Bobby explained. "I have seen the one you made to Commander Seers. I take it you prefer not to say more at the moment?"

Lord Adour scowled again, pulled open a drawer of his writing table, took out a piece of paper, and threw it across to Bobby.

"There you are," he said. "That's the cheque Itter Bain gave me. He asked me not to present it till he had paid in enough to clear it. No good now, of course, except as evidence of debt. For that matter, I'm not sure the sale itself is good now. Strictly speaking, I doubt if it had been completed. It was all more or less a friendly, informal arrangement. There was a memorandum of agreement, but that was all. I think Itter's death destroys that, too. Terms not carried out, never put into execution. I'm not sure. Not that that's of much importance if the *Seagull* has been stolen. If it has been taken across to the Continent, there's not much chance it will ever be found."

"We'll do our best," Bobby promised. "You never know your luck. There is a suggestion it may have been taken out to sea and sunk."

"Not very likely," Lord Adour said. "At current prices, she is probably worth much more than I asked. Two thousand. One doesn't sink two thousand pounds," and he had the air of being slightly shocked by the suggestion.

"Not without good reason," Bobby agreed. "I must put another point to you—under reserve, of course, of your full right to refuse to answer for any reason whatever or for no reason at all. My information is that a man named Thibaut, believed to be of French nationality, was seen in this neighbourhood, apparently on his way to this house. He is understood to have inquired his way here. We are trying to get in touch with him, but have not been able to do so as yet, though we hope to shortly. Do you care to make any comment?"

That this invitation Bobby let fall quite casually had a most disturbing effect on Lord Adour was very apparent. His jaw dropped, he shrank back in his chair as if he had received some heavy blow. Nor at first did he make any attempt to answer. Bobby got up and went across to that shelf on which he had previously noticed such works of navigation and seamanship as the *Admiralty Manual*. He picked up the chart case in which, on his earlier visit, he had found that chart whereon had been traced a course from Toad-in-Hole Harbour to a spot on the French coast where was shown no indication of any village, of any human habitation indeed.

"I think I should like to keep this," Bobby said. "I will write out a receipt."

Lord Adour, still silent, still pale, watched while this was done, Bobby passed the receipt across. Lord Adour took no notice. He said gloomily:

"How do you know all this?"

"I've been getting to know a good deal in one way or another," Bobby explained. "Police work is like that. Adding little bits and pieces together till at last you begin to see a coherent pattern taking shape. 'Information received' is what we say. It would help, of course, if you would care to give me your side of it. Might prevent me drawing false conclusions."

Lord Adour was still silent. Easy to tell that he was doubtful, confused, hesitant. Bobby waited patiently. He could see a decision was coming, one way or another. At last Lord Adour spoke:

"You seem to know so much," he began, "I suppose I had better explain, though I can't say anything to help about the murder. I have big commitments in France. I was extremely anxious to get news of how my business affairs stand there. Most unfortunately, some of my pre-war associates seem to have compromised themselves during the German occupation."

"Collaborators?" Bobby asked.

"That is what is being said, apparently," Lord Adour admitted. "If any of the concerns in which I am interested worked for Germany, I regret it, but I can't feel responsible. I should certainly have done what I could to prevent it, had I known. Of course, that was impossible. But it was important, vital, for me to know how matters stood."

"I can see that," Bobby said, "but was there still difficulty once the war was over and communication opened again?"

"All I could learn," Lord Adour answered, speaking with some care, "was that investigation was proceeding. A suggestion was made that I should go to Paris. The idea seemed to be that I should appear as a witness before the tribunal set up. I did not choose to do so. I had no wish to submit my private affairs to the questioning of a prejudiced court, only too anxious, I felt sure, to find a scapegoat—above all, a foreign scapegoat. I might easily have found myself accused also of being a collaborator. I might have been held responsible for transactions of which I knew nothing. My record is entirely clear. There is nothing I have any reason to hide. I certainly shared the confidence felt by many highly responsible, highly placed persons, persons in the confidence of the Government, that there would be no war, that war was incredible. Utterly incredible. I can hardly believe even now in such madness. But I do see that some things had happened that could be twisted to my disadvantage. On the outbreak of the war—I was in Paris at the time—I was induced to take part in a meeting in Switzerland. I have learned since that some of my French colleagues went further than I knew at the time or could have approved. It seems my name was used without my knowledge. Naturally, I informed the Foreign Office on my return and no objection was raised. It was realized in the highest quarters that the German offers made could be considered, but unfortunately there seemed no really satisfactory official guarantees. Assurances, but no undertaking that action would follow. I had reason to believe the matter might be raised in the French courts if I went to Paris now, and there might have been highly undesirable political repercussions. I happen to know that was the view taken in the Foreign Office."

"That is all very clear and understandable," Bobby agreed, "but at the moment I don't quite see the connection."

But this remark was not altogether true, for already he was beginning to guess where all this careful explanation and defence was likely to lead. There was a brief pause before Lord Adour, still speaking with slow caution, went on with his story. He said: "The very urgent need still remained for me to know exactly how things stood. Itter Bain knew the position. That came about when he suggested my advancing money to his firm to carry them over the very difficult peace period. I explained my own difficulties and he then suggested he might be able to put me in touch privately with some of my former associates. Irregular, perhaps, but not, I think, in any way criminal or disloyal. The war was over."

"That's all quite outside my province," Bobby said. "Did you know Itter was engaged in smuggling or black market activities of some kind or another?"

"I never had the least suspicion," Lord Adour declared, so earnestly that Bobby was inclined to believe him, difficult though it seemed.

"Surely," he said, "you must have realized that Itter had to have some connections of some sort over there?"

"Of course, of course. What he told me was that his uncle, a man who writes most objectionable, subversive propaganda under the nom-de-plume of Jack Cade, Junior, was in touch with members of the French Resistance who would be able to help." A doubtful explanation, Bobby thought—one accepted only because acceptance was desired. Quite obviously, members of the Resistance were not exactly persons to whom one would apply for an introduction to suspected collaborators. As an excuse, it might serve perhaps, though lamely. He made no comment, though that might be necessary later. Lord Adour continued: "Bain suggested that if I let him use the *Seagull* he would go across in it and try to get me the information I needed. I hesitated at first. I felt I did not care to run the risk of being further implicated. He suggested that my name could be kept out if he became the owner of the *Seagull*. I didn't like the idea, but in the end I agreed. It was becoming almost a matter of averting ruin. I may have been too anxious, too worried to make an entirely wise decision."

"It is only the actual facts of what really took place that is any business of mine," Bobby said gently. "Itter Bain was running a big risk, both of a French prison and of serious trouble with our own authorities. For what consideration?"

Lord Adour hesitated again. He looked even more uncomfortable than before, though now his former pallor was giving place to something like a blush. Embarrassed and hesitating, he said at last:

"Well, the fact is ... I had to think of Helen's future ... unless I could save something from the wreck of my French interests ... Helen is hardly fitted for business ... it would be very difficult for her without a secure background ... her looks, her temperament. It was chiefly of her I was thinking."

"Yes?" said Bobby when Lord Adour paused.

"I told Itter," Lord Adour said with a rush, "that if he helped me in this way I would raise no objection to his meeting Helen or to their marriage if he got her consent. I suppose what he expected was that I would do my best to persuade Helen to listen to him and that I would see he had opportunities to meet her." With an air both of defiance and defence, he said: "I was sure Helen would have nothing to do with him."

CHAPTER XXVIII
NEARING THE TRUTH

BOBBY RECEIVED this story in silence. It troubled him, for it seemed to bring back into prominence, as a compelling factor in the case, Helen's strange, disturbing beauty. But he could not as yet see clearly how it affected his main problem, the identification of the murderer. Clearly Itter Bain, secure of the father's encouragement, might have felt himself entitled to press his wooing with a greater urgency, an urgency that Helen, or Jane for her, might easily have resented or been frightened by— that is, if Jane had really entered the spinney and there met the waiting Itter, who could so easily have taken her for an emissary acting on Helen's behalf. It was even possible that the kingfisher had been merely an excuse seized upon to persuade Helen into the spinney where Itter would be waiting for a chance to press his suit. But had Helen gone there? Had Jane? Had either or both? If they had done so, what had happened? Dark possibilities seemed envisaged. Bobby could only hope they would recede into the limbo of discarded theories under the light of the further information he hoped for.

For some few moments this silence continued, Bobby deep in uncomfortable thought, Lord Adour still flushed and embarrassed. It was clear he felt he had played an undignified and unworthy part in thus making use of his daughter's name. No doubt the temptation had been strong, the inducement overpowering. Presently Bobby said:

"Did you mention this promise or arrangement to Miss Adour?"

"Certainly not," came the prompt and emphatic answer. "I made it perfectly plain that Helen would naturally decide entirely according to her own feelings and wishes. All I promised was that Itter Bain should have opportunities to come to the house—an invitation to dinner, perhaps. Something like that. Or a business talk and then a cup of tea. Nothing more. I made that plain," and these last words were delivered with even greater emphasis.

But Bobby wondered whether it had been equally plain to Itter. Itter might well have read into Lord Adour's acquiescence more than Lord Adour had intended. With eager wishes and hot passion to inflame his desires, Itter could easily have supposed that Lord Adour knew Helen had in some way shown herself inclined to regard his suit favourably. If she had entered the spinney, he might have gone to her with all the ardour and passionate eagerness of an accepted suitor; and she, bewildered and alarmed, might have let her fears master her so far as to snatch up her father's gun for protection. Or much the same thing might have occurred if Jane had been taken for Helen's messenger. It seemed to Bobby that Lord Adorn: had, however ignorantly or innocently, prepared meticulously all the elements of tragic misunderstanding.

He reminded himself that all this remained theoretical. But it had certainly become even more necessary that Helen should be questioned. Jane, too, would have to be interviewed once more. He said slowly:

"There are still one or two points I should like to be a little clearer about. About this man, Thibaut. I suppose you had known him previously?"

"I think I had met him once or twice. I knew his name. Vaguely. As a kind of confidential agent—a go-between useful in business deals. Preparing the ground beforehand. That sort of thing."

"Was he himself compromised as a collaborator?"

"I don't know. He denied it strongly. He did say once that it is easy for activities perfectly proper and legitimate at the time to be represented as criminal in the light of later events. Perfectly true, of course." Lord Adour paused, and Bobby knew he was thinking of deals he had himself had some part in—deals perhaps even less innocent than those carried through in the City of London when only a day or two before the outbreak of war copper, rubber, and other munition material had been dispatched to Nazi Germany. One felt so sure there would be no war, and even after war had broken out, was it not proudly announced by a responsible statesman that a new way of waging war without bloodshed had been found? The impregnable Maginot Line, the impeccable neutrality of the border states Hitler had pledged himself to respect, the British blockade! As a sensible, realistic people, the Germans were sure soon to realize the futility of war, and since that was so, why not continue business relations with associates who, even though temporary enemies, would be good friends again very soon?

Easy to see how plausible all this had seemed in the period of the "phony war," and how easily such beliefs could have led to deals that now would bear a treasonable air. Another theory was pushing itself into the foreground in Bobby's mind. Suppose this had been so, and Itter Bain knew it—from information supplied by his uncle perhaps or possibly through Thibaut—and suppose he had used his knowledge for some sort of blackmail, crude in monetary form, subtle in pressure on the father to secure the daughter's hand?

Bobby felt his mind was becoming less a thinking, observing, calculating machine than a mere hive of buzzing, conflicting, contradictory suppositions, all probable, all lacking any confirmation of the solid fact, proof, evidence, for which he found himself longing with almost passionate intensity. He said at last: "Was Thibaut able to tell you anything?"

"Nothing," Lord Adour answered gloomily. "He knew nothing. Or said he didn't. What he had come for was to get me to use what he called my influence to induce our Government to ask the French authorities to stop the investigation they've started. Strings can be pulled, I know," admitted Lord Adour still more gloomily, and Bobby suspected he had done his share of string-pulling in his time, "but not like that. Not to mention that I've no influence at all with any of the people now in power. I'm suspect rather. And nothing Thibaut could tell me, or so he insisted, beyond what I knew already—that all books and papers had been seized. Not that that affects me personally. There's nothing I ever signed they can take exception to."

"I suppose the arrangement was for Itter Bain to take Thibaut back across the Channel in the *Seagull*?"

"Yes, but there was some sort of unpleasantness. Apparently they quarrelled on the way here. I don't know why. I didn't ask. But it seems Bain lost his temper, put Thibaut ashore safely, but then told him to 'hop it' without telling him how to find his way here. 'Hop it' was a new expression to Thibaut and he thought it was meant for an insult. Unfortunate, for that is why he had to ask his way and was noticed."

"I see," said Bobby. "How did he manage to get back, then? Or is he still here?"

"No. There were people in London he wanted to see. He went on there. I let him use my flat. He had great hopes of persuading what he called 'powerful British interests' to help his friends. Quite impossible, of course. No one here could interfere even if they had wanted to. He was very disappointed and I believe in the end had to pay some fishermen heavily to smuggle him across again. He had had warning that he was going to be questioned and was likely to be expelled under arrest. So he got out while he could—in a hurry. He wanted to avoid questioning."

Like, Bobby could not help thinking, like Lord Adour himself, who also it seemed had been in no way eager to undergo questioning. Bobby asked a few more questions. The answers were clear, were supported by one or two letters and telegrams, and showed that Thibaut had been in London at the time of the murder. An alibi as well established beyond reasonable doubt on the strength of independent evidence, as, for example, that of Prescott Bain. So the theory of Thibaut's possible guilt had to be put aside. Some of Bobby's questions had allowed Lord Adour to guess that this had been in Bobby's mind, and Lord Adour made it clear that he thought it a most extravagant and far-fetched notion— he made it equally clear that he held the same opinion of the rest of the theories on which Bobby was working.

"To my mind," he declared, "there's no real doubt. Haile is the man. A common trick, to pose as the detective when you are really the criminal."

Bobby suggested meekly that it was hardly common. He did not think he himself had ever known such a case. Lord Adour smiled, implied that Bobby was comparatively young and inexperienced, remarked that he had often read of the trick. As for motive—Bobby having hinted he had found none—why, in Lord Adour's opinion, Haile had almost certainly been concerned in, or at least known something about, Itter Bain's cross-Channel activities. A quarrel over the division of profits was likely enough or even an attempt at blackmail. Anyhow, to Lord Adour's personal knowledge, Haile had been seen hanging about in the neighbourhood before the date of the tragedy, and what was that for? Bobby made no mention of Miss Lambert and merely remarked that all these considerations were being carefully studied. Lord Adour's expression showed very clearly what value he attached to that assurance. Bobby said:

"All you've told me makes it still more necessary I should have a chat with Miss Adour. I hope you'll agree it has become essential." Lord Adour made no comment. Probably he realized that that could no longer be avoided. Bobby continued: "I want to ask you once more to give us permission to post a man here. I consider it a necessary precaution."

"I prefer to take my own precautions," Lord Adour retorted with renewed defiance. "There's enough gossip and talk going on already without police hanging about to make everyone believe that we are all under arrest or being watched for fear we de-camp."

"Do you mind telling me what precautions you are taking?"

"Unnecessary," Lord Adour pronounced. "The question is closed."

"I regret it," Bobby said stiffly. "As soon as I get back, I shall make a formal written request to Commander Seers, asking him to take all possible steps to persuade you to change your mind."

"Quite useless," snapped Lord Adour. "Besides, I've told Seers and he fully agrees."

"I shall still wish to put my view on record," Bobby said quietly. "As far as possible I must free myself from all responsibility for anything that may happen. And now, if Miss Adour is still incapacitated by this unfortunate headache, would it be possible for me to have a little further talk with Miss Felgate?"

"Oh, come, really, no, decidedly no," Lord Adour exclaimed. "You've put her through one cross-examination already to-day. That's enough."

"Sorry," Bobby answered, "but it seems necessary to ask her to clear up one or two of these fresh points." Lord Adour still looked obstinate and did not move. Bobby went across to the fireplace and pressed the bell. "You will forgive me, I hope," he said.

"You take unpardonable liberties, sir," exclaimed Lord Adour, going very red in the face, sitting very upright.

"I am conducting an inquiry into a murder," Bobby answered. "I am beginning to feel I am drawing nearer the truth."

CHAPTER XXIX

BOBBY INSISTS

IT WAS JANE HERSELF who came, rather hurriedly, to answer the insistent clamour of the bell on which Bobby had continued to hold his finger longer than was perhaps necessary. The Kindles household was one of the more fortunate as regards domestic help. One elderly maid had stayed on from pre-war days, declaring herself too old to change over to factory life. There was also a woman from a neighbouring cottage who came in for an hour or two in the morning and would have been willing to stay longer had food been available to provide her with a meal. For the rest, Helen did most of the cooking—she was never so much the normal feminine, so little the earthly embodiment of an unearthly beauty, as when, tying an apron round her middle, she presided over her pots and pans. Jane's province was the management of rations and points and the giving of a helping hand where help was needed. Now, knowing the elderly maid was out and the daily woman gone home, she came, hurrying and uneasy, as soon as she heard the prolonged summons of the bell. Her uneasiness increased when she saw the heavy frown on her uncle's face, the grave expression Bobby wore.

"Oh, what is it?" she asked nervously, and still held open the door by which she had just entered, as though instinctively keeping clear a line of retreat.

"Lord Adour has given me a little fresh information on one or two points," Bobby explained. "Won't you come in? Please sit down." He waved her to a chair and she obeyed though very much as if against her will. Bobby could see plainly that Lord Adour was trying to signal to her to be cautious and that these signals merely puzzled and alarmed her. As well, Bobby told himself, that Lord Adour had had no opportunity to speak to her in private. He went on: "So I want to ask you to help check up on a few details. There's one thing though I must make quite clear. It is necessary I should see Miss Adour. I hope I shan't have to consider taking steps to enforce an interview."

His voice hitherto had been hard and official. Now he made it warmer and more friendly as he continued: "I am sure you both understand nothing, nothing at all, can be allowed to interfere with the course of justice. It is essential I should have an opportunity of hearing Miss Adour's personal story."

"But there's nothing Helen can tell you," Jane protested. "I can't either. Commander Seers said so."

"Telling nothing often means telling a great deal," Bobby replied. "Of course, we've learned a good deal since Commander Seers said that. I'm sure he wouldn't say it to-day. Lord Adour tells me he called out to you that he had seen a kingfisher in the spinney. That was when he was hurrying back to get his camera. Please tell me precisely, in every detail, what you did."

"But I didn't do anything," Jane answered. "Helen had come back from the River Farm with Mr. Winstanley, and he had gone home, and she came out again to see if she could get some vegetables for dinner. I was rather excited about the kingfisher, so I ran across to tell her."

"Was she excited, too?" Bobby asked.

"Oh, yes. At least, not very. Helen never is. Except about cooking."

"Sufficiently excited though," Bobby suggested, "for her to hurry to the spinney to see the kingfisher herself?"

Jane, a little flustered under the double strain of Bobby's questioning, and Lord Adour's winks and frowns, of which she could not understand the meaning, answered hesitatingly:

"Yes. Why shouldn't she? I don't see—"

"No reason at all why she shouldn't," Bobby interposed. "Very natural. I suppose you went, too?"

"Yes. I wanted to see the kingfisher as well."

"Of course. You and Miss Helen went together?"

"I ran back first for my bag. I was getting some flowers for the house, and it was rather difficult, because of all the rough weather we've had, and I had left my bag on the grass. It has all our ration cards in it, and I never let it out of my sight, so I went back to get it, and a good thing I did, because the puppy was playing with it. He nearly had it open."

"Miss Helen didn't wait. She went on alone to the spinney?"

"Oh, yes. The kingfisher might have flown off any moment. I only waited to make sure the ration books were all right. It's so awful if they get lost or anything."

"As soon as you had done that, you followed into the spinney?"

"Yes."

"Did you or did Miss Helen see Itter Bain's body?"

"Oh, no," Jane cried. "Oh, what a horrible idea. We had no idea, not any, not till next evening. We were both out all next day, visiting Great Aunt, and we only got back late. That was the first we heard of it. The next day Commander Seers came to see us and we told him everything, and he said it was only what he knew before."

"Yes, but," Bobby explained again, "we know a great deal more than we did when Commander Seers said that. Quite true at the time," Bobby said and added to himself: "Or so the fat headed old blunderer believed." Aloud he said: "Things that seemed unimportant then mean a good deal now—or may. When you followed Miss Helen, had you any difficulty in finding her?"

"Oh, no. It was only a minute or two. I ran along the path and she heard me coming and called out from where she was."

"She wasn't actually on the path, then? She had left it? Why? What was she doing?"

"Well," Jane answered uncomfortably, "she was looking for the kingfisher where Uncle said, and she saw Uncle's gun, and she picked it up, because she couldn't think why he had left it there like that. I told her to put it down. I thought it might go off."

"Did she?"

"Well," Jane answered still more uncomfortably, "Helen said it had been let off already, and she showed me where it was when she saw it, underneath a bush, as if it had been pushed there out of the way, and what had Uncle done that for? I said again to put it down in case it went off, and she said it couldn't, and she made it open to show there wasn't anything in it, but you never know, do you?"

"Had neither of you heard any report?" Bobby asked.

"If we had, we hadn't taken any notice," Jane explained. "There's always shooting going on—rabbits or scaring birds or something, the soldiers, perhaps, and then it wasn't for two days that we were asked. We couldn't be sure, either of us. Or about the time exactly.

Commander Seers said it only showed again what he knew already—that someone had found Uncle's gun and killed Mr. Bain with it."

Bobby listened silently. No doubt all this had seemed of no great importance to Commander Seers with his preconceived certainty of conviction that people of the social standing and position of the family of Lord Adour and Avon could not possibly be mixed up in violent crime. Bobby had no such certainty. There was a clear picture in his mind of the two girls talking together, the murder weapon in the hands of one of them, close by the still warm and bloody body of the murdered man. What other picture might not presently become equally clear? he asked himself fearfully. He did not like the thought of the one, which, just possibly might begin presently to take shape and form. Then with immense relief he remembered one detail that seemed to suggest this picture would never formulate itself into any semblance of reality. Even Jane noticed, and was puzzled, that his voice was a good deal more cheerful as he turned to her uncle and said:

"Did Commander Seers ask you where you left your gun when you put it down?"

"Oh yes," Lord Adour answered. "He said the murderer must have pushed it there under the bush where Helen saw it. He must have been somewhere quite near. Seers said it was the mercy of God Helen didn't see him, or find the body, or she might have been murdered, too. After the two girls went away, the murderer must have thought he had better find a more secure hiding place for the gun."

"I told Helen to leave it there," Jane interposed. "She isn't a bit frightened of guns and things, but I made her. Helen says it's silly and she doesn't mind a bit, but then she is used to them. She used to go out with the men sometimes before the war, when there were shooting parties."

This was said quite simply. Evidently Jane herself saw no special significance in her remark. Lord Adour looked glum and muttered something inaudible. Bobby told himself that he was certain Jane spoke the truth as far as she knew it. But then the question remained: How far did she know it? Had there been other happenings, of which she knew nothing, happenings before her arrival on the spot where Helen stood with a recently discharged gun in her hands? He did not know. Impossible to say. One thing alone seemed clear. He must give all he had just learned the most careful consideration before taking any action. Obviously all this should have been known long ago. The questions asked by Commander Seers would assuredly have been of a very different and far more searching character had they been addressed to cottagers. Not that Seers had been in the least conscious of any partiality. The conviction was simply ingrained in him that certain things were "not done" in the best circles, and as they weren't "done," they couldn't happen.

"A respecter of persons without knowing it," Bobby reflected, "and that's the worst kind of all."

Then he said aloud, speaking directly to Lord Adour:

"Commander Seers is an extremely capable officer, but he hasn't any very great experience in detective work. Neither he nor the young ladies may have realized the importance of their stories. I am wondering, Lord Adour, whether you did. I think you must have done. I think the truth is you went to the spinney to meet Itter Bain. Most unfortunately, as things turned out, you took your gun with you as a kind of excuse, camouflage, to suggest you were only going to see if you could get a shot at a rabbit, though I don't think the middle of the afternoon is the best time for rabbit-shooting. It was because you were afraid that if you admitted you knew Itter was waiting for you, you might have to go on to admit that you had been in touch with him and had encouraged his hopes about a possible marriage with Miss Adour—"

"Oh," Jane cried out, interrupting, "oh, he didn't—oh, Uncle never did; did you, Uncle?"

Bobby saved Lord Adour the need for replying by the gesture with which he imposed silence upon Jane.

"Never mind that," he said. He continued, still speaking directly to Lord Adour: "I expect it was because the gun was only a kind of camouflage that you forgot it so entirely. You are quite clear in your mind where it was you left it?"

"I've shown you exactly where," Lord Adour answered at once, though sulkily enough. "What does it matter? It's clear it was taken by the murderer. I didn't go to look for it till much later on. It was getting dark. The gun was gone. I made sure someone had seen it and gone off with it. I told the police at once. I rang up. Sergeant Gregson answered. He said they would attend to it. I didn't suppose there was much chance of getting it back."

"Did you see Itter Bain's dead body?"

"No. I didn't." Lord Adour answered violently. "I've told you. It was getting dark. What did bother me was that Helen said nothing about him. I thought he must have gone away without having spoken to her."

"Although," Bobby said, "although he was there for that very reason, waiting for the opportunity you had promised him of seeing her alone? Did that seem likely?"

"It was possible, anyhow," Lord Adour answered, ignoring a fresh exclamation of surprise and disbelief from Jane. "Helen— sometimes I think she frightens people. You never know what anyone will do when she's been there. I'm her father, but I know it has the oddest effect, watching her. Of course, we're used to her. I thought most likely Itter hadn't dared to speak; I thought he must just have slipped away. How was I to guess he was lying dead close by?"

Bobby got up to go.

"Thank you," he said. He added: "I hope I've made it quite clear it will be necessary to ask Miss Helen for a statement. On that, I must insist. I think Commander Seers is out of hospital. I will ask him to come with me. It would be wise, perhaps, if you asked your solicitor to be present. I shall also want you both to put in writing what you have just told me. You will tell Miss Adour to expect us to-morrow?"

"I will tell her," Jane said; and a faint smile touched her lips as though she thought that it was all very well to talk in this easy way of interviewing Helen, but that perhaps the proposed interview might take a course very different from that Bobby expected. "I'm sure it's very much better to bring Commander Seers with you," she remarked.

Bobby felt very annoyed. It almost seemed as if she thought he was bringing the Commander with him as a kind of safeguard, a sort of chaperon.

"Hang it all," he reflected indignantly, "she might be thinking that if I'm not careful I shall be going down on my knees begging the girl to elope with me," and in point of fact it was something like that, less crude but in essence much the same, that Jane was thinking.

CHAPTER XXX

LAUNCH FOUND

THE FIRST THING Bobby did on leaving Kindles was to try to get in touch with Commander Seers. Yet another drifting mine had been reported, however, and then lost sight of, so Seers was out in a motor launch looking for it, as in the prevalent conditions of wind and tide there was considerable risk of its coming ashore.

Bobby had to content himself with writing a note explaining that in the light of recent developments he felt it had become necessary to insist on securing a statement from Helen Adour. It also, he wrote, seemed to him desirable, indeed essential, that when this was done Commander Seers should be present. He added that he was making a report to that effect to the Home Office. He wrote also another letter, this time to Lord Adour, in which, in stiff, official terms, he asked permission to place men on guard on the Kindles property "as a matter of extreme urgency." To this he managed to get added, in addition to his own signature, that of the senior officer under Seers. Then he sent it to Kindles by Sergeant Gregson, hoping that possibly delivery by hand by a sergeant might impress.

It failed to do so. Gregson returned with a curt refusal. Lord Adour preferred to take for himself such precautions as might seem desirable, the brief message ran, and indeed Bobby had not expected any more favourable reply. He wondered a little what precautions had been taken, if any. Lord Adour had never been willing to explain their nature, and Bobby was inclined to doubt if they existed and was sure that even if they did they were not likely to be very effective. He decided that all he could do in the circumstances was to have the road near Kindles patrolled all night.

"His lordship won't like that either," Bobby remarked. "He has got it firmly into his thick head that if any of us are seen anywhere near his place, then everyone will take it for granted he is on the point of being arrested."

"Yes, sir," agreed Gregson. "He said something about not wanting police hanging round as if he were being watched for fear he decamped." Not without some understanding of this point of view, Gregson added: "Worst place ever for gossip, this is."

"Did you ever know," Bobby asked, "any place anywhere that wasn't the worst ever for gossip?"

Leaving Gregson to muse upon this, Bobby went off to bed. He felt very tired, for the emotional strain of his long talks at Kindles had been considerable, nor was he as yet quite clear in his mind as to the conclusions that should be drawn therefrom. But he was not destined to enjoy much rest, for he had scarcely closed his eyes, and that happened as soon as his head touched the pillow, when the sergeant came knocking on the door.

"There's Billy Soper here," Gregson called as soon as he heard Bobby answer. "He says they've spotted her and will you come at once?"

"I'll be down in a jiffy," Bobby called; instantly alert, for this might mean that at long last he would be able to test, and perhaps to prove, the theory which he had been steadily pursuing, in spite of all cross-currents and alluring and divergent sidepaths.

He dressed hurriedly. Below the young harbour man was waiting.

"She's there all right, sir," he said. "We're getting on with the job."

"Good," said Bobby. "You're sure?"

"Oh, yes," Soper answered. "It's her all right. I don't know how you knew, but that's where she was."

"I'll get the car," Bobby said.

"I've my motor-bike," Soper said. "It would be quicker. She can go along the bank where a car couldn't. That is, if you don't mind getting up behind."

Bobby didn't, even though it was not easy for him to tuck his long legs out of harm's way. In a few minutes they were off, speeding through the heavy darkness, for the moon was not yet up and the night was cloudy. Before them the beam of the cycle's head lamp threw a lane of light. Behind followed Gregson on a pedal cycle, annoyed that the car hadn't been used, since then he could have ridden in comfort instead of having to push along in the dark.

Soon the last houses of the little harbour town were left behind. From the smooth highway they turned to the rough path that ran by the river-side, bumping and jolting their way along. On one side flowed the river, dark and silent in the night. On the other hand brooded the quiet fields, still and solitary. Alone the chug-chug of their busy engine disturbed the silence and the dark. Presently there grew into visibility before them a strong, clear light and as they drew nearer there came to them the sound of men working and talking.

"They'll soon have her up," Soper said over his shoulder. "The crane's there and it'll do the job in quick time."

They arrived. Bobby jumped down. The Harbour-master's assistant greeted him. The Harbour-master himself was out with Commander Seers, trying to find the mine reported floating inshore. It might be necessary to warn people to leave their houses near the beach if the thing did drift in with the tide.

"Lucky the wind's dropped," observed the Harbour-master's assistant, "but there's a swell on and she keeps popping up and down, so it's hard to see where she is."

Natural enough that the mine, with its latent threat of destruction to the town and to their homes, should seem of more pressing interest to them than did the work on hand, especially as they had little idea of its purpose or significance. But they got on steadily with the job. Soper, who had gone to speak to them, came back to Bobby. He said:

"There's a bloke on the other bank."

"What's he doing?" Bobby asked.

Soper did not answer. He seemed uneasy. Bobby went to the bank to look. Soper threw the beam from his head lamp across the broadly flowing river. But all they could see was what appeared to be a shadow that moved and vanished as the beam from the lamp approached. The Harbour-master's assistant said: "There isn't anyone."

Soper said:

"I saw him clear. He was watching like."

"Wondering what we're up to?" suggested one of the other men who had heard what they were saying.

"Who is there?" Bobby called across.

"He won't answer," Soper said. "He just watches."

"Well, never mind," Bobby said. "It's too dark to do anything. If we tried to get over there he would be off at once." After a moment's pause, he added, a little uneasily: "Whoever it is."

He turned away to see how the work was progressing. A barge carrying a small crane was moored in the stream. A strong searchlight was in operation. A diver's head appeared from the water. He announced that he had the chains fixed.

"She's about ten foot under," Soper said. "I reckon it's the deepest pool there is. Took some finding I reckon."

"I expect so," Bobby agreed.

"Someone else coming," the Harbour-master's assistant remarked. "We shall have 'em all here soon," he grumbled.

The sound of an approaching motor cycle was now quite plain. They went on working. From the dark water they saw slowly lifting the bow of a small boat. Bobby could read the name *Seagull*. The motor cycle, coming at speed, bumping over the rough towing path, was close now. It stopped. The rider jumped off. He called out loudly: "What's going on here?"

Nobody answered. They were all intent on watching the crane as it pushed and lifted and guided the rescued *Seagull* towards the bank its bows were already touching. The newcomer said:

"That's the *Seagull*."

Bobby turned.

"Oh, it's Mr. Prescott Bain," he said. "Yes, it's the *Seagull*. We've found her at last. Is Mr. Mauley Bain with you?"

Prescott did not answer. He came nearer and seemed to wish to make sure that it really was the *Seagull*. The water was pouring from her stern now that she was lying higher up the bank. Prescott said:

"How did you know where she was?"

"She had to be somewhere, hadn't she?" Bobby remarked. "At the harbour they seemed pretty certain she hadn't been taken out to sea. She might just possibly have been loaded on a lorry and carted away somewhere inland, but it didn't seem likely. Somebody, somewhere, would be sure to have noticed a launch on a lorry. We made inquiries and heard nothing. So with sea and land ruled out, there was only the river left, and as she wasn't on the river, it struck me she might be in it. Obvious idea. Simple job. Nothing like being simple and obvious when you've something to hide. So I got help to have the river searched wherever the water seemed deep. Surprising what a number of deep pools there are."

"More than you would think till you came to try," Soper put in. "I reckon whoever sank her there meant to leave her for a time and then get her up again on the quiet. Tough job though, without—" and he nodded towards barge and crane.

Bobby had been watching the water flow away from the interior of the launch. He said to Prescott:

"What was it brought you along?"

"Those lights show," Prescott said. "I wondered what was going on."

"Does that mean you knew where the *Seagull* lay?"

"Certainly not. How could I?"

"She's nearly free from water now," Bobby said.

"Well, it's a relief to know she's been found," Prescott said, but he spoke nervously. "She's worth money. In my idea, she belongs to the firm. Bought with the firm's money. Mauley wants to make out she is part of Itter's private estate."

"Where is he?" Bobby asked.

"Who? Mauley? I don't know. Why? In bed, most likely."

But Bobby looked doubtfully across the river at the opposite bank the darkness veiled. He said:

"Was it Mauley told you something was going on here and asked you to come and see?"

"No, it wasn't. I told you," Prescott answered angrily. "I saw the lights here. They show up. I wondered what they were for. We use water transport a lot. If anything was wrong, I wanted to know."

Bobby climbed into the launch and disappeared. Soper followed, taking tools with him. A noise of hammering and knocking was soon heard. Bobby reappeared. He climbed down to the bank again. He had a gun in his hands.

"We found it under the cabin floor," he said. "I think it must be Lord Adour's gun, the one used to kill Itter Bain. It will have to be identified." Prescott began to move towards the spot where he had left his cycle. Bobby said sharply: "Please stay here, Mr. Bain."

"What for?" demanded Prescott. "It's nothing to do with me." His voice had grown high and shrill. "I didn't know the gun was there. How could I?"

"I remember once," Bobby said, "you told me exactly where Lord Adour put down his gun by the oak the day your cousin was shot and I wondered then how you knew."

"I didn't," Prescott cried. "I mean ... what's it matter, anyhow? I've an alibi. You know that. I was with the Coastal Bank men all the time. You know I was. You've asked them. They've told you."

"Yes, I know," Bobby agreed. "You've a perfect alibi. The perfect alibi." He turned to Gregson. "Sergeant," he said. "Mr. Bain is to stay here. See that he does. If necessary, arrest him on a charge of obstruction. He is to be held at all costs. Understand?"

"Yes, sir," said Sergeant Gregson and moved silently to Prescott's side.

CHAPTER XXXI
HASTE! HASTE!

WITH BOTH great anger and an obvious terror, Prescott Bain attempted to protest, at times with loud vehemence, at times with threats of legal action. Gregson listened stolidly—and watchfully. Bobby did not listen at all. He was giving other instructions, making other arrangements, all with speed and efficiency, for it was in his mind that there might be need for haste. On the highroad that here, in a great arc, came within a few hundred yards of the river, they saw the headlights of a car coming at speed. They heard it stop.

"Spotted the lights and want to know what it's all about, and so they're coming to see," Soper remarked.

"It's the searchlight," the Harbour-master's assistant said. "It shows up."

The newcomers were making their way across the fields that lay between road and river. They were using electric torches. One of them as they came nearer shouted out something. Bobby could not catch the words, but he thought he recognized the voice. He called back:

"Is that Commander Seers?"

"What's all this? What's all this?" came the reply. The speaker, running now, broke through the hedge that divided field from towing path. The searchlight showed him as Commander Seers. He said: "Is that you, Mr. Owen?" His voice did not sound very cordial, very pleased. He went on: "Is this some fresh development? I don't think we had been notified, had we?" That was true. Bobby had gone on the useful and undeniable principle that those who don't know, can't tell. He was not without experience of the mischief that can be done to careful plans by even one incautious word—by, in fact, that "careless talk" of which we heard so much during the Second World War. He was prepared with his answer though. He said quickly:

"I tried to get in touch with you, but I was told you were out mine-chasing again. Any luck?"

The question was a useful diversion. Every man within earshot stopped what he was doing to listen for the reply. The tension of their eagerness could almost be felt, for it was the safety of their homes that was in question. The Commander felt the pressure of their anxiety, of their attention. He said:

"There oughtn't to be any danger. She was just where the tide and the Westways current meet, caught between them, so she ought to drift off again when the tide turns. Then we'll explode her as soon as she is out of range. We've made a light fast, so we shall be able to tell if she starts to drift inshore again."

Sounds of relief came from the listeners. Bobby said: "Good. Good work." Prescott Bain came up, Gregson at his heels. Prescott said loudly:

"I protest against this outrage. I warn you all, all of you, I shall hold you all responsible. I shall consult my solicitors."

"What? What's all this?" demanded Seers, turning to Bobby. "I take full responsibility," Bobby said. "I think it necessary Mr. Bain should be detained for the time. I will explain later. I think we had better get on to Kindles as quickly as possible. Trespassing or not, I'm going to spend the rest of the night sitting on the Kindles doorstep."

"But ... but ..." began Seers, quite bewildered.

"I'll borrow your car if you don't mind," Bobby said.

"Yes, but—" began Seers, trying by a gesture to stop Bobby, who was moving away. "Do I understand you're charging Mr. Bain? His alibi ..."

"I know," Bobby interrupted. "The perfect alibi. Come to Kindles with me. I'll explain. There's no time to lose ... I think."

"But—" began Seers once more.

"No time now," Bobby repeated, and, ignoring Seers's gesture of upraised restraining hand, set off at a run towards where on the high road the headlamps of the car were visible.

"But—" Seers called after him and then followed, running, too, half-bewildered and wholly angry.

Bobby was running fast, but with caution, for the ground was rough, and it would be easy to trip and fall. He flashed his torch to show where the ground was smoothest. Seers was running, too, trying to overtake him, but not with much success. Seers tried to shout to Bobby to stop, to wait for him, but had no breath. Behind him followed a constable who had accompanied Seers and who now was not sure what was happening or whether it would be either wise or respectful to outrun his chief. In the car, another constable was waiting, sitting at the wheel. He heard their running, and, guessing there was need for haste, was ready to start. Bobby reached the car first. He jumped in.

"Kindles," he said. "Wait for the Commander. He's there." Seers came charging up. He was elderly, not in the best physical condition, but he had made good time. Only he had no breath left.

"But—" he panted.

"Jump in. Hurry," Bobby said, and almost pulled him in.

The constable, following close behind, scrambled after. Bobby repeated "Kindles" to the driver, and added the injunction: "Quick as you can—quicker." The car shot away. Seers said,

"But—" and paused.

Bobby said, "Hurt yourself?" to the constable, who, imperfectly prepared for the sudden jolt of that abrupt departure, had been sent sprawling.

"But—" repeated Seers, and this time managed to get out with an angry gasp: "I insist—"

"Of course," agreed Bobby. "Naturally. I shall make a full report. That was the *Seagull* we got up. You remember? Mauley Bain reported her stolen. She had to be hidden. All they could think of was to sink her in the deepest river pool. I asked the harbour people to help get her up again. I couldn't let you know as you were in hospital, and I didn't much want to have to explain to your subordinates. I didn't know if you would approve."

"But," began Seers afresh, half-placated, it is true, yet still suspicious of this young man who was always so reasonable and so conciliatory, but who yet always went his own way first and only explained afterwards, who seemed positively to enjoy taking that full responsibility for his actions which most are only too glad and happy to push on to others.

"But—" he repeated, and then paused, and then he said "But—" so that to Bobby the memory of that swift, brief drive in the night is punctuated by a series of "But—" as if no other word could get itself pronounced by the huddled, puzzled figure at his side.

To Bobby indeed the moment seemed unsuitable for explanation and chiefly to prevent the issue of more "buts," he said:

"Jolly good, your spotting that mine. If they turned me on mine-hunting, exploding the things, sticking lights on them, I think I should resign and go in for poultry-farming—risky, too, but not the same kind of risk."

"Nothing to it," the Commander declared. "The things don't go off—at least, not often." They had come to the top of a rise in the ground where they had to turn to the west in order to reach the Kindles entrance. "There she is," the commander said, pointing, as the whole stretch of coast and sea to the south came into sight. "See that light? That's her." He said uneasily: "She looks to me nearer in, as if the tide had got her."

"Hope not," Bobby said.

The driver leaned back, speaking over his shoulder.

"Kindles," he said. "The gate's open. Do I drive through, up to the house?"

"No, stop here," Bobby said, and started to alight as the car slowed down.

"But—" began the Commander once yet again.

Two figures came running up, flashing torches. It was the patrol Bobby had asked should be placed on this stretch of road that ran by the low wall bordering the Kindles grounds.

"Good men," Bobby said. "Seen anything? Heard anything?"

"No, sir. Quiet as the grave," one of them answered.

Seers and the second constable had alighted, too. Bobby flashed his torch on the ground. He saw what he had expected, feared, to see. Traces of fresh footprints on the damp earth by the side of the road where someone had stood to open the gate to the Kindles drive Bobby knew was always kept closed at night.

"Got here first," Bobby said and started to run.

"But—" said Seers as he followed, and the others followed after him.

CHAPTER XXXII
IT HAD TO BE

THE KINDLES DRIVE was of no great length. Bobby had run but a few yards along it, and the house was already visible as a dark mass against the night, when he saw and heard a movement behind the trees and bushes that lined the avenue. He swung the ray from his torch towards whence the sound seemed to come, and now there came towards him Mauley Bain, still moving with that slow step of his which always seemed somehow to give such an impression of restrained and latent speed.

"I thought it was you," Mauley said. "I was expecting you. You waste your time. You have nothing to do here."

"Haven't we?" Bobby asked. "What are you doing here?"

"As to that ..." Mauley said and seemed to think the answer sufficient.

"Your shoes look wet and the ends of your trousers," Bobby remarked. "Was that when you crossed the river so as to get here before us?"

"I hadn't noticed," Mauley said vaguely. Then he said: "You can go. You have nothing to do here."

Commander Seers interrupted.

"Mr. Owen has found the gun, Lord Adour's gun," he said. "The gun that was used in your brother's murder. It was in the *Seagull*, and your cousin, Prescott, was on the spot when it was found."

"Prescott?" Mauley repeated, as if puzzled by the name. "Oh, yes, I told him there were lights along the river bank. I asked him to go to see what was happening." Abruptly he added. "There was no murder."

"No murder?" Seers repeated, staring.

"It was a thing that happened," Mauley said. "That's how it was. It happened. What does it matter through whom it happened when it had to be?"

"What's he mean?" Seers said bewilderedly to Bobby.

"Let him talk," Bobby said.

"You're the detective they sent from London," Mauley said. "You are trying to do your best, I know, but your best is not enough. You don't understand, you never could or will."

"Has he been drinking?" Seers asked.

"I don't think so," Bobby answered. "Only thinking. That is often worse." To Mauley he said: "What is it I don't understand and never could or will?"

"The thing that happens," Mauley said. "It is so different, the thing that happens from the thing that's done."

"We've had enough of this," began Seers, annoyed.

"No," Bobby said sharply, now that hard note of dominance in his voice that sometimes came there though often he was unconscious of it. "Let him talk. Never stop a witness talking." To Mauley he said: "What difference is there between what happens and what's done?"

"What is done," Mauley answered, "need not have been, but what happens is what had to be."

"I don't understand all this," Seers protested.

"That's what I told you," Mauley said, "even though it's perfectly simple. It's because it's so simple it's so hard to understand."

"Mr. Bain," Bobby said, "I think I must tell you, before you say anything more, that it is my intention to charge you with the murder of your brother, Itter Bain. Anything you say may be used in evidence."

"But, man alive," cried Seers in a crescendo of bewilderment, "you've just arrested Prescott."

"No. I only had him detained to prevent his saying anything to Mauley. Unnecessary precaution apparently, as it's turned out. It must have been Mauley who was watching from the other bank, so he knew all about it. But I wasn't sure of that at the time."

"Do you mean Mauley killed Itter?" Seers asked. "Oh, now then," he muttered, "it couldn't be, his own brother." He said to Mauley: "Are you your brother's murderer?"

"No," Mauley answered at once. "I'm quite innocent. When I saw him lying there I said to him, 'I didn't do that.' He heard me. He understood. I could see that by the way he looked at me before he died."

"How did Lord Adour's gun come to be in the *Seagull*, where it was found?" Seers asked.

"I put it there," Mauley answered. "To keep it out of his way." He nodded at Bobby as he spoke. "Has he nosed it out? Police." Again he looked at Bobby, frowning and thoughtful. "Police," he repeated. "I dare say he's a good policeman. Much better than you, Seers, much better. But police have no part or lot in this." In a loud voice and now speaking directly to Bobby, he said: "You've found the gun that killed my brother. Well, then, do you think the gun is the murderer?"

"No, but who pulled the trigger?"

"It was done through him," Mauley agreed, "it was done by him. So also it was done through the gun, by the gun. But neither did it."

"Who did, then?" Seers asked.

"It was the thing itself that got itself done," Mauley repeated. "But that is just what you will never understand. How could you? Not to be expected. But Itter understood. I told you. I could see it as he looked at me when I was holding his hand before he died."

"You ... you held his hand?" Seers gasped.

"Then I kissed him as mother used to make us do when we were little after we had said our prayers," Mauley went on, "and I took the gun away and put it where I thought it was safe. Because I knew that finding it would only make it all so much more difficult to understand. So it will now it's been found," and he paused to look rebukingly at Bobby.

Seers threw up his hands in a gesture of complete bewilderment.

"He is certainly mad," he said in a baffled voice.

"I think no one who kills is ever wholly sane," Bobby said, "but I think Mauley is sane in his own way, if not in ours."

"You mean you believe he did kill his brother?" Seers asked.

"He must be charged," Bobby said. "That's clear, anyhow," but there was still a faint touch of hesitation in his voice as he turned to stare in a troubled way at the great mass of Kindles, looming darkly in the distance in the dark night.

"I've told you already I am innocent," Mauley said angrily. "Even you police, you don't call the gun a murderer, do you?"

"No, only the means," Bobby said.

"That's it," Mauley agreed. "You begin to see ... don't try to pretend I murdered Itter when we are brothers, and I never could or wanted to. A means," he repeated. "A way. No more."

"A means to what need never have been, but for the will behind," Bobby said. Then he said: "Whose was the will?"

"The whole question is there," Mauley said. "That is the one intelligent thing you have said so far. I had no will to kill."

"This is all beyond me," Seers said. "It's too deep for me."

"I think at any rate," Bobby said, "it is going deeper than we need to follow." There was a grimness in his voice as he said: "We are policemen and all we have to think of is our duty. The rest is for others." To Mauley, he said: "You have told us a great deal. Will you tell us now exactly what happened—the bare facts, and never mind how they came to be?"

"Even though how they came to be is all that counts?" Mauley asked with pity for such simplicity, yet half-amused by it. "The way those two men from the bank talked and talked, they and Prescott never stopping, that's how it began when I knew all that mattered was that Itter was waiting there and that she did not know. Because he had told me he had arranged everything with her father, and he would send her where Itter would be waiting and then it would be all right because, Itter said, she could never stand out against him and all the force and passion in him. But I knew it must never be, and I told him so and he laughed. It was a pity he laughed, foolish. Because then I knew. It wasn't that I wanted her for myself. I had hardly even spoken to her, only watched her as she went by, and the strangeness and the beauty that went with her, and what would have become of that if she had merely been a woman like another? When I thought of that, I seemed to see her there among the trees and Itter ... well, then I knew what had to be. I passed a note to Prescott to say I was bored with all the talk and I wanted to get on with what was waiting for me. That was true, but not in the way he thought I meant. I said in my note that if the bank people wanted me told anything or to be sure I agreed, then Prescott could pretend to ring me on the house 'phone and make up any reply he liked. That gave him a free hand, which was always what he wanted. Later on, when he heard about Itter, he asked a lot of questions, and he went into a panic because of being scared of what might happen to the business and his money in it."

"You found Itter in the spinney?" Bobby asked.

"That was the meeting place, where Itter waited for her where she came. I was too late. A little sooner and it would never have happened. But it had happened already."

"What do you mean?" Seers cried, horror and dismay in his voice. "You don't mean ... not Helen Adour ... ?"

"If I had been earlier," Mauley said, speaking slowly and very thoughtfully, "then I think it need never have been and Itter would still be alive. But it had to be, for when a deed has to be done it can't be stopped. And I was too late. He would not listen, he could think of nothing but that she was coming for he had seen her through the trees, and he did not know she was coming for his death. He fetched the gun. To make me go. But he let me take it from him, for that was how it had to be. We were all innocent. She did not wish his death. Was it Itter's fault he could not understand she was for no man's privacy? Was it my fault I was too late in getting there? Was it her fault that she dazzled like the sun, so that nothing was the same when she went by? Or was it perhaps the fault of the gun that it was there, waiting? But it is necessary that it must not happen again, never again get itself accomplished. Never again must her beauty kill. The instrument must be broken, the gun hidden away, and blood paid for in blood, as it has been from the beginning and always shall be."

Bobby turned and began to run towards the house. He shouted over his shoulder as he ran:

"Don't let him get away."

A light shone in the house, in one of the windows, then in another and another. Against the blinds there could be seen shadows of people running to and fro.

Seers said:

"That was her room, Helen's room, where the lights showed first," and in the thoughts of all their minds, in Bobby's mind, too, as he raced towards the house, ran the unspoken question: "Has then another deed got itself accomplished?"

CHAPTER XXXIII
AN EPITAPH

BOBBY, RACING UP the Kindles avenue, paradoxically driven on by the fear, the knowledge, that it was too late and speed all unavailing, reached the entrance to the house. The door was open. He ran in and called aloud. Somebody, he could not see who it was, was running down the stairs, but as he entered turned and ran up them again. From the rear of the house, Lord Adour appeared.

"Is it the doctor?" he called. He saw Bobby. "Oh, you," he said. "Have you brought a doctor? I can't get through."

Without waiting for an answer, he rushed away again, back to his study, and Bobby could hear him shouting into the 'phone. A woman came from the back regions. Bobby recognized the elderly maid who formed the whole of the resident domestic staff. Her hair was in the curling pins he had been told were an obsolete relic of a past and forgotten age, she clutched an ancient dressing gown about her. Bobby said:

"What's going on here?"

But he thought he knew and perhaps his question was an unconscious effort to postpone assuring himself by sight and touch.

"It won't burn up," the elderly maid answered. "There's no oil. Shall I use sugar? It's rationed."

She disappeared again. Bobby ran up the stairs. There was a light burning in the corridor. Jane came to the door of a room almost opposite the head of the stairs. It was the room Bobby knew from its position must be that occupied by Helen. Without showing any surprise at his appearance, Jane said:

"Can you help? Can you get a doctor? I think it's too late."

She went back into the room. The window was open and the dressing table near it had been pushed aside. On the small bed lay a still form. The bedding had been turned back and on the sheets were crimson spots. There was a dreadful contrast with the dainty furnishings, the soft colour harmonies the room displayed. Jane was speaking again. She said:

"He must have got in through the window. Can't you get a doctor?"

"Lord Adour is trying," Bobby said. "He is 'phoning." He heard footsteps in the hall below and someone calling out. Seers and the others had arrived. Bobby ran to the head of the stairs and shouted: "Send the car for the nearest doctor. Very urgent." Lord Adour rushed out of the study.

"I've got London," he called. "They've promised to get through here."

He disappeared again. Seers was giving instructions as Bobby had requested. Bobby went back into the room. Jane repeated: "He'll never get here in time."

Bobby went nearer to the bed. He stared unbelievingly at the still, quiet figure lying there. He said:

"That's not her. That's Wayling." Then he said: "Is he wounded?"

"He is dying," Jane said, "and there is no doctor." She came to the bed and stood by Bobby's side. She went on: "I did what I could There wasn't much bleeding. I think that makes it worse. I tore the sheet for bandages to keep out the air. I don't know what else to do.

Do you? I've told them to get the fire going. I got my hot-water bottle. Helen's too. It's all no good."

"I don't understand this," Bobby said. "I never expected this. How did it happen?"

"There was no light," Jane said. "Both bulbs had been taken out. I had to put one in to see by. He must have done it on purpose, to prevent any one knowing."

Seers came hurrying into the room, up to the bed.

"That's not Helen," he said.

"Is there anything—anything at all we can do to help?" Jane said to Bobby.

Bobby was bending over that still, quiet form.

"I don't know," he said. "There's no bleeding—not much, I mean. I've a brandy flask, but there's a stomach wound."

"Two," Jane said. "There are two."

"I think we can do no more than try to keep him warm and wait for a doctor," Bobby said.

"That's Wayling," Seers told them challengingly, almost protestingly. "That's not Helen. It's the fellow who was at that what d'ye call it pub. How did he get here? Where's Helen?"

"She is in our room," Jane answered. "I sent her away. She wanted to help, but she couldn't. No one can. I must go to her. She's terrified. I thought she was going to faint."

"Thank God she's safe," Seers said; and, as if his relief were so great he could no longer stand, he sat down on the nearest chair and then got up again, not sure such fragile daintiness would endure his weight. Pointing to the bed, he said: "How did he get here? What was he up to? Is he badly hurt?"

"I think he is dead," Bobby said; but, as he spoke, Wayling opened his eyes.

"Hullo, Owen," he said. "On the spot as usual. Smart boy, and what's the good? My note-book ... in my breast pocket."

"Who did this?" Bobby asked him.

"My note-book," Wayling said again. "I want it. In my coat pocket." He began to cough and a little blood and froth showed on his lips. "My note-book," he repeated, but much more feebly. "I want it. Damn you," he whispered, "can't you see I've no time to spare?"

His clothes were in an untidy, sprawling heap on a small silk and golden chair. Bobby picked up the coat and took the note-book from a pocket. He said:

"Never mind all that now. How are you feeling? Have you any pain? We're trying to get a doctor. Who did this?"

"It's all there," Wayling said, whispering still so that Bobby had to bend to catch what he said. "All I ever borrowed. I always meant to pay back every penny."

"It will be," Jane said. "Every penny, if I have to sell my last frock to do it."

"Thank you," Wayling said, and smiled, and the smile seemed touched with some strange and sudden glory. "O.K.," he whispered and closed his eyes.

"Did Mauley Bain do this?" Bobby asked and, when Wayling made no answer, he said again: "Who was it? Who?"

Wayling opened his eyes again and chuckled. He said very loudly and clearly:

"I fooled him beautifully, didn't I? With the bulbs taken out, he couldn't see, and he never thought to look, and so he thought that I was Helen. That's damn funny, you know," and the chuckle became a delighted laugh, and as he thus laughed with delight, he died.

"It is finished," Jane said, and, to the two men: "You can go. I will do what must be done."

"But what was he doing here?" Seers asked, still in utter amaze and complete bewilderment.

Jane answered:

"He told us Helen was in danger and we must let him sleep in her room and she could sleep with me; because then she would be safe and it was the only way to make sure and know for certain who it was, so it could be proved. And he said it would be quite all right, because no one wanted to hurt him, and so there wasn't any danger for him. But, of course, that wasn't true and he knew it wasn't, and I expect we knew, too, only somehow you always believed what he told you even when you didn't really, only he made you think you did."

"Yes, I know," Bobby said.

"Well, anyhow," Seers said, his voice full of an enormous relief, "you're sure Helen's all right? Quite safe and well?"

"She is safe and well," Jane answered, "but he is dead."

"Yes, I know," Seers echoed Bobby; and his voice was still all one great relief. He looked in a puzzled way at the dead man on the bed. "He was potman at the 'Good Haul,' wasn't he?" he said. "There've been complaints ... getting money ... false pretence ... that sort of thing. Nothing you could lay hold of in a criminal sense, civil proceedings generally. He seemed to be an unscrupulous little scamp."

"It will do for an epitaph as well as another," Bobby said. "He did what he did and he was what he was, and he died well."

CHAPTER XXXIV
MAGNIFICENT SUICIDE

ONE OF SEER'S MEN was posted at the door of the death chamber. It was explained to Jane that for the present nothing must be touched. She went back to join Helen in the room they shared together. The elderly maid, having got the fire going at last, made tea, which she and Lord Adour shared together in friendly companionship. Lord Adour had finally succeeded in getting in touch with a local doctor. Through the London exchange, a second doctor had been told that his services were badly required at Kindles. The police car sent off by Commander Seers was returning with a third. It seemed likely all three would arrive together. The Commander himself was hurrying down the avenue with Bobby, on their way to where they had left Mauley Bain in the charge of the two remaining constables.

"Wayling never told us who it was," Seers was saying uneasily. "Is there enough to justify a charge?"

"Enough on both counts," Bobby answered grimly.

"His own brother," Seers said. "I can hardly believe it."

"Not the first time," Bobby answered, "that brother has killed brother for a woman's sake."

"It is the mercy of God," Seers said, "that Helen is safe."

"Don't forget Wayling," Bobby said.

Seers did not answer. He could not quite co-ordinate his memory of the potman at the local pub, the unscrupulous little scamp about whose conduct he had received complaints, with his memory of the man who had died in Helen s room to save Helen from danger. The inconsistency was too great and he was still half-unconsciously seeking for a comfortable explanation.

They came to where Mauley Bain and the two constables were waiting. Mauley was sitting on the ground, his knees hunched up, his hands clasped about them. The two constables left to watch him were standing near. They had moved the police car so that its headlamps shone full upon them all, so making around them a little island of light. As Seers and Bobby came up, they stiffened to attention. Mauley, seated, immobile, staring out across the darkness at the lighted Kindles windows, might have been unaware of the return of Bobby and the Commander, so utterly did he ignore it and them. Even when Seers spoke to him he took no notice. There was something a little frightening about this intense abstraction, as though, still living, he had yet withdrawn himself into another world. Only when Seers laid a hand upon his shoulder did he look up. He shook off the Commander's hand, not impatiently, but as if it were irrelevant, and would have relapsed again into whatever dark sea of thought and memory had absorbed him, had not Bobby called him sharply by name.

"Mauley Bain," he said. "Mauley," he repeated, for somehow he understood that it was the first name—his private name, as it were—that was important and that best could reach him, "we have come back from Kindles and we have seen what you did there."

"Is she still beautiful?" Mauley asked.

"What a thing for you to ask," Seers gasped.

"It was a beauty that was never right, never in its place, not in this world," Mauley said.

"If you mean Helen Adour," Bobby said, "it was not her we saw."

"Now no one ever will," Mauley said. "A loveliness like hers was only here to make men mad."

"It was for worship and for love," Seers said loudly; and then stopped and looked surprised, astonished to hear what he himself had said, not quite sure indeed that it was really he who had spoken. Then he said: "I think I was in love with her myself."

"No one ever loved her as I loved her," Mauley said.

"My wife said once I was," Seers continued, pursuing his own troubled line of thought. "I was angry. I must tell her she was right."

"I only spoke to her twice," Mauley said. "The first time I said, 'How do you do?' The second time I said it was a fine day. She looked surprised because it was raining hard. I hadn't noticed. I hurried away as fast as I could. I expect she was used to that sort of thing—people behaving strangely, I mean. How could they help?"

"I put this to you," Bobby said. "You climbed into the room you believed was occupied by Helen Adour. The room was dark."

"I hadn't thought to bring my torch," Mauley said, "and the electricity wouldn't come on. There must have been something wrong. It didn't matter. I knew where the bed was and I knew what had to be done. Death must answer death and Itter's death required another Death always does. Why do you say you did not see her. The lights came on in her room."

"Helen wasn't there," Seers interposed. "She was safe somewhere else, thank God. It was Wayling you killed, the potman at the 'Good Haul.' I can't make out how he got there. He was in the bed."

"Oh, no," Mauley said. "It was her. It was her room, her bed."

"Her room," Seers agreed. "But she wasn't there. She had moved out. Wayling was sleeping there. It should never have been allowed."

"That's nonsense," Mauley said. "It couldn't be. I know the man you mean. An ugly little brute, more like a gargoyle than anything else. How could he be taken for Helen's loveliness?"

"It seems you did," Bobby said. "I think he found it funny. I think he saw the joke. That his ugliness should answer for her beauty."

"He died laughing," Seers said.

"You're lying," Mauley said. "Liars both of you. It couldn't happen."

"Only it did," Bobby said, "and nothing now can alter it."

"It's all a lie," Mauley repeated. "That ugliness of his and her high beauty. It couldn't. It would be too funny."

"So Wayling thought," Bobby said. "It is why he died laughing."

"Oh, well," Mauley said. "Now then."

"You must come with us," Bobby said. "You will be charged with the murder of Alexander Wayling and with the murder of your brother, Itter Bain."

"Well, now then," Mauley said. "What next?"

Suddenly, unexpectedly, with a lightning and an astonishing activity, he was on his feet. The change from the perfect immobility of his previous attitude to this of intense action, movement, was baffling in its rapidity. It took them all entirely unawares. Before any one of the four men around could so much as raise a finger he was racing away. They followed, followed hard upon him for their momentary paralysis of surprise lasted but the fraction of a second.

Swift and straight he ran, unfalteringly, taking every obstacle as it came, hesitating before none. It might have been the cinder track of athletic grounds on which he fled, so heedless did he seem of where he trod. Behind him, hard upon him, the gap between measured only in feet and inches, the others followed fast. One of the two constables was, as it happened, an athlete, only just released from service as a Commando, and still in first-class training. He was so near as he ran that he was almost within arm's length—but not quite. Bobby was only a foot or two behind, and he ran as not even he had often run before. Behind them were the second constable, less agile, falling slowly behind, and Seers who, despite age and lack of condition, kept gallantly his place.

So they ran and fled and thudded through the night and ever the former Commando was so near to the fleeing Mauley, he was almost within arm's length—but not quite. And Bobby, though he called on every ounce of energy he possessed, was still that foot or two behind, and still he could not close that tiny gap.

For all the reckless speed with which they three fled un-hampered through the night, they might have been three static figures, so little did their positions change in relation to each other. But for the trees and the bushes and the night that fled by, they might have seemed as immobile as when Mauley was sitting hunched up on the ground and Bobby and the Commander talked with him.

For Mauley ran as one possessed, and for all the hindering night, the treacherous dark, he ran as strongly, as securely, with as assured a foot, as though it were full day. So, too, ran the former Commando, ran Bobby. Further back, the other constable slowed to a trot. He told himself he was no half-mile champion. Seers more or less kept his place, only a few yards behind the foremost three. But then he ran on his will and the second constable only on his feet.

It came to Bobby that they were heading for the sea, direct for the sea. Its immensity was drawing near, the sound of its restless waves was plainer every moment. Nothing save an open stretch of sandy beach was before them now. The former Commando slackened speed a fraction. He gasped out to Bobby:

"He'll have to turn. If you go right and I go left, we'll cut him off."

Bobby made no answer. Already the ex-Commando had dropped behind, losing time and speed by speaking. Very certain was Bobby that that swift, direct race, unswerving to right or to left, would end in no turning aside. Straight Mauley had run, and straight and direct he would continue. Bobby made yet another effort to increase his speed. Possibly he did gain an inch or two. Certainly no more. The former Commando tried, and tried in vain, to regain the few yards he had dropped behind, now he saw that neither of the others slackened or swerved, but fled straight on to the sea. Nor did Mauley pause or hesitate or alter his wild rush, even when the first small waves lapped his hurrying feet.

Straight on he continued; and splashed and struggled through the water and Bobby was knee deep in the water, too, when the Commando caught him by the arm.

"Plain suicide, that's what he means," the Commando said. "Don't you, sir. No man could live long in that sea, not with tide and current the way they are. And even if we did follow up, he could drown us easy, grabbing hold."

Bobby knew well this was true. He stood still, the water lapping about his feet. The next wave hardly reached them, for the tide was running strongly seawards. Seers came running up, panting heavily. He said between gasps:

"He's a class swimmer. He means to try to swim in again, somewhere up or down the coast."

"He could never make it," the Commando said. "No man could. Not with this tide running."

"He's a strong swimmer," Sears repeated. "In the front rank." Bobby said:

"What's that light—straight in line?"

"Which?" asked Seers. "Oh, that. It's the mine, closer in than I like. We fastened a burning buoy to her."

"I think we ought to give a warning," Bobby said.

"Why?" Seers asked. "She won't go off. Why should she? She's being watched. In case she drifts nearer. But she won't, not with this tide. There's no danger."

"I think there is," Bobby said. "But there's no time to do anything about it. Not if I'm right."

"God in Heaven," the Commando cried, and turned as if to run, and checked himself. "No time," he said a little wildly. "Not if he means—that."

"Means what?" Seers said irritably. "No time for what?"

The Commando said once more:

"He'll never make it, not with this tide running, not at night, and in his clothes and all."

But this time he spoke without conviction.

"See that?" Bobby said. "Did you see?"

"Yes sir," said the Commando. "Him right enough."

"See what?" demanded Seers, still more irritably. What it is now the fashion to call his sub-consciousness knew well that his sight, once so keen, was no longer what it had been. But this had never admitted, not even to himself, not even in the small wakeful hours of the night when in the quiet darkness so many things grow so crystal clear. "You can think you see anything when it's dark like this," he complained.

"There was the figure of a man," Bobby said. "He showed for a moment clear against the buoy fight. He was climbing on the mine."

"Oh, that," Seers said, trying to persuade himself he had seen it, too, and remembering in fact that for a moment the light of the burning buoy had been obscured. At the time he had supposed it was merely the movement of the sea that had hidden it. He said: "What I told you. Wants a rest. Or to take off his coat and shoes. Then he'll try to swim in somewhere along-shore. There ought to be a lookout. I ought to 'phone."

But he made no attempt to move away. What he had said had brought no conviction even to himself, for he was beginning to understand. They stood waiting, three still and silent figures in the night, and before them the sea drew itself slowly away. The second policeman arrived. He said to the ex-Commando:

"Swam out to sea, didn't he? He'll drown; sure thing he'll drown. His body won't come in yet awhile, not this tide. What's the big idea, waiting?"

No one told him.

They were still standing there, in the same small silent group, when it happened, and the sea rose up in fire and flame, and all the air rushed together and then apart again, and over the little town and harbour roared the wind, as it were the breath of the Lord in anger.

"Magnificent suicide," Bobby said when they four, whom the blast had thrown here and there, had come together again and found they were unhurt. "We had better go see what help is needed."

Bobby wrote the next day.

"... So with poor Mrs. Gregson in tears and in despair over fallen ceilings, glassless windows, a gaping roof, broken crockery, and all the rest of it that the raided towns know so well, I have had to move, and, as you will see from this address, Seers is putting me up. I hope his offer means he has forgiven, if not forgotten, the way in which I was dumped upon his doorstep, like an outsized and most obstreperous foundling.

"Though now, I am more than happy to say, the case may be regarded as closed, I shall have to hang on here a bit longer. I shall have to appear at the inquest on Wayling and possibly at the adjourned inquest on Itter Bain. There can be little doubt of the verdict in both cases—wilful murder against Mauley Bain. Whether there will be an inquest on Mauley seems uncertain. The point has been raised that there is no corpse and no certain proof of death. The argument seems to be: No corpse, no inquest. But I'm told that's not valid and that there are precedents for inquests without corpses. The other suggestion is that though a man was seen to go into the sea and a man was seen to climb out of the sea on the floating mine, there is no proof of identity. To my mind, that is merely a technical point over which lawyers can have a bit of professional fun if they want to. The courts will certainly give leave to presume death, if that is required.

"As so often happens, Mauley went out of his way to draw suspicion on himself. The first time I had a talk with him here, he said that when I saw him earlier he had been to the harbour to have a look at the Seagull *launch, but had not gone on board as her engines had broken down and would have to be repaired. He made that statement twice over. Clearly he wanted me to believe that he had not, in fact, boarded the launch, But when a possible suspect— not that till then I had had any special suspicion either of him or of anyone else—clearly wishes one thing to be believed, it is a sound rule to believe the opposite. Moreover, while a broken-down engine*

is a sound reason for not taking a motor launch out to sea, it seems less adequate as a reason for not boarding her while she is lying at anchor in harbour.

"So I began to think rather seriously about Mauley, but at once met with a snag, for it was Prescott Bain who betrayed knowledge of the exact spot under the oak where Lord Adour had left his gun when, according to his own story, he had put it down to run off for his camera on seeing the kingfisher no one else saw but himself.

"Guilty knowledge, Prescott Bain seemed to be showing; and so there was a switch to him as first suspect and probably a quarrel over the firm's finances as murder motive. But Prescott had an alibi that seemed unbreakable and in fact was so, since it was genuine. Moreover, his alibi seemed to cover Mauley as well; since apparently Mauley had been either in the room with the two bank officials, or available over the house 'phone, during the significant time. That could be explained by complicity on the part of Prescott; but complicity between Prescott and Mauley against Itter meant the cousin and the brother lined up against another brother, whereas all the evidence suggested that what differences existed were between the cousin, the finance man, on the one hand, and the two brothers, the operative side, on the other. Again, such a prearranged plan to murder Itter would have involved previous knowledge of Itter's presence in the Coldstone Spinney at that particular time—though such knowledge was unproved and unlikely.

"Anyhow, I had also to consider the possibility that Lord Adour was guilty, according to the theory put forward by the Bain uncle—the pamphleteer who calls himself Jack Cade, Junior, and who was Haile's employer. I mean the suggestion or belief that his lordship's guilt was being covered up and with the underlying idea that, if that could be proved, it could be used as a spur to prick on our socialistic Government to more extreme measures. It was, of course, quite clear from Seers's attitude and his pukka sahib complex he showed at our first talk that he would never believe a peer of the realm guilty of crime, not even if he had himself been an eyewitness. It was plain his faith in the House of Lords would always transcend any belief in his own eyes. Not conscious or deliberate, of course. It was merely that in his mind crime—especially violent crime—was for the 'lower classes' *alone. Of course, he knew very well there were many instances to the contrary, but for him they were merely the exceptions that confirmed the rule. Lord Adour continued in his mind—or his unconscious if the unconscious exists—to be above suspicion.*

"That much seemed clear. What seemed less clear was whether there existed any good reason why his lordship should in fact be regarded with suspicion. The gossip that he had shot Itter as an unwelcome suitor for his daughter didn't seem convincing. One doesn't shoot the unwelcome suitor; one shows him the door.

"But then it began to appear that there were in fact transactions, though of a different nature, nothing to do with the girl, between Lord Adour and the dead man. There was the sale of the Seagull, *which began to take on the air of a bogus transaction. There was the chart I found showing a course picked out to a solitary spot on the French coast.*

"Love and jealousy began to my mind to fade out of the picture as the murder motive, and money to appear instead. There is a good deal to be made just now by black market smuggling between here and the Continent.

"But once more, a snag. On that new theory, where did the kingfisher business come in? For by this time I was feeling fairly certain that the kingfisher yarn was an invention.

"Why? What for?

"It took some pretty hard thinking to worry that out, but it did begin to seem that it might have been an invention to persuade Helen to enter the spinney and so give Itter, waiting there, a chance to urge his suit. Later facts that turned up made this likely, and so brought the motive swinging back to love and jealousy. I think now that Lord Adour told Jane about the kingfisher, feeling sure she would tell Helen and they would both go at once to look for the bird themselves—the almost certainly non-existent bird. I think it probable that Itter Bain, in talking to Lord Adour, had shown a disturbing degree of excitement and that the idea in Adour's mind was that Jane's presence in the spinney would be a precaution, while at the same time Itter would not be able to complain that the promise had not been kept. The undertaking was he should have a chance to see Helen and talk to her. There was no promise that Jane

should not be somewhere near. The letter would be honoured, if not the spirit.

"I feel it was most likely the same underlying uneasiness that made Lord Adour leave his gun where he did, leaning against the oak tree—another precaution. For one thing, though his story was that he put it down in a hurry, on the spur of the moment, yet he remembered the exact spot. Itter was young and an athlete. Lord Adour was elderly and none. On my theory, the obscure uneasiness he experienced over the inner excitement he felt Itter was betraying at the prospect of meeting Helen, made him wish to have his gun handy—-just in case. Not that I imagine he felt this consciously or would now or at any time have acknowledged it.

"But now the more the case developed, the more facts I collected, the more it began to seem that everything was consistent with the guilt of Helen herself. Easy to suppose that Itter Bain had frightened her, that she had seen her father's gun and that she had used it to defend herself and that much of the difficulty and obscurity surrounding the case was due to lying by friends determined to protect her. From what I could learn of her, her strange, aloof and solitary character, her attitude of almost religious awe towards her own beauty as of something to be guarded for itself alone, it seemed likely she would resort to any extremity to protect it from even the semblance of a threat. For a time, then, everything I got to know appeared consistent with her guilt. Then Jane mentioned that, though she did see the gun in Helen's hands, Helen told her she found it lying under bushes and that it had already been discharged. But her father had left it standing against the oak, so there was proof the gun had been previously used by someone else and pushed away by him under the bushes where Helen found it.

"Unless, of course, it was a clever, made-up yarn. But I was quite unable to believe that Jane was lying or that Helen had been cool enough, immediately after killing a man, or Jane either, for that matter, to invent a story to meet a contingency not yet arisen. How could she or either of them know that it would turn out of such importance whether the gun had been standing against a tree or lying under bushes?

"Plainly, then, if the gun had been used by another person before Helen found it, then that person was the criminal, not Helen.

"Plainly, too, it was of ever-growing importance that the gun should be found.

"Three alternatives apparently.

"If Lord Adour or Helen were in fact guilty, then the gun might be hidden at Kindles and so out of my reach unless I could get a search warrant. And that I knew I should never be granted against a man in Lord Adour's position unless I could show grounds for suspicion so strong that the discovery of the gun would be almost superfluous. A sort of vicious circle. No search for the gun without evidence. No evidence without the gun. That's the sort of thing that makes a detective old before his time.

"Secondly, the gun might, as was freely suggested, have been stolen by some stray tramp or vagabond. In that case, if recovered, its value as evidence would be nil.

"Thirdly, the murderer had himself hidden it somewhere. Only where? I'm afraid I rather jumped to conclusions and felt sure it would be at the bottom of the sea. It seemed so obvious and easy, and, of course, if that was it, would never be found. Then it struck me that for safety it would have to be taken out a good distance from land. I remembered the weather had been bad for small boats. Not impossible, but bad enough to make it noticeable and to be remembered if any small boat had gone out. And I remembered the time I talked to Mauley and his apparent wish to stress that he had not boarded the launch. Perhaps he had, I thought, and perhaps he had boarded it to hide the gun, or even had it hidden there already, in preparation for taking out the launch to sea and getting rid of the gun. I held off for a while, on the chance that Mauley might try to remove the gun and could be caught in the act. Instead, the launch disappeared—first upriver to the factory and then, when I still showed an interest in it, altogether. And a wholly improbable story that it had been stolen. Not difficult to think out where it might be; and that is what brought about the climax when Mauley realized the gun had been found and his liberty of action was likely to be soon and seriously curtailed.

"Before that, though, there had been another diversion. The sudden production by Prescott of a large sum of money, with no very convincing explanation of where it had come from. That brought back the idea of the money motive and Prescott as the

murderer in order to secure cash to save the business. But there was always that alibi of his there was no way of getting round. Also it seemed certain that the money was the product of Itter Bain's black market smuggling undertaken with the very object of getting the cash needed to tide over the Bain Products concern during the outbreak of peace difficulties. Itter must have hidden it somewhere and Prescott found it and was using it for that same purpose. It seemed, therefore, that he was probably within his rights. Anyhow, Mauley had made no objection, though he must have known or guessed. No complaint received and no apparent connection with the investigation. In no way a police matter and no cause for action.

"Of course, all the time I had to keep an eye open for other possibilities. I knew I might well be working on the wrong track. There was Prescott with his convenient and unbreakable alibi that always seems so suspicious, but that this time was really genuine and conclusive. There was Haile, and there was evidently something that was making him uneasy. It might be consciousness of guilt. In fact, he was afraid that his intrigue with Miss Lambert might come to light and with it his connection with the contemplated illegal operation, about which he was very nervous. But his pose as a private detective and his anxiety to help me might well have been camouflage. Martin Winstanley soon faded out of the picture, but I knew might appear again at any moment. By the way, Jane and he are engaged now, so I suppose there's a happy ending for him. And for Haile and Miss Lambert, too, for I think her influence, and his new sense of responsibility as husband and father, will sober him down a bit; and he seems to have really got the new job he talked about, though I was half inclined to suspect it was merely an excuse for borrowing a little cash and fading out. A mistake to be too suspicious. Then there was poor little Wayling who told me so fiercely he would always be willing to kill for Helen's sake, and who might have done so, but who, in the end, died for her instead.

"Mauley's motive, of course, was simply plain, old style jealousy, though that, I think he never realized, so overlaid was it in the secret places of his mind, in such a world of suppressed feelings and unrecognized emotion had he come to exist.

"There ought to be a possibility of different verdicts in such cases. Our simple 'guilty' or 'not guilty' is much too great a

simplification. There should be something on the lines of murder in the first or second degree or something like that. Mauley killed, but he did not kill 'of malice aforethought.' That is what he meant when he declared with such force and evident conviction that he was innocent. He felt himself a driven man, a mere instrument. In his mind, circumstances had conspired and he had been their innocent and unconscious tool to carry out what through them had become necessary and inevitable. The same thought or belief or idea, or whatever you like to call it, has been displayed by others; others who undoubtedly killed, but who still, to the very end, protested their innocence because they knew they had never willed or intended the dreadful thing that happened through, but not by, them.

"The psychology of the murderer should be given much more serious study than it has ever yet received. I wish I had the necessary qualification. It is quite different from that of the ordinary, commonplace criminal who simply matches his wits against society outside the law, and who is no worse or other than the unscrupulous business man who does the same within the law.

"In Mauley's case—and there are parallels in the records of criminology—his inner self, his unconscious, whatever you like to call those deep urges that sometimes rise from the depths of our being to master us, was unable to bear the burden of his brother's blood. He had to seek relief, to shift the guilt, as it were. In primitive man, this took the form of the need to placate the angry ghost; and that that still survives was shown most curiously in the United States when gangsters, killed by other gangsters, were given most elaborate funerals, with silver-mounted coffins and many expensive wreaths. The same idea of averting the dead man's anger. With Mauley this deep sense of a guilt that had in some way to be redeemed—the expression he used was that 'death needed death'—took the form of transferring that guilt to Helen's beauty, which to him began to seem alone responsible.

"Since he knew, and most deeply felt on that primitive level of emotional crisis which is far stronger than any form of reason or of logic, that his brother's death must have its equal consequence, its necessary compensation, it was from her, or rather from her beauty, that the due penalty must be exacted. Not otherwise could the eternal balance be restored.

"In this way, in the fantasy he created for himself under the awful weight of his brother's blood, he transferred himself from the role of murderer to that of avenger.

"Strange enough, too strange perhaps for the normal mind to grasp. But there is nothing more strange than the human heart and nothing in the dark and tangled labyrinth of its ways that is beyond belief."

The rest of the letter is of purely private interest.

THE END

Lightning Source UK Ltd.
Milton Keynes UK
UKOW04f1404260716

279281UK00001B/20/P